BEYOND HER REACH

ALSO BY MELINDA LEIGH

Echo Road

BREE TAGGERT NOVELS

Cross Her Heart

See Her Die

Drown Her Sorrows

Right Behind Her

"Her Second Death" (A Prequel Short Story)

Dead Against Her

Lie to Her

Catch Her Death

On Her Watch

Track Her Down

MORGAN DANE NOVELS

Say You're Sorry

Her Last Goodbye

Bones Don't Lie

What I've Done

Secrets Never Die

Save Your Breath

Scarlet Falls Novels

Hour of Need

Minutes to Kill

Seconds to Live

She Can Series

She Can Run

She Can Tell

She Can Scream

She Can Hide

"He Can Fall" (A Short Story)

She Can Kill

Midnight Novels

Midnight Exposure

Midnight Sacrifice

Midnight Betrayal

Midnight Obsession

The Rogue Series Novellas

Gone to Her Grave (Rogue River)

Walking on Her Grave (Rogue River)

Tracks of Her Tears (Rogue Winter)

Burned by Her Devotion (Rogue Vows)

Twisted Truth (Rogue Justice)

THE WIDOW'S ISLAND NOVELLA SERIES

A Bone to Pick

Whisper of Bones

A Broken Bone

Buried Bones

The Wrong Bones

BEYOND HER REACH

MELINDA LEIGH

This is a work of fiction. Names, characters, organizations, places, events, and incidents are either products of the author's imagination or are used fictitiously. Otherwise, any resemblance to actual persons, living or dead, is purely coincidental.

Text copyright © 2025 by Melinda Leigh
All rights reserved.

No part of this book may be reproduced, or stored in a retrieval system, or transmitted in any form or by any means, electronic, mechanical, photocopying, recording, or otherwise, without express written permission of the publisher.

Published by Montlake, Seattle

www.apub.com

Amazon, the Amazon logo, and Montlake are trademarks of Amazon.com, Inc., or its affiliates.

EU product safety contact:
Amazon Media EU S. à r.l.
38, avenue John F. Kennedy, L-1855 Luxembourg
amazonpublishing-gpsr@amazon.com

ISBN-13: 9781662516986 (hardcover)
ISBN-13: 9781662522086 (paperback)
ISBN-13: 9781662516979 (digital)

Cover design by Shasti O'Leary Soudant
Cover images: © Mohamad Itani / ArcAngel; © lzf / Shutterstock; © sutipong / Shutterstock; © Smileus / Shutterstock

Printed in the United States of America

First edition

*For Rosie.
I think Ladybug would approve.*

Chapter One

The perceived safety of suburbia was an illusion.

Or maybe delusion *is a better word. We believe what we want to believe.*

Sunlight glimmered on a few inches of fresh snow as Sheriff Bree Taggert drove her official SUV down Oak Street. The upstate New York neighborhood wasn't extravagant—average-size houses built on average-size lots—but the properties were well kept. It was quaint enough that Bree felt as if she were driving into a TV show. Half of the properties bore holiday decorations. Red ribbons waved from wreaths. Lighted reindeer adorned lawns. A thin layer of snow covered neighborhood imperfections. But the scene's idyllic perfection wasn't any more real than a Hollywood set, because Bree was responding to a report of a probable homicide.

Easing off the gas pedal, she rolled past two patrol cruisers that sat at the curb, lights swirling, sirens silenced. One of her young deputies, Juarez, stood next to his vehicle, interviewing a man in a navy-blue parka. A witness, Bree presumed.

She drove past them and parked. Exiting her vehicle, she stepped into two inches of fresh snow, but she didn't mind. In early December, she still enjoyed snow. In another month or two, she'd curse at every flurry in the forecast. She inhaled a lungful of damp air, as if imprinting the clean smell into her nostrils in preparation for the sensory onslaught to come.

Walking to Juarez's cruiser, she couldn't decide who was paler—her deputy or the witness. Juarez was one of her younger deputies. He'd seen some things since joining her department, but he didn't have the experience yet to compartmentalize the horror show that sometimes came with the job.

"Sheriff." Juarez gestured toward the man. "This is Antonio Santori. He found the victim."

Antonio, a lean man in his sixties, had thick, wavy salt-and-pepper hair. He exploded into a language Bree didn't understand. It wasn't Spanish. Calloused hands punctuated his speech with frantic motions.

Footsteps crunched on rock salt. Bree turned to see Deputy Renata Zucco crossing the street toward them from the direction of the house. Zucco calmed the man in what sounded like the same language.

Zucco glanced at Bree. "Italian. I'm good with languages."

Antonio took a long breath, then shuddered. He zipped his coat closer to his chin. "I'm sorry. I speak English, but when I'm upset, sometimes I forget." His words carried a slight accent.

"Understandable," Bree said. "Just tell me what happened."

Antonio gestured toward a dark-blue van emblazoned with the words THE TILE GUY parked on the other side of the street. "I came to meet with Mrs. Gibson. She didn't answer the door. I heard a voice inside, like maybe she was calling me. The door wasn't locked, so I went in." Antonio's breath caught. Then he blew out the words with a puff of steam. "The voice was the TV, and she was . . ." His Adam's apple bobbed as he swallowed hard. He stared at his hands for a few seconds, then lifted his eyes. The deep brown of them swam with horror and bewilderment. "Who could do such a thing?"

Isn't that always the million-dollar question?

Antonio shifted his weight from one work boot to the other. "May I go?"

"Not just yet." Bree sized up the exterior of the house.

Antonio pulled a phone from his jacket pocket and checked the time. "I have other jobs to bid on later today."

"I understand," Bree said. "We'll try not to keep you too long. If necessary, we can call your employer and explain."

Antonio shook his head. "It's my business, but I need to know if I should have my wife reschedule my other appointments for the day."

Bree glanced at Zucco's grim face. "I think that's a good idea. We appreciate your cooperation."

With a nod, Antonio raised his phone.

Bree lifted a hand. "I'm going to ask you not to give out Mrs. Gibson's name. It's better if the family hears about this"—she gestured toward the house—"from me rather than sees it on the news."

Antonio pressed a hand to his heart, as if the thought pained him. "Of course."

Bree took a step toward the house, then paused. "One more question. Did you touch the body?"

Antonio's eyes opened wide in revulsion. "No. No *no*."

"It's OK," Bree soothed. "We just need to know."

As Antonio moved toward his van, he crossed himself, muttering something that sounded like a prayer in Italian.

Bree turned to her deputies. "Zucco, you were first on scene?"

She nodded. "Juarez helped me clear the house."

Juarez blinked and swallowed. His pale face grayed, but he said nothing.

Bree motioned toward Antonio, standing next to his van and talking on the phone. "Juarez, stay with the witness. Zucco, show me."

Zucco turned and headed back toward the house.

Glancing sideways, Bree assessed her deputy's face. Deputy Renata Zucco had come from the NYPD. She'd worked patrol and vice, including some undercover work. Not much fazed her. Now, her cop mask shielded her expression. But beneath it, her eyes were hardened, and her lips were pressed into a thin, bloodless line. Keeping her mask in place appeared to be taking effort.

She's definitely shook.

Two trails of footprints marred the soggy slush in the driveway.

Zucco pointed toward the double track on the left. "Those are Antonio's footprints." The imprints going into the house were normal. The prints leaving were spaced wider and showed places where Antonio had slipped. Bree imagined him running, sliding, panicked.

"Did you get photos?" Bree asked. Already the prints were disappearing as the snow melted.

"Yes," Zucco confirmed. Her finger shifted to the right. "Those tracks are mine and Juarez's."

Once a suspicious death had been noted, Bree's deputies knew to minimize their impact on the scene. They'd stuck to one path through the snow to the house. The rest of the slush was unmarred. If there was a car in the garage, it had been there since before the snow accumulated.

As if following Bree's train of thought, Zucco said, "There were no footprints in the snow on the grassy areas when I arrived. Not anywhere around the house. That single trail circling the property is mine. I have pictures of that as well."

Bree was grateful her deputy had enough experience to recognize the precarious nature of the outside scene and had prioritized preserving the evidence at risk of disappearing as the day warmed and the snow melted. She thought about the previous evening. She'd checked the horses at eight thirty. The ground had barely been covered. "The snow started around seven p.m., but it was a slow storm and took a while to accumulate."

"Still." Zucco stepped onto the covered front porch. "The killer must have either arrived before the snow started or they left early enough for their tracks to have been covered."

Bree donned gloves and reached for the front door handle.

Zucco stopped her with a hand on her elbow. With a grim look, she pulled shoe covers from her pocket and handed Bree two. "It's messy. I'd put these on out here."

That bad . . .

They slipped on the booties. Bree bent to examine the door lock and hinges but saw no sign of forced entry.

With a gloved hand, Zucco opened the front door. "The front door was unlocked and partially open when I arrived. Antonio says it was unlocked but closed when he got here. I assume he ran out so fast he didn't shut the door. The body is in the family room."

Bree stepped across the threshold. The smell of death drifted toward her, a foul blend of blood and other bodily fluids. The bowels and bladder often evacuated upon death. Bree removed her coat, leaned out the front door, and dropped it on the concrete. Fabric absorbed the odors of death. She could change her shirt and trousers. She didn't have a second winter uniform coat.

Zucco led the way past a formal living room and a stairway. The hallway floors, a medium-toned hardwood, looked new. The walls were freshly painted in a buttercream color. They followed the same wood floor down the hall toward the kitchen. A cluster of framed photos hanging on the wall caught Bree's attention. Two kids, a boy and a girl, shown in their school pictures throughout the years. The photos ended with high school graduation pictures. Bree's heart ached. These two kids had just lost their mother, and they didn't even know it yet.

The foul smell intensified as they entered the room. The backsplash and countertops were not yet installed, and drop cloths covered the floor. Pendant light fixtures looked new. A manufacturer's label hung from a cabinet door. The appliances still bore the clear-blue protective strips. Folded sheets of clear plastic, a tool bag, and various power tools sat in front of a set of sliding glass doors.

The family room adjoined the kitchen. An old leather couch faced a TV mounted above a fireplace. On the screen, a loop of streaming previews played.

Bree stopped short. The body wasn't in sight yet, but arcs of blood streaked the creamy walls, disconcertingly reminding Bree of one of her artist brother's paintings.

"She's on the couch." Zucco showed no inclination to move closer.

Bree watched her step. Her boots were covered, but she didn't want to disturb biological evidence on the hardwood. And it was, frankly, everywhere. She rounded the side of the couch.

Holy . . .

The victim lay sprawled on her side. Her neck gaped with a deep slash wound, so deep that the neck's internal structures were visible. Bree scanned the scene. No sharp instrument in sight or within reach of the victim. "Well, it definitely wasn't an accident."

The medical examiner had already been summoned. She would need to give the official declaration, but the damage was clear enough. Bree's gaze was pulled to the blood-splattered lamp and ceiling. Separate from the arterial spray, these smaller spatters had been flicked from the bloody murder weapon after it left the victim's flesh.

"That's one nasty wound," Zucco said from the kitchen. "And what's the deal with the position of her head? It almost looks like they tried to rip it off."

The victim's head was tipped backward and twisted at an odd angle, as if the killer had tried to make her bleed more—or faster—or possibly tried to break her neck.

She was a petite brunette with shoulder-length hair. She wore pale gray lounge pants and a matching loose sweater. Blood had soaked her lovely outfit, run from the cushion, and dripped to the floor, where it had spread in a large puddle and dried. Her feet were bare, but a pair of sheepskin slippers sat between the couch and the square cocktail ottoman. A wooden tray on the ottoman held a single mug. A tea bag string and tag dangled next to the mug's handle.

She spotted a possible smudge from a shoe at the edge of the blood puddle, but no bloody footprints walking away. Either she was wrong about the smudge and the killer had moved backward as the blood spread, or they'd removed their shoes before stepping out of the puddle.

Bree leaned forward to get a better look at the victim's face. One cheek was pressed into the leather. Her face looked fine, but Bree wouldn't want to show the remains to a family member for identification purposes, not with that wound. "Are we sure the victim is the homeowner?"

"The tile guy said it was."

"Did you see a purse anywhere?" Bree glanced around.

Zucco jerked a thumb over her shoulder. "On the table by the glass doors."

Bree backtracked to the kitchen. A folding snack table stood behind the power tools. The purse on it was black, medium-size, and appeared stylish to Bree, who admittedly had no sense of style whatsoever. Bree released the metal clasp. The contents were organized. She withdrew a black leather wallet and opened it to view a driver's license. "Kelly Gibson, age forty-five, brown eyes, five feet, three inches tall. Description fits." She carried the wallet back to the family room and compared the photo to the victim. Kelly's cheeks were a little thinner than in her license photo, as if she'd lost weight, but her features were the same. "Looks like her."

Bree looked through the rest of the wallet. "Cash and credit cards are still here."

"Purse was in plain sight," Zucco said. "Not a robbery."

"No." Bree retreated to the kitchen and returned the wallet to the purse. "The ME should be here soon. Chief Harvey and Investigator Flynn are both on their way."

Matt Flynn was Bree's part-time investigator. The rural sheriff's department budget didn't allow for a full-time detective, but Matt worked as a civilian consultant whenever a difficult case popped up. He was also her live-in . . . boyfriend? *Boyfriend* sounded casual—and young. What did people in their thirties call the man who shared their life and their home? They weren't engaged, but they were definitely in a committed relationship.

"Start recording the scene. I want pictures and videos of everything. Check all doors and windows for signs of forced entry."

Bree went outside and gulped the cool, damp air. Two more patrol vehicles had arrived. Her chief deputy, Todd Harvey, walked toward her. She summed up the scene. "The snow is almost gone. The yard is going to be a muddy mess in a few more hours."

"I'll get a couple of deputies to search the surrounding area ASAP."

"Include the whole block in case the killer parked in front of another house and walked over here."

Todd nodded. "We'll do a door-to-door too. Maybe a neighbor saw something or captured the killer on a home security camera."

"Kelly Gibson has a doorbell camera. Let's get access to it."

"Have you seen her phone?" Todd asked.

"Next to the body," Bree said. "Rory should be able to gain access." Rory MacIniss was the digital and tech expert in their forensics department.

Todd gestured toward Antonio. "What do you want to do with the tile guy?"

Bree glanced at Antonio, who stood in the street between his van and Juarez's cruiser. His hands were shoved into the pockets of his parka, his shoulders hunched. "Have a deputy accompany him to the station. Get him to sign a statement. We need his fingerprints and shoe tread impressions for elimination purposes. Run a background check. If nothing relevant pops up, he's free to go."

"Do I need to make any calls?"

"The ME is on her way. Matt should be here any minute. I'll call forensics now." Bree glanced back at the house. "We're going to need more deputies. As soon as we have an approximate time of death, we'll start that neighborhood canvass. Have Marge check real estate records on the house. Copy me and Marge on everything you're doing in case you have to leave suddenly. How's Cady?"

Cady was Todd's girlfriend—and Matt's sister. She was ready to have a baby any day.

"Uncomfortable but good. Scared but excited."

Bree smiled. "If you need to go, you go." She waved a hand to indicate the crime scene. "This is not as important."

"No worries. I won't hesitate. She's my world." A dazed look crossed his face. He shook it off. "But the doctor said it could be another two weeks, so I'll get back to work now." He pointed to the house. "Because that woman deserves justice."

Kelly Gibson had been killed in a horrific act of brutal violence. Whoever had killed her could not be allowed to get away with murder.

An angry male voice yelled, "What is going on here? Kelly!"

Chapter Two

Bree turned to see Juarez blocking the path of a large man walking up the driveway. He was at least six four, both lean and wide-shouldered, with a poofy *Duck Dynasty* beard and a baseball cap sporting a fish on the front. A long scar ran down his left cheek.

Juarez stopped him politely. "I'm sorry, sir. You can't go inside."

"Why not?" The man's posture emanated belligerence as he glared down at Juarez, whose ability to remain calm impressed Bree. The man drew back his shoulders. Towering over Juarez, he jutted out his chest like a WWE wrestler about to do a body slam. "I have a right to know what's going on!"

Juarez didn't budge, but he didn't seem intimidated either. "This is a crime scene, sir. I cannot let you through. Please step back."

"I will not! What do you mean, it's a crime scene?" The man glared over Juarez's head and spotted Bree. "Sheriff!" he yelled. "What happened? Where's Kelly?"

He knew the victim.

Bree headed for him. "Can I help you, sir?"

She gave Juarez an *I've got this* nod.

Juarez stepped aside, and the man brushed past him, attempting to blow right by Bree as well.

Yeah. Not happening.

Juarez moved into the man's path again. "Sir, you need to stop right there."

"I have rights. You can't stop me." He dropped his upper body and attempted to plow a shoulder into Juarez's body, but Juarez dodged him. Unfortunately, the man's momentum carried him toward Bree. She sidestepped and twisted, getting out of the way just in time to avoid a tackle. His shoulder brushed past her midsection, and his elbow clipped her in the jaw. Her teeth snapped together. Pain zipped through her lip, and the coppery, salty taste of blood flooded her mouth.

Son of a . . .

Deflecting his shoulder with a hand, she kicked out in a boot-to-boot leg sweep. He might have an eighty-pound weight advantage over her, but she had learned and trained to take down larger suspects. He couldn't muscle over the laws of physics. In fact, his broad-shouldered build made him top heavy. His momentum—and excessive confidence—carried his upper body forward while her maneuver took his foot in the opposite direction. He went down fast and hard. His body hit the concrete driveway like a sack of horse feed. Slush sprayed on Bree's boots and pant legs. He landed on his belly, the air bellowing out of his lungs with an audible "Oof."

To keep him down, Bree crouched, folded his arm into a chicken wing, and carefully applied a knee to the back of his hip.

He struggled for a few seconds, but Bree just waited. If he'd had leverage, he could have easily overpowered her. But with his cheek pressed into the driveway and his arm behind his back, he had exactly none. Still, she cuffed him for extra assurance.

"What the . . ." He stopped himself, going quiet as the click of the handcuffs forced his brain to process the reality of the situation.

"I didn't see that coming. I'm sorry," a distressed Juarez said over her shoulder.

Bree shook her head. "I didn't see it coming either."

"Do you need help?" Juarez asked.

She patted down the man's pockets, which were empty except for a cheap cell phone. Bree shook her head. "I don't think so, but don't go anywhere."

"Yes, ma'am. Your mouth is bleeding." Juarez shot an angry glare at the man on the ground.

Bree ran her tongue over her teeth and lips. She found a small cut on the inside of her lip. "Bit my own lip."

"Do you want me to take him in for assaulting an officer?" Juarez narrowed his eyes at the man.

"Not just yet." Bree wanted to know how well the man knew the victim. She leaned closer to him. "If I let you get up, will you cooperate?"

A sigh heaved through his big body. "Yeah. I'm real sorry, ma'am. I would *never* strike a woman."

"Except you just did," Bree pointed out, thinking of the dead woman in the house.

"That was an accident." He sounded sincere.

Though Bree noted that he offered no apology for attempting to bulldoze Juarez.

She warned, "If you don't behave, I'll have to arrest you."

"I won't do anything. I swear." Regret deflated his body.

"OK." She released his arm and stood back. Her posture was deceptively casual. One hand rested on her duty belt—right next to her Taser and baton.

Her takedown seemed to have snapped his self-control back into place, but she made mental notes regarding his agitated state, sense of entitlement, and poor emotional regulation. Those three traits could possibly lead to an impulsive act, like slashing a woman's throat.

"I'm Sheriff Taggert. What's your name?"

"Jeff Burke." He jerked his chin toward the house across the street. The smaller home was white with navy-blue shutters and a black cat in the window. "I live there."

Bree touched her mouth with a fingertip. "As my deputy pointed out, I could arrest you for assaulting an officer right now."

Burke frowned at her face, then stared down at his toes, scraping one boot on the concrete, his demeanor suddenly that of a kid in the principal's office. "I apologize for that. I shouldn't have done it, but I was—am—upset at seeing all this police activity at Kelly's house."

"Because she's your neighbor?" Bree asked.

"Yes." A red flush brightened his cheeks over his scraggly facial hair. "Kelly is more than my neighbor. She's also my . . . friend." The slight hesitation before *friend* made Bree wonder if that was the extent of his relationship with the victim.

Neither of those relationships gave him the right to access the crime scene. But Bree had no desire to argue. She needed information, and she was willing to let his little tantrum slide if he proved useful.

"Did Kelly get robbed or something?" he asked.

Bree didn't answer. "When was the last time you spoke with Kelly?"

He jerked a shoulder. "I don't know exactly. A few days ago maybe? I was coming home from work and she was at her mailbox."

"And what was the nature of that conversation?"

Burke's steel-toed construction boot scraped on the concrete again. "The usual. I said hi. She waved back."

"So you didn't have a *conversation*?"

"No, ma'am," he admitted. Irritation flashed in his eyes but disappeared in an instant. Had he been annoyed that Kelly didn't stop to talk to him? Or that Bree had made a note of it? Both?

"And that's the last time you saw her?" Bree asked.

"Yes." He expanded his chest and let all the air out in a huge sigh.

"When was the last real conversation you had with her?" Bree asked. "Something more than a neighborly wave."

He glanced at his own house. Thinking back or thinking of the best way to respond? "Last week we talked about her renovation."

"Where did that conversation happen?"

"In her house." Burke nodded, as if affirming his own statement.

"Did she invite you over?" Bree asked.

"Not exactly." Burke frowned. He clearly did not like Bree highlighting the superficial nature of his relationship with Kelly. "I got a letter of hers by mistake. I delivered it to her."

"Did you talk at her door or inside the house?"

"Inside. I wanted to see her new kitchen cabinets."

Bree wondered if Kelly had offered to let him in or if he had pushed his way in, using that sense of entitlement he'd already exhibited with her. She didn't bother to ask. He wouldn't admit it. Instead, she asked, "How did she seem?"

He shrugged. "Normal. A little stressed, but that *was* normal for her."

"What was she stressed about?"

Burke shifted his weight again. His inability to remain still was a tell of discomfort. Whatever he said next might not be the complete truth. "The renovation was taking longer than she wanted. The costs were higher, the usual stuff."

"Did you exchange any phone calls or texts with her?"

He ground his molars. "I don't have her phone number."

So they weren't close.

"Did she mention being afraid of anyone or anything?" Bree asked.

"Afraid?" Burke stiffened. His gaze shot to Kelly's house. "What the hell happened to her?"

Bree spotted a news van coming down the street toward them. No point in holding back now. The media would pull Kelly's name from the property address. As soon as they saw the ME van arrive, they'd know someone had died here. "Kelly was murdered."

Burke fell back a step as if she'd pushed him. His gaze darted back to the house, then refocused on Bree. "What?"

"Kelly was murdered," she repeated.

His jaw sawed from side to side as if protesting the news his brain was processing. "When did it happen?"

"I don't know yet," Bree said. "Did Kelly mention receiving any threats?"

Burke shook his head. "Not to me."

"Does she have a significant other?"

Burke's face scrunched up in distaste. "She and her husband are separated. Harrison is a douche. He never deserved her."

"Why do you say that?" Bree left the question intentionally open-ended.

Burke huffed. "He's the kind of guy who buys a sports car, dyes his hair, and chases younger women because he's approaching fifty, like any of that is going to keep him from aging."

Bree guessed Burke was probably fifty-fiveish. His beard was shot with gray, and the silver Ford F-150 that stood in front of his house looked to be about ten years old. "You don't like Kelly's husband."

"No," he said without hesitation. "He dumped Kelly for a younger woman after the last kid left for college. That's not the way you treat a good woman."

"When did they split up?"

"Last spring? Dunno exactly."

"What about Kelly? What was she like?" Bree asked.

Burke's eyes went misty. He blinked. "She was sweet. Smart. Good mom. Kept the house nice, yard too."

"Did she work outside the home?"

Burke shook his head. His face filled with admiration. "No. She was happy to be a homemaker. It's the most important job, after all." His tone was wistful. Was he single? "So many rude kids out there, but not Kelly's. She brought them up right."

Bree didn't comment, but a tinge of guilt crept up her spine. She was raising her niece and nephew, but a fresh homicide case would lead to more time away from them. But they didn't need a stay-at-home mom to turn them into good kids. They were already good kids. Bree's sister had been a single working mom. Why did she let people get to her? "Is there a Mrs. Burke I could speak with?"

He stared down at his battered boots. "No. I was never lucky enough to find the right woman." Sadness filled his eyes, wiping out any trace of his earlier aggression. His moods were more volatile than the weather between seasons.

Bree noted that Burke's front door was directly across the street from Kelly's. "Do you have a doorbell or security camera?"

Burke snorted. "Hell no. I won't give Big Brother any more opportunities to watch me." He pulled his cell phone out of his pocket. It looked like a prepaid model. "No smartphone for me either. Nobody's listening in on my conversations."

Disappointed, Bree moved on. "Did Kelly have issues with any of the other neighbors?"

Burke shook his head. "Not that I know of. Everybody loves—loved—her. I just can't wrap my head around her being gone. Why would anyone want to hurt her?"

Bree had no answer for that. "How about family? Did you ever witness any fights or loud arguments?"

"No." He paused. "Yes," he corrected. "I saw Kelly and Harrison argue more than once."

"Recently?"

"Yeah." His nod was enthusiastic. "He came over here a while ago. I don't remember exactly when, maybe like a month or two? She wouldn't let him in. He was real mad that she'd changed the locks. Good for her, though. I mean, *he* moved out. Why would he think he could just waltz back in whenever he wanted?"

Why indeed?

"What did they argue about?" Bree asked.

Burke shrugged. "The divorce. He wanted her to sign the papers, but she wasn't happy with the settlement, said he was being stingy. No surprise there."

"Did you ever see him threaten or strike Kelly?"

"No," Burke admitted reluctantly. "Have you talked to *him* yet?" Burke said *him* with vehemence, his face flushing with temper again. "Because if I were you, I'd look at him pretty hard."

"Was there anyone else in Kelly's life?"

"She has a lady friend I see here regularly. Don't know her name. She's average height, fit, dark hair." Burke rattled the handcuffs behind his back. "Are you going to arrest me?"

Bree sighed. "Not at this time." Yes, he'd tried to knock her over, but he'd been distressed. She circled a finger, and he turned around. She removed the cuffs. "I'm going to cut you a break. I won't give you another one."

Burke turned to face her. "OK." He looked appropriately penitent as he rubbed his wrists. Suddenly, he froze. "Wait. A man brought her home one day last week. I don't remember which night, and I didn't recognize him. He opened her car door and walked real close to her, like it was a date or something." He frowned, his eyes narrowing. Jealousy?

"But you don't know who it was."

"No." Burke looked thoughtful. "Tall guy. Dressed fancy." He rolled his eyes. "Drove a slick black sedan."

"Do you remember anything else about him or his car?"

"No, but I wish I did." Burke brightened. "His number must be in her phone. You should probably look for him."

Bree nodded. "We will investigate everyone in Kelly's life."

Including you.

Chapter Three

Matt Flynn stopped to wipe the slush from his boots before entering the victim's house. Last night, Matt, Bree, and her nine-year-old niece, Kayla, had watched the big, wet flakes drift from the sky. They'd made hot cocoa, eaten cookies, and played cards. Excited, Kayla had chattered about building a snowman after school with her friends. At the rate the snow was melting, the kids would be constructing a mudman.

Seeing Bree's coat on the porch, Matt removed his own and left it with hers. Then he donned shoe covers and stepped over the threshold. The too-familiar smell of death slapped him, immediately clogging his nose and coating his throat. He spotted Bree in the kitchen at the end of the hall and walked toward her. His booties slid on the polished hardwood floor.

Deputies surrounded her, each one listening to her instructions with serious concentration. She was an average-size woman, though her duty belt and body armor added a bit of bulk to her trim frame. But she seemed larger than her physical size. She commanded the room. She projected intelligence and experience like an aura. The deputies she'd trained since taking the job of sheriff nearly two years before operated like the well-drilled team they were.

As a cop and detective, she kicked ass. No question. But it wasn't just her competence that commanded the respect and loyalty of her staff. She was full of common sense and compassion. No matter how many criminals she put away, she never lost hope in humans. Matt wasn't sure how she accomplished it, but she still believed most people were inherently good. She cared about the community. She valued her deputies as human beings as much as for the work they did. These qualities did not make her weak but rather enhanced her strengths as a leader.

After her sister had been murdered, she'd moved to upstate New York to raise her niece and nephew. She'd walked away from a solid career as a homicide detective in Philadelphia without a second thought. She kicked ass as a guardian too, especially considering she'd taken on the parenting job with no preparation or experience, and while in the middle of grieving the loss of her sister.

Her success was about effort and intention, he decided. Bree cared enough to put aside her own needs. She worked hard to help the kids understand and process their trauma, the same way she put aside her own ego to keep the citizens of Randolph County safe. She never shirked the hard work. Instead, she took on more than her share of the burden every time.

He made no sound, but Bree's head whipped around as if she sensed his presence. Their eyes met. Neither of them believed in PDAs on the job, but his response to her threw him a little, as always. It blew his mind that eye contact alone was comforting. The grimness in her expression softened. The change was almost imperceptible. Probably no one else noticed. But he did. She took the same comfort from his presence as he did from hers. She swallowed, breaking the moment, her focus returning to her task, her professional mask sliding back into place.

He walked closer, taking in the messy murder scene. He passed the couch, giving it a wide berth and placing his feet with care, until he had a view of the body and the horrific injury that had been inflicted upon it.

How could someone do that to another person?

He'd seen some terrible things in his law enforcement career. He'd been a deputy, an investigator, and a K-9 handler for the sheriff's department before being shot in a friendly-fire incident. Damage to his right hand had messed with his handgun aim and ended his career as a deputy. A settlement from the county took care of his financial needs, but he'd been floundering personally. The shooting had stolen his purpose. Then he'd met Bree.

After she'd solved her sister's murder and been appointed sheriff, she'd talked him into working investigations on an as-needed basis. For a while, he'd been satisfied, his life purpose restored by his work. Now, he wasn't so sure that was the case.

He felt more useful and fulfilled in his relationship with Bree and in helping her parent the kids.

Not what he would have expected.

The world had shifted under his feet like a floating dock. He still valued his work. Bringing criminals to justice would always be important. But it wasn't all he had now. Investigating crimes was a part of his life rather than the central focus.

Turned out the experts were right. It did indeed feel healthier to be a well-rounded individual with their priorities in the proper order.

Bree dispatched her deputies. Then she turned to Matt. "I'm glad you're here."

Matt looked down at the victim and tried to see beyond the horror to the evidence. "Who was she?"

"Looks like the homeowner, Kelly Gibson." She summarized the case so far. "We're waiting on the ME and forensics now."

"The ME is here," Dr. Serena Jones's low voice called out.

She was a tall Black woman with the long, easy stride of an athlete. Her assistant trailed behind her. Both carried medical kits that looked like tackle boxes. Dr. Jones unzipped a knee-length coat to reveal maroon scrubs and rubber boots topped with shoe covers.

"Dr. Jones." Bree gestured toward the body and gave her the info on the victim's ID.

Snapping on gloves, Dr. Jones approached the body. She lifted one of the corpse's hands. The muscles in the arm and shoulder resisted movement. She tested the remaining limbs. "Rigor is set." Rigor mortis, the stiffening of the muscles after death, followed a rough twelve-twelve-twelve pattern at ambient temperatures. Twelve hours to stiffen fully, twelve hours to remain locked, and twelve hours for the muscles to release. She lifted the victim's sweater and examined the underside of the torso. "Lividity is fully fixed. She doesn't appear to have been moved since death."

Lividity referred to the settling of blood in the body after the heart stopped beating. Gravity caused blood to pool at the lowest points, creating purple stains on the skin. This process was typically complete in six to eight hours after death. The pattern of lividity on the skin could reveal not only the time since death but also the position of the body in the hours immediately following it. A discrepancy between the staining and the body's position was sometimes the first clue that a victim had been killed elsewhere and dumped in the current location.

The ME used a scalpel to cut a small incision in the torso. She inserted a thermometer to record the body's temperature via the liver. She conferred with her assistant, pulled a clipboard from her kit, and did a few quick calculations. Looking up, she twisted the corner of her mouth and tilted her head. "Considering rigor, lividity, and body temp, my initial estimate of time since death is eighteen to twenty-four hours."

Matt checked the time—it was Tuesday just after noon—and did his own math. "So she died Monday between noon and six in the evening."

Dr. Jones leaned closer to the victim's head. "I expect the cause of death—barring any unusual findings—to be exsanguination caused by the obvious neck slash."

The ME shined her light on the victim's hands, checking the fingertips and nails. "She has two broken nails and a bit of fabric under one of them." Sliding Kelly's sweater sleeves above her elbows, she examined the woman's forearms. "But I don't see any other defensive injuries. She would have been bleeding heavily. Shock and blood loss would have rendered her helpless fairly quickly."

"What about the twisting of her neck?" Bree asked. "That doesn't look natural."

"No." Dr. Jones rocked back, then leaned closer to the neck wound. "The cut is deep, but the angle of the blade was turned. The carotid wasn't fully severed. It appears as if the killer turned her head to open the wound farther."

Matt surveyed the blood-soaked couch. The killer was impatient. "They wanted her to bleed harder, die faster."

"But why the rush?" Bree asked. "Anyone can see that wound is not survivable."

Dr. Jones tilted her head. "She would have died in under ten minutes."

"But that wasn't fast enough," Matt said. "Was it desperation? Rage?" He viewed the arcs of blood on the wall, the flicks from the blade. "I vote rage."

Bree nodded. "Now we need to find out if that rage was random or directed at Kelly Gibson for a specific reason."

"Were they covered in blood when they left?" Matt asked.

Bree pointed to the wall. "There are no interruptions in the initial blood spray. They were standing behind her."

Matt looked down at the expanse of the blood puddle. "But they didn't get away without getting blood on their shoes."

"Any idea what kind of weapon was used?" Bree asked the ME.

Dr. Jones pulled a small flashlight from her pocket and shined it on the wound. "I'll get you precise measurements during autopsy, but you're looking for something thin and sharp." She adjusted the light.

"There's some debris in the wound, but I'm not going to remove it until autopsy."

"Debris? Maybe a tool?" Matt gestured toward the kitchen. "There's a tool bag full of possibilities." He walked into the kitchen to visually inspect the selection. The top of the bag had been left open, its unzipped edges gaping like the wound on the victim's neck. On the outside, fabric loops held pliers, wrenches, screwdrivers, and all the other tools Matt could think of. "Scissors, razor blade, handsaw, knife."

"Not a saw." The ME shook her head. "Not a serrated edge."

Matt made a note to have all the sharp tools bagged and sent to the lab for testing.

Bree propped a hand on her duty belt. "The front door was unlocked, and we haven't seen any sign of forced entry elsewhere. Maybe she knew her killer."

Matt turned back to the family room. "Kelly was sitting on the couch, facing the TV. Let's say the weapon was in the tool bag in the kitchen. The killer grabbed it and walked up behind Kelly." He mimicked the action, walking toward the couch. He raised his empty fist, feigning a grab-and-slash. "All it took was that initial, well-placed cut to take Kelly out."

"*If* that's the way it went down, our killer is right-handed." Bree shifted her feet. The drop cloth was plastic coated on one side and rustled under her boots. "This plastic is noisy. The killer didn't sneak up on her."

"So she probably knew them," Matt added. "If you turned your head and saw a stranger in your house, you'd likely get up to run or face them or something."

Bree continued his thought. "She potentially knew them well enough that she knew they were in the house, and she felt comfortable with her back to them."

Matt envisioned the crime again. He lowered his arm to brush his thigh. "The killer could have held the weapon down and kept it mostly out of sight. As long as Kelly was distracted and not feeling threatened, she might not have noticed."

Bree nodded. "Because if she'd seen the weapon coming down, she would have instinctively raised her arms to block it. We would see defensive injuries. She'd have cuts on her hands, not just a couple of broken nails."

"Yes," Matt said. "Did the killer come here planning to kill her, or did they argue?"

Technically, the answer could mean the difference between first degree murder and manslaughter, a cold and calculated crime versus a heat-of-the-moment act.

Bree shook her head. "If they were arguing, Kelly would have been facing the other way."

Matt pictured the blow coming down. "Then I suppose it looks more like murder."

Across the space, Dr. Jones stepped back from the body. "I'll let you know if I come up with anything else interesting." Her assistant began photographing the body, starting in the far corners of the room and moving toward the victim in a spiraling pattern.

Matt and Bree left them to work.

They spent the next couple of hours searching the house, starting in the kitchen. Matt donned fresh gloves, though he was careful to not touch anything unless absolutely necessary. Bree changed hers as well. Gloves needed to be swapped often at a crime scene to avoid cross contamination between surfaces. Also, everyone scratched an itch eventually. It was important for responders to minimize leaving their own DNA on evidence.

He took in the home as he moved through it. He estimated the house to be thirty years old, based on the neighborhood. Whoever had designed the renovation had stuck to a neutral palette of gray, cream, and white. Matt was no carpenter, but he was handy enough. The work looked to be quality.

The new kitchen cabinets were empty. Boxes were stacked chest high in the walk-in pantry. Labels indicated their contents belonged in the cabinets. Neither the living nor dining room contained anything that seemed relevant. Furniture was covered with dustcloths. Matt doubted the rooms had been used recently. More kitchen supplies were boxed in the two-car garage next to a blue minivan. The vehicle was registered to Kelly Gibson, but they found nothing of interest in it. Given the snow, the vehicle was probably parked in the garage before the murder.

Upstairs was more lived in. Matt ducked into the hall bath, which had clearly been renovated. An electric toothbrush sat next to each of the two sinks. One drawer held shaving gear, acne cream, and an Old Spice deodorant. The rest of the drawers held a billion hair, skin, and feminine products. He looked in the tub/shower combo. On one side of the space, a bottle of Old Spice bodywash stood alone. The opposite side looked like a Bath & Body Works had exploded.

Bree joined him in the hallway. She gestured toward the two doorways. "Looks like two kids, teens or older."

Matt jerked a thumb over his shoulder at the bathroom. "Same in here."

"Lot of empty space in the closets and drawers. College pennants on the walls. Kids are probably away at school."

"Makes sense."

The fourth bedroom had been set up as a home office.

They gave the space a cursory look-through, and then Bree said, "We'll take the laptop and go through the papers in here later."

Matt closed a drawer. "The paperwork looks old. Most people keep records digitally now. The laptop will be more useful."

Bree stepped into the primary bedroom. "I wish we had this much space."

The bedroom they shared at her house was half the size of this one. Every night, they squeezed into a queen-size bed with two large dogs and a cranky old tomcat who hissed if the dogs didn't give him enough room. Sometimes Matt woke with his limbs at odd angles and pins and needles in a hand or foot, his blood flow impeded by a heavy canine head.

Outside, a vehicle door slammed, and voices sounded. The primary bedroom overlooked the street, and Matt peered through the blinds. A county van parked at the curb. "Forensics is here."

"Good."

"We should consider an addition," Matt said. "It's not like we don't have the land."

Bree had inherited her sister's farm when she'd assumed guardianship of the kids. The house was smallish, but there was plenty of space to add on.

"We should." She flipped on the light in the adjoining bath. "Could you imagine having a bathroom this big?"

A quick glance showed him a roomy, gray-tiled room with a freestanding tub and a huge shower. Two mirrored medicine cabinets were mounted over double sinks. Bree opened one. "This one's empty."

Two doors flanked the bathroom. Matt opened one to reveal a walk-in closet, fully outfitted with a fancy organization system. Women's clothes filled shelves and hangers. Luggage was stored overhead. Purses and shoes lined up like colorful soldiers. Matt backed out and tried the other door. The second walk-in closet was mostly empty. A few boxes and a coating of dust occupied the higher shelves. Only a few men's clothing items remained: snow boots, gloves, a parka. "Looks like her man moved out."

Bree appeared at his side. "The neighbor mentioned he'd moved out last spring."

Matt surveyed the items in the closet. "He hasn't needed his cold-weather gear yet."

They went downstairs and stepped out in the damp air. Matt retrieved his jacket and handed Bree hers. Despite the cold wind, the sun shone from a clear and brilliant blue sky, melting snow as its rays spread across the ground. Matt shaded his eyes with a hand. An act of brutality had been committed in this pretty neighborhood with its neatly shoveled sidewalks, barn mailboxes, and lopsided snowmen. Had the killer stopped to admire the twinkling lights on the house across the street? Kelly Gibson hadn't put up any decorations yet. Had she planned to? Would her kids be devastated by her death?

The year before, neither Bree's seventeen-year-old nephew, Luke, nor his sister, Kayla, had shown any interest in decorations. They hadn't been ready to celebrate a typical holiday season, not the first Christmas without their mother. But this year, they both seemed excited. Matt had brought the boxes of lights down from the garage attic the day before. But he was thinking of taking the kids out to select some new things too. Kayla had oohed and aahed over a light-up penguin on a lawn in town. A mix of old and new seemed right.

Did the murder occur while Matt had been enjoying a relaxing family evening? He thought of Kelly's kids, likely away at college. They would never look at the holidays the same way again.

Todd met them on the front porch. From there, Matt could see several news vans parked on the street. Reporters appeared to be giving sound bites with the house in the background. "Deputies have completed their outdoor sweep. They didn't find anything. Forensics is working inside. Real estate records indicate the house was purchased by Harrison and Kelly Gibson twenty-one years ago. The deed is unchanged."

Todd pointed to the house next door. "The elderly lady who lives there hasn't seen Kelly in a couple of days. When I told her what happened, she said it was probably the husband. She isn't a fan."

"Does the elderly neighbor know where Harrison is staying?"

Todd nodded. "She says he's living with his mother. She doesn't know the address, but Kelly once mentioned that her in-laws had a farm and it smelled like shit—literally. Marge found an Elaine Gibson on Rural Route 87. She runs a small chicken farm."

"I know where that is." Bree peeled off her gloves, then stooped to tug off the shoe covers. "It's Tuesday. In case he's at work, do we know where that is?"

"Farris Corporation," Todd said. "On Morris Road."

Matt dropped his own gloves and booties in a receptacle just outside the front door, then headed outside. "Let's go talk to the husband."

"You know what the statistics say," Bree said.

Matt did. Women were usually killed by someone they knew. "There's a reason the significant other is always the primary suspect."

Chapter Four

Bree headed for her SUV as Matt kept pace at her side. She sniffed her shirt. As expected, she smelled like death. "I need to stop at the station for a fresh uniform." Bree had an aversion to smelling like the corpse when informing the family of a loved one's demise.

Matt lifted an arm and sniffed his own sleeve. "Ugh. Same."

"Follow me? We can leave your vehicle at the station."

At his nod, she climbed into her SUV and drove the seven minutes to the sheriff's station. After she parked in the fenced rear lot, she walked through the back door, grateful that the recent renovation had been completed. When she'd taken over the job nearly two years before, the station hadn't had a locker room for women. But then, the department hadn't had a single female deputy either. The former, now deceased, sheriff had been sexist as well as corrupt.

Bree had cleaned house in more ways than one.

She no longer had to change her uniform in the restroom or commandeer the men's locker room if she needed a shower.

Bree's administrative assistant, Marge, stood guard at the office door. Marge was in her sixties, with box-dyed brown hair, a thick cardigan, and sensible shoes. She wrinkled her nose and raised her precisely drawn eyebrows. "I'll bring a fresh uniform to the locker room."

Marge was nothing if not efficient. By the time Bree completed a five-minute shower, the uniform hung next to her locker. Bree dressed, blasted her hair with the dryer for a couple of minutes, then pinned it up still damp. As usual, she skipped makeup. She didn't need to be pretty. She just needed to not smell like a dead body.

When she emerged, Matt was waiting in her office. He smelled like soap, but his reddish-brown hair was short enough that it was nearly dry. A broad-shouldered six three, he was an imposing figure, and the thick, trimmed beard over Scandinavian cheekbones lent him a distinctly Viking look.

Bree stopped to update Marge on her agenda, then she and Matt headed back out to her vehicle.

While Bree drove, Matt used the dashboard computer. "Harrison Gibson is forty-six. He drives a black Corvette. He's accumulated six points on his license with speeding tickets within the last year. His mother, Elaine Gibson, has owned the property for over forty years."

Bree slowed the vehicle. "There it is."

The small farmhouse sat the center of what appeared to be five or six acres of open fields. There was more square footage in outbuildings than in the residence. A large barn, a few sheds, and a detached garage sprawled on the land behind the house. Everything looked to be in working farm condition: function over fancy. A fence surrounded the barnyard and adjacent field. Chickens pecked the ground. A few alpacas grazed among the birds.

Bree cruised down the bumpy driveway.

"There's his vehicle." Matt pointed to a low-slung black convertible parked in front of the garage. "He must hate this driveway."

Next to the sports car sat an ancient pickup truck and a ten-year-old gray Ford Taurus.

"Then he's probably home." She glanced at the computer screen, where Harrison's photo stared back at her. He was clean-shaven, with thinning brown hair salted with gray.

Matt made a disappointed sound. "Sometimes, it's nice to catch them at the office, where their coworkers are on-site to confirm or deny their whereabouts."

"We can't change where he is right now." Bree stepped out. There was no snow left in sight, but the day was damp and cold. The odor of animal waste hung in the air.

She waited for Matt to fasten his body armor vest and join her in the driveway. Typically, he wouldn't wear his vest to perform a death notification, but in this case, the next of kin could also be the killer.

They walked to the front door and knocked. A tall woman in her midsixties opened the door. If Bree had to describe a farmer's wife, Elaine Gibson could be the model. Her sturdy frame was dressed in jeans, a thick wool sweater, and practical boots. Short gray hair poked out from under a knit cap. She tugged on a worn barn coat and joined them on the porch.

She squinted at them. "How can I help you?"

A cold, damp wind swept across the open meadow. Bree shivered. "Are you Elaine Gibson?"

"Yes." Deep crow's-feet framed her clear blue eyes as she assessed them. She didn't seem impressed.

Bree started to introduce herself and Matt. "I'm Sher—"

Mrs. Gibson waved the air. "I know who you are. I've seen you on the news, and you're in uniform." *Obviously* was implied by her tone.

"We're looking for Harrison," Bree said.

Mrs. Gibson buttoned her coat. "Why?"

Bree kept her answer vague. "I really need to talk to Harrison."

"Oh." Mrs. Gibson cocked her head, her eyes narrowed with curiosity for a few seconds, then she poked her head inside the house and yelled, "Harrison! The sheriff is here to see you." She turned back and searched her pockets. "I'm sure he'll be out in a minute. He's on a business call. I have to feed the animals and put the chickens inside before it gets dark. I haven't lost as many to predators since I got the alpacas, but it pays to be careful. I'm a small operation. I can't afford to lose good laying hens."

Curious, Bree had to ask. "How do alpacas help with predators?"

"They'll stomp a fox or coyote to death. Those cute puffballs are wicked protectors," Elaine said.

Bree eyed the placid-looking beast blinking at her from the other side of the wire fence. Between the poof on its head and its long neck, the animal looked like a walking Q-tip. "I would not have thought that." They looked so innocent and chill.

"The wool makes great sweaters and socks too," Mrs. Gibson said.

"How many chickens do you have?" Matt asked.

"About a hundred." She paused at the pasture gate.

"I suppose it's helpful to have your son around to help with the work," he said.

Mrs. Gibson shrugged. "I've been running this farm by myself for a couple of decades. I enjoy my son's company, and he's always willing to pitch in when I need him, but his heart isn't in farming. Plus, I never mind hard work. Farmers don't need to go to a gym." She bent her arm, as if making a muscle under the bulky coat.

"So true," Matt said.

Mrs. Gibson tugged on her gloves.

"How long has he been living here?" Bree asked.

"Since last March?" Mrs. Gibson rubbed her chin. "No, maybe it was April. You'll have to ask him."

"Was Harrison home yesterday?" Bree tried to sound casual.

"Why do you ask?" Mrs. Gibson propped a fist on her hip, clearly onto Bree's attempt to grill her about her son's whereabouts.

When Bree didn't respond immediately, Elaine asked, "Why are you here?"

"Just to ask him a few questions."

Suspicion narrowed Elaine's eyes. "Again, you'll have to ask Harrison. I was busy in the barn all day and not paying attention to where he was." Without waiting for a response, she walked away, passing through the gate toward the barn. The chickens and alpacas flocked to her. As Mrs. Gibson opened the rolling barn door, three cats emerged and serpentined around her ankles. Just like at Bree's farm, all the animals knew the dinnertime routine.

Matt leaned close to Bree's ear and spoke in a low voice. "Well, she was suspicious and vague."

Did her son have something to hide?

The door to the house opened, and a man about six feet tall faced them, Bluetooth earbuds in place, a puzzled expression creasing his brow. Bree recognized him from his driver's license photo, except the gray had disappeared from his hair, as Jeff Burke had surmised. Harrison wore expensive-looking black joggers and a long-sleeve gray T-shirt snug enough to showcase decent biceps. His clothes were not typical farmer attire. They were athleisure.

Despite a small paunch, Harrison seemed to be fairly fit. Standing next to Matt, though, he looked average. Most men did in comparison.

Bree opened her mouth to introduce them, but Harrison held up a douchebag finger, then pointed to one earbud and mouthed, "I'm on a call." Focused on his conversation, he gestured for them to enter and turned back into the house. Bree exchanged a *get a load of this guy* look with Matt as they stepped through the doorway onto worn parquet floors. The house smelled musty, and everything in sight looked like an antique.

A set of french doors stood open to the dining room, where Harrison had set up an office on the fancy old table. "Mm-hmm. Mm-hmm."

Most people were alarmed to have a sheriff knock on their door—alarmed enough to stop what they were doing to find out the reason for the visit.

But Harrison was determined to finish his business first. "Let me research those numbers and get back to you this afternoon." He signed off, then turned to face Bree and Matt. Harrison wore a salesman expression, hopeful and slightly aggressive but also assessing. "You must have the wrong address."

"Are you Harrison Gibson?" she asked.

His brown eyes grew wary. "Yes."

She introduced herself and Matt. "When was the last time you saw your wife?"

"Kelly?" Harrison's pleasant mask slipped for a second, and his eyes shone with irritation before he composed himself again. "I met her at her attorney's office a few weeks ago."

"Do you see her often?" Matt asked.

Harrison shrugged. "Once in a while. We're still working out the details with the divorce."

"Who is her attorney?" Bree asked.

"Kurt Martin in Scarlet Falls." Harrison's eyes narrowed with suspicion. "What's this about? Did Kelly say I did something?" His tone turned defensive.

Bree ignored his question. "Has she accused you of things in the past?"

He didn't answer. Lines bracketed his mouth as he clamped his lips shut, as if he knew better than to answer the question honestly. His gaze shifted to Matt for a few seconds, then back to Bree. "I asked what this is about."

Bree said, "We're here to give you bad news." Unless he hated his estranged wife or resented any financial difficulties the divorce was causing him—then he might consider the news good. "We regret to inform you that your wife was found dead this morning." Bree watched him closely.

His face didn't change, not at all, for several seconds as he appeared to absorb her words. Then his head shook back and forth once. His gaze slipped to Matt, his expression questioning, as if Bree weren't making any sense. "What?"

"Kelly is dead," Matt said without preamble.

Harrison's jaw went slack, and his lips parted. Something flickered in his eyes, a revelation perhaps, some mental puzzle pieces sliding into place. Then he blinked it away. "I can't believe it."

Bree reworded her question. "When did you last speak to her?"

He paused, calculating his answer. Caution shuttered the emotions from his face. They were still standing in the dining room. He took two steps sideways and lifted his phone from the table to scroll. When he spoke, it was clear he'd chosen his words carefully. "We spoke on Friday." He gave no details.

His evasion spurred Bree's suspicion. "What did you talk about?"

"As I said, we're still ironing out the divorce settlement," he said.

More evasion.

Bree shifted course. "What prompted the divorce?"

He shrugged, but the casual gesture seemed stiff. "Empty-nest syndrome? Our youngest left for college, and we realized we were like two strangers sharing a house. We'd been focused on raising kids for twenty years. Kelly and I no longer had anything in common."

His explanation sounded good, though clichéd, but Bree wasn't feeling sincerity. His words felt flat.

Rehearsed?

Suddenly, Harrison took a step backward and eased onto the couch. "I have to tell the kids. How am I going to break it to them?" His words weren't directed at Bree or Matt. It sounded more as if Harrison were thinking out loud.

Ironically, Bree thought these were the first completely honest sentences he'd uttered and the first authentic emotion he'd expressed since they'd arrived.

"Where are they?" Matt asked.

"Sierra is a junior at Boston College. Shane is a freshman at the University of Miami." Harrison opened the calendar app on the phone still in his hand. "They'll both be home for winter break soon. They're in the middle of finals. This news is going to derail their studies."

What the fuck? The death of their mother would devastate most people, especially when the death was violent and shocking. Sierra and Shane were young. Assuming they didn't hate their mother for unknown reasons, this would—or at least *should*—derail more than their schoolwork. Bree had been shepherding her niece and nephew through their own grief for nearly two years. Like Kelly, their mother had been violently murdered. Bree had shielded them from as many of the horrific details as possible, but Grey's Hollow was a small town with the typical gossip chain. Luke and Kayla had had to process more details about their mother's murder than children should have.

Kelly Gibson's kids would have it worse. They were young adults. They would hear it all. If there was a trial, they might attend. They might see the crime scene photos and pictures of their mother's injuries. The trial would traumatize them all over again. And if the case wasn't solved, they'd have to live with the knowledge that their mother's killer was out in the same world as them.

Free.

Free to kill again.

No. Bree would do her best to make sure that didn't happen. She'd do everything in her power to at least give them closure, like she had for Luke and Kayla.

"Maybe I shouldn't tell them until they finish their exams," Harrison said, again seemingly to himself. "It's only another week."

Bree cleared her throat. "It'll be in the news."

Slumped on the couch, he looked up, his eyes blank, as if he'd been so lost in his own thoughts, he'd forgotten she and Matt were there.

Again, it was Matt who said what needed to be said with the bluntness Harrison clearly required. "Kelly was murdered."

Bree was off her game this afternoon. Maybe she needed more coffee.

She suddenly realized Harrison hadn't asked how Kelly had died. Bree had been so distracted by the parallels to her own past that she'd missed his omission. Frustrated, she exhaled. She'd been too connected on her last case and had nearly blown it. She supposed it was better to realize what was happening now and correct for it. *Live and learn.*

"Murdered?" Harrison's voice echoed with disbelief. "I assumed she'd been in an accident or something. Was she, like, mugged?"

Bree said, "She was attacked in her own home."

Harrison sat upright. "Someone broke in?"

"We don't know." Bree wasn't giving him any details at this point. If Harrison had killed Kelly, Bree needed to leave enough slack in the metaphorical rope for him to hang himself.

He fell back against the cushions, dragged a hand through his hair, and breathed out. "Fuck."

That about sums it up.

Bree fired the heavy cannon. "Where were you yesterday between noon and six p.m.?"

Harrison's head snapped up. His nostrils flared. Was he angry? Indignant? He suppressed his emotions with a deep breath. "My girlfriend's two boys had a half day at school. She had to work, so I took the afternoon off and took them to the indoor trampoline park."

"You didn't have to work?" Bree asked.

He shrugged. "I have a flexible schedule. I work in the accounting department for Farris Corp."

Bree nodded, hoping some rapid-fire questions would have him answering without thinking. "And you work from home?"

"Some days," he answered.

"What time did you pick up the kids?"

"School ended at twelve twenty."

"What time did you leave the park?"

Harrison lifted a shoulder. "Around four thirty. I had the boys home by five o'clock."

"What time did you leave their house?" Bree pressed.

"I don't remember exactly. Probably sixish."

"What's your girlfriend's name?" Bree pulled out her notepad and pen and waited expectantly.

Harrison gritted his teeth. "I'd rather not involve her."

Next to Bree, Matt snorted. "That's really not an option, not if you want an alibi."

Harrison gave them another slack-jawed look to note the second surprise of the conversation. "I'm a suspect?" His tone was incredulous.

"At this time, everyone close to Kelly is a person of interest," Bree said vaguely. She tucked the pen into the spiral metal edge of her notepad. "Look, if you have a solid alibi we can easily confirm, then we can check you off our list and move on to other suspects. I don't want to waste time and effort chasing an innocent person."

Her answer seemed to pacify him. He huffed. "Her name is Marina Maxwell." He read off a phone number.

"Thank you." Bree wrote both down. "How long have you been seeing Ms. Maxwell?"

"I don't know exactly." Harrison glanced down at his phone. "Six months or so."

Again, Matt went with blunt. "Were you seeing her before or after your marriage broke up?"

"After." Harrison made the staring kind of eye contact that was a deliberate attempt to sell his answer. One eyelid twitched.

Liar.

Did he realize his phone records would probably give him away? Bree underlined his answer in her notepad and marked it with a question mark.

Harrison rocketed to his feet. "How fast will this be on the news?"

"I can't say for sure," Bree said. "The media usually picks up on murder cases quickly."

Matt frowned. "I would assume the case will at least make the local news today."

Harrison shoved his hand through his hair again. "I have to call my kids. Would you give me time before you contact them? It might take me a couple of hours to get in touch with them. They have to turn off their phones for classes and exams. I don't want them to hear it from anyone else."

The cop in Bree wanted to see or at least hear the reactions from the kids when they got the news. But the parent in her agreed with Harrison. The parent won, but Bree didn't love it. "Yes. I'll give you until tomorrow before I contact them."

Harrison sagged in relief. "Thank you."

Bree remembered Kelly's fuller face in her driver's license photo. Had she been ill? "Did Kelly lose weight recently?"

Harrison nodded. "She started a strict exercise and diet plan about a year ago." He frowned. "It worked. She lost a bunch of weight."

"But?" Bree prompted.

"But she was no fun. None. She wouldn't eat a crumb that she didn't allow in her calorie budget. She completely gave up alcohol. Before that, we used to go to wine tastings and have a nice dinner out once a week. She stopped doing all of that. All she made for dinner was salad or chicken breast and broccoli." He made a disgusted face. "Don't get me wrong. I was the one who encouraged her to get healthier, and I commended her for her discipline, but you have to have some balance, you know? A glass of wine once in a while would have loosened her up. When we first dated, she was a party girl."

Bree made a noncommittal sound.

"I didn't mind that as much as I hated the lectures." He changed to a falsetto, clearly impersonating Kelly. "'Wine destroys your metabolism,'" he mocked. "That sort of thing. I like a nightcap after a long day of work, but Kelly was suddenly a nag about it. She acted like alcohol was the devil." He rolled his eyes.

Bree had grown up with a drunk for a father. For some people, alcohol *was* the devil. Did Kelly struggle with substance abuse? Did her husband not support her efforts to be sober? Or was Harrison a nasty drunk?

"Does Kelly have any friends?" Matt asked.

Harrison nodded. "Yeah. Her best friend is Virginia Hobbs. She's local. I don't have her number. It'll be on Kelly's phone." He straightened. "She was seeing someone new."

"Kelly was dating?" Bree asked.

"Yeah." Harrison's head bobbed. "He has a stupid name. Trevor? No. Troy!" He sneered as he pronounced it.

Troy sounded like a normal name to Bree, but she suspected Harrison was biased. "Did you meet this Troy?"

"No," Harrison said.

"Then how do you know she was dating him?"

"She told me." Harrison's tone turned sullen. "Apparently, he's rich. I guess she wanted me to be jealous or something."

Which is exactly what he seems.

She left him with a final thought. "I'm sure I'll have additional questions for you as the investigation proceeds."

He frowned, clearly not appreciating her parting words.

Outside, Matt strode straight for the SUV. "I love my parents, but I can't imagine living with them as a forty-six-year-old. That is a small house."

"The lack of privacy would drive me up a wall," Bree said.

Matt paused, one hand on the door handle. "He didn't ask how Kelly died."

"Nope." Bree walked around the front of the vehicle. "He could have been so shocked that he wasn't thinking straight. Accidents are common. Murder is not." She slid behind the wheel.

Matt climbed in the passenger seat. Closing the door, he stared through the windshield. "He considered not telling his kids so they could finish their exams. That was either clueless or cold."

"I could believe both." Bree started the engine. "Let's talk to the girlfriend. Can you get her address? I'd rather drop by than call first. Unrehearsed answers are best, when possible."

"He could be on the phone with her right now," Matt suggested.

"Making sure her answers will match his?"

"Wouldn't be the first time."

"No kidding." Bree drove out of the lot toward the station. "How much do you want to bet he's been seeing the girlfriend since before he left Kelly?"

"Not a penny," Matt said. "He was lying so hard when he answered, his pants should have self-combusted."

Bree snorted. "Glad you saw it too."

"And he was definitely jealous of her new boyfriend."

"Ironic, isn't it?" Bree asked. "He left her and now he resents the man she's dating."

"Some guys want to have it all." Matt woke the dashboard computer. "Maybe Harrison didn't ask how Kelly died because he already knew."

Because he killed her?

Chapter Five

Harrison's girlfriend did not answer the door of her little bungalow.

"We'll try again tomorrow." Frustrated, Bree drove to the station, where Marge greeted her with fresh coffee. Bree issued instructions to her deputies and administrative staff, divvying up information-gathering tasks. Warrants needed to be requested for phone and financial records. Background checks would be run on the Gibsons and Harrison's girlfriend, plus the neighbor, Jeff Burke. Something about him didn't sit right with Bree. Now that they had an approximate time of death, they'd need to interview Burke again and get his alibi. Todd was still at the Gibsons' house, working with forensics to finish processing the crime scene.

Matt poked his head through her office doorway. "Do you want me to order dinner?"

Bree glanced at the time on her computer. Almost time for the press con. "No." She pulled a mirror out of her desk drawer. She smoothed her hair. *Good enough.* She pushed her chair away from her desk. "After the press con, I want to go home and eat with the kids. We're waiting on a ton of information. We might as well enjoy one last family evening before the case really gets rolling. We can work from the home office after the kids go to bed."

She faced the press in the station lobby and began with a prepared statement. "The body of Kelly Gibson was found in her home early this morning." She gave only the basic details about the victim.

A reporter asked, "Do you know the cause of death?"

"The medical examiner has not yet completed the autopsy," Bree said. "But the victim's throat was slashed."

Another reporter shouted, "Is this another serial killer? Should the public be frightened?"

Bree chose her words carefully. She didn't want to panic the residents of Randolph County, but she always exercised caution. "We have no reason to believe the crime was anything but personal or that the public is in any immediate danger. That said, we always encourage residents to take care with their personal safety. Lock your doors. If you have an alarm system, use it."

Bree didn't have many details, and the press conference wrapped up in a speedy twenty minutes. She returned to her office to collect her messenger bag. Her desk phone beeped, and the red light from Marge's line blinked. Bree picked up the handset.

"Jager is on her way back." Marge had barely finished her warning when someone knocked on the office doorframe.

"Thank you," Bree said before replacing the handset in its cradle. She turned to face the woman who'd just entered her office and perched in one of the chairs facing Bree's desk.

Madeline Jager led the county board of supervisors. She was a caustic, opportunistic, ruthless politician. She also controlled the county budget, including the funding for Bree's department. With her ultra-thin frame and dyed hair, Matt had dubbed Jager a redheaded Cruella de Vil. The nickname was seared into Bree's brain, but she was trying to abolish it. After many months of being adversaries, Bree and Jager had come to a sort of truce. They weren't exactly friends, but they weren't enemies either. *Frenemies* was probably a better description, but whatever Bree called it, a less antagonistic relationship with the board of supervisors made her job easier. So why the unannounced visit to Bree's office? Jager was obsessed with appearances, and Bree prepared herself for criticism of her handling of the press conference.

"Good press con." Jager's words were a surprise. "I'm glad you took my advice about getting in front of the camera as often as possible."

Bree sighed. "I didn't do it to further my career. I called the press con to inform the public. It's my job."

Jager shrugged. "Tomato, tomahto."

"It's not the same thing at all." Bree didn't know why she was arguing. She'd given the public important information. Jager was pleased for an entirely different reason, but maybe she would stop hounding Bree to make more public appearances. Two birds, right?

So why did Jager's praise feel . . . icky?

Jager asked, "Do you have any other information on her murder?"

"Not much."

"I'm glad to hear the murder was personally motivated."

Bree raised her brows.

Jager rolled her eyes. "Because it means it was probably a one-off. And with a personal motivation, you're more likely to catch the killer."

"No guarantees." But Bree hoped all that was true. She'd like nothing more than to solve Kelly's case quickly.

Jager cocked her head. "If the killer knew the victim, then the link should be in their life somewhere, which sounds much easier than trying to find some rando whack job with zero connection to his victim."

"You make a valid point."

"Good. I have complete confidence that you'll catch this killer ASAP." Jager rocked to her feet with enthusiasm. "You'll keep me updated?"

"Yes." Bree didn't specify how often.

Jager laughed. "I'll call you and check in."

Great.

After Jager left, Bree took two ibuprofen tablets, slung her messenger bag over her shoulder, and left her office. She collected Matt and relayed her conversation with Jager on the drive home.

"Not sure how to reclassify Jager," Matt mused. "It was easier when she was a Cruella."

"Gray areas are harder to pigeonhole, but not having the board of supervisors on my butt 24/7 has been nice."

Matt stroked his beard. "I'm going to hold off judgment. She hasn't earned your trust yet."

"Agreed." Bree turned into their driveway and parked.

She led the way into the kitchen. She and Matt toed off their boots and left them in the tray by the door. Ladybug, Bree's chubby pointer mix, body-slammed her in the knees to say hello. Laughing, Bree shed her coat and crouched to give the aggressively affectionate dog a full-body rub. Ladybug wagged her tail stump. Brody, Matt's former K-9 partner, waited like a gentleman, and offered a polite paw. Matt scratched the German shepherd behind the ear. Bree's black tomcat, Vader, watched with disdain from across the room.

"Hey," Kayla said without looking up from her schoolwork. Hunched over a notepad, tongue between her teeth, she worked her pencil furiously. "I have one more problem, and then I'm done."

Bree remembered the little girl running to hug her at the door in the past, but now she had to be content with the dogs' greetings. The kids were growing up too fast. She straightened. "Where's Luke?"

"Barn." Kayla pointed in the general direction with her pencil.

"Feeding the horses." Dana, Bree's former homicide partner, opened the oven. "You're just in time. Dinner will be ready in ten."

"I'll go help Luke." Matt stepped back into his boots and exited the room.

When Bree had left Philadelphia, Dana had come with her to help with the kids. She'd been retiring anyway and had no plans on what to do with the rest of her life beyond taking some time to decompress from a long career in law enforcement.

Bree went upstairs to change out of her uniform and lock up her weapon. By the time she reentered the kitchen, Kayla had cleared away her books and was setting the table.

Bree grabbed napkins and helped her finish. "How was school?"

"Good. Multiplying fractions is fun."

Laughing, Bree put a hand on her niece's forehead. "Do you feel OK?"

Kayla giggled. "Would you take me to the library after dinner? I need a new book."

The nine-year-old went through books like her seventeen-year-old brother went through food.

Bree checked her watch. "What time does the library close?"

Kayla didn't miss a beat. "Eight."

Bree nodded. "We should be able to make that." She marveled at how much the child had matured over the past few months.

"Yay." Kayla bounced to the counter to retrieve the salt and pepper shakers.

Bree transferred a basket of Italian bread, the butter dish, and a salad from the counter to the table.

Luke and Matt returned from the barn and washed their hands before the whole family sat down to eat. Brody stretched out on the floor a few feet away. Ladybug stayed close to the table, ever hopeful for a dropped morsel. Vader maintained his position. He looked relaxed, but if any of the animals were to successfully steal food, it would be the cat.

For the first five minutes, everyone focused on filling their plates.

Bree should have started with salad, but instead buttered a slice of bread. "How was your day, Luke?"

Luke chewed a shovelful of lasagna. After swallowing, he reached for his milk glass. "I confirmed tours of Boston College and BU for January."

Bree's eyes grew hot. She blinked away the impending tears, covering up the unexpected burst of emotion by drinking some water. "Great. I blocked off that whole weekend on my calendar."

For a change, Luke—not Kayla—did the chattering through the rest of the meal. He was also applying to several other East Coast schools, sticking with the larger institutions because he wasn't sure about a major yet, and he wanted to have options.

She couldn't believe he would be starting college in the fall. While she was happy and relieved to see his excitement, the thought of him moving away left her with an onslaught of conflicting emotions she was having trouble processing.

She'd taken this parenting/guardianship job under the worst possible circumstances: her sister's murder. The kids' biological father was worse than useless. Not only had he not had anything to do with them for most of their lives, he was a criminal currently serving time for fraud. The first few months after Erin's death had been hell on all of them. Juggling her own grief and helping two young kids navigate the loss of their mom was the hardest thing Bree had ever done. And soon she'd have to let go of one of them.

She suspected that might be just as hard.

Clearing her throat, she packed away her feelings until her therapy session later in the week. Luke was not her therapist. It wasn't his job to handle her emotions. He should be able to enjoy his journey with no guilt over Bree's sadness. She would not ruin this for him. She would deal with her own shit.

She'd always known that parenting was the hardest job in the world, but until she'd actually been responsible for the well-being of two young humans, she hadn't appreciated the sheer amount of sacrifice it would require.

After dinner, Dana stood and brushed her short, gray-and-blond hair back from her face. "I have a date. Someone else will have to do the dishes."

"We're going to the library." Kayla shoved back her chair and sprinted out of the room.

"Luke and I have got this." Matt stood. "Tell Nolan hey for me."

Dana was currently in a relationship with Matt's older brother.

"Thank you." Bree helped clear the table while she waited for Kayla.

Matt gave her a look. "You don't have to thank me for possessing and performing basic life skills. If you're going to thank anyone, make it my mother, who insisted I be self-sufficient."

The little girl returned, lugging a loaded tote bag, the weight of which rendered her lopsided.

Bree relieved her of it. How did the kid even carry it? "This bag weighs as much as you do." They donned coats and went out the back door. "How many books do you have in here?"

"Seven." Kayla skipped toward the SUV. "If I don't like one, it's good to have another ready. I always have a book with me. Just in case."

"In case of what?"

"An emergency." Kayla fastened her seat belt. "Actually, I like to have two books, in case I finish the one I'm reading."

"I get it. I was a bookworm when I was your age."

Bree drove to the library, barely ten minutes away. She took Kayla's hand to cross the parking lot. As they walked through the sliding glass doors, Bree had a flashback that weakened her knees. Bree was maybe eight. She looked up. Her mom had her by the hand. She was young and beautiful, smiling down at her. Bree could feel the warmth of her mother's palm. Hot air from the heat vents near the door blasted on her cold cheeks. A sudden chill swept over Bree as she knew—somehow—that this memory was from shortly before *it* had happened.

"Aunt Bree?"

Bree shook herself.

Kayla stared up at her, her thin face scrunched in a slightly quizzical expression. "Are you OK?"

"Yeah." Bree almost brushed it off. No. Memories of her mother had been surfacing over the past months, and not just the nightmare ones of the night she'd died that had haunted Bree her entire life. The night her father had murdered her mother, then turned the gun on himself while Bree hid her younger siblings under the porch. She waited for the nightmare to take over. For the shock of the first gunshot, the panic of trying to suppress her baby brother's cries, listening for the sound of his boots, the terror of waiting for him to find them.

To kill them.

But this time, the recollection of her mother's death didn't immediately block out all other memories. She could still feel the squeeze of her mother's fingers, hear the sound of her voice as she said, *Go on to the kids' section. I'll catch up.* Horror didn't take over. Bree's brain simply let her experience a good memory, a bit of her childhood that was actually pleasant. She'd forgotten most of those moments.

She gave Kayla's hand a little squeeze. "I used to come to the library with my mother when I was your age."

"Really?"

"Yep. I loved books. To me, they felt like friends." Bree's childhood had been a violent storm to weather. Her father's unpredictable rage had rolled in like thunder, and his fists had lashed out as quick as lightning.

"They *are* friends," Kayla said, obviously delighted with the comparison.

For much of Bree's childhood, before and after *it* happened, books had been her only friends. She'd hidden herself in their pages, taken refuge in their worlds, escaped her own miserable life.

"I'll return these." Bree lifted the bag. "You only have about thirty minutes until closing. Do you know what you want?"

"Yes!" Kayla skipped across the worn commercial carpet.

Bree stacked the books on the return counter and exchanged a polite greeting with the librarian as she collected the books. Bree turned to look for Kayla, and her eyes fell on a cluster of tables in the center of the space. She could clearly see her mother sitting at one of the tables. An older woman sat across from her. The woman had a file open in front of her. The two women were bent close, clearly having a hushed and hurried conversation. Bree's mom kept raising her head and looking around, her posture that of someone waiting to get caught.

Was she afraid Daddy was going to find her? That he'd followed her? Daddy's voice played inside Bree's head. *You be back by eight, you hear?*

Her mom's face snapped around, as if she felt eyes on her, her own eyes full of fear, like a prey animal. Relief relaxed her features as she spotted child-Bree and stood. The older woman leaned across the table and said something, grabbing Bree's mom's jacket sleeve to stop her from leaving. The child-Bree would not have recognized the urgency in her body language, but the adult-detective Bree did. Her mother shook her head and brushed off the woman's grip. The older woman sat back, disconcerted, frustrated.

Worried.

"I'm ready, Aunt Bree." Kayla's voice startled Bree out of the memory, but she held on to it. The little girl shoved a stack of books onto the checkout counter.

"You have more books than you returned."

"I know!" Kayla grinned.

Bree carried the heavy book bag to the SUV and drove home. They went in the back door. The scent of lasagna lingered in the warm kitchen.

Kayla tossed her jacket at a peg on the wall and missed. "I can't wait to start my new book."

Bree hung her own jacket and retrieved Kayla's from the floor.

Kayla lugged her even heavier bag of books toward the steps.

Bree called after her, "Shower first!"

Once Kayla started reading, the child lost all track of time.

"OK." The child thundered up the steps, her footfalls sounding more like those of a mini horse than a small human.

The kitchen was empty. Luke's light had been on, so he was probably studying. Dana wasn't home yet. The dishwasher hummed softly as Bree made a cup of tea and headed for the home office.

Matt sat behind the desk, hunched over his laptop. "How'd it go?"

"Good." Bree told him about the memory.

Matt leaned back, his brows knitted. "What do you think it means?"

"I don't know—yet. Maybe nothing." But she instantly knew dismissing the memory was the wrong move. It had resurfaced for a reason. "But somehow it felt . . ." She searched for the right word. "Significant. I can't explain why."

"You don't have to," Matt said. "It's a decades-old memory. Does it matter how long it takes for you to sort out what it might mean?"

"No, and good point. It can marinate for a while." She sat down in the chair facing him and opened her messenger bag to slide her own laptop onto the other side of the desk. "What are you doing?"

"Basic google and social media searches on Kelly and Harrison Gibson. Jeff Burke and Marina Maxwell are next."

"Find anything interesting?"

"Possibly." He stroked his beard. "I can't find Kelly on social media at all, and I've tried the four major services."

"What about Jeff Burke?" Bree asked.

"No social media," Matt said.

"Makes sense, considering his distrust of technology."

"Yep," Matt said. "But that isn't the most interesting thing."

"No?"

He shook his head. "The woman Harrison has been dating? Marina Maxwell? She's been his social media *friend*"—Matt emphasized the word with air quotes—"for over a year. There's even a picture of them together."

"Which is several months before he and Kelly split up," Bree mused. "So, your *liar liar, pants on fire* suspicion was accurate."

"I have a knack for smelling bullshit." Matt closed his laptop. "I wonder what else Harrison could have been less than truthful about."

"Once someone lies, it's hard to believe anything they say."

Chapter Six

Wednesday morning, Matt started a whiteboard for the case in the conference room. The task didn't take long. They had little information, except likely cause and time of death. They had only two suspects so far: Kelly's estranged husband, Harrison Gibson, and her neighbor Jeff Burke. He added both names to the board, plus *unknown new boyfriend, possibly named Troy.*

Bree came in carrying a notepad and a fresh mug of coffee. Todd entered the room, laptop in hand, and sat at the table. Fidgety, Matt preferred to pace. He capped the marker and tapped it on his palm.

"Where are we with background info?" Bree asked.

Todd opened his laptop. "Let's clear the kids first. We verified that both are currently at school. Sierra is in Boston, and Shane is in Miami."

"Let's eliminate them as suspects," Bree said. "But we should also verify neither flew recently, and we still need to talk to both of them. I'll make the calls. They might have knowledge of their mom's life she wouldn't share with anyone else. We'll check in with Harrison to find out when they're coming home. I would expect them to come back immediately once they get the news, but you never know."

Matt didn't ever like to think someone's kids could kill them, but he'd seen it happen. He'd seen a lot of things happen he wouldn't have believed before he started his career in law enforcement. He wrote Sierra's and Shane's names in the interview column. He added Virginia

Hobbs beneath the kids' names and tapped on the name with the marker. "We also need to question Kelly's best friend."

"Let's drop in on her today," Bree agreed. "Forensics finished processing the scene, and the ME expects to complete the autopsy this afternoon." She turned to Todd. "We need to call Kelly's attorney, Kurt Martin, in Scarlet Falls. He'll be privy to divorce details. Did anyone check Kelly's doorbell camera?"

Todd nodded. "The battery was dead. We're charging it now. We're still canvassing the neighborhood, but no one's front door lines up with Kelly's except Jeff Burke's, and he said he doesn't do technology. The warrants are in. We've requested phone and financial records on Kelly and Harrison Gibson, Marina Maxwell, and Jeff Burke. Criminal background checks are clear on everyone. Rory figured out Kelly's phone passcode in about five minutes. We found Kelly's dating app, Date Smart, which shows her connecting with a man named Troy. Their in-app messaging progressed and then they exchanged actual phone numbers. Their conversations then migrated to calls and texts. The number she communicated with is registered to a cell phone belonging to Troy Ryder from Scarlet Falls."

"Troy Ryder sounds like a Disney character." Matt was very well versed in Disney lore, having watched many, many movies with Kayla since he'd moved in with them.

"What were the nature of these texts?" Bree asked.

"Mostly romantic." Todd scrolled. "Troy first appears on Kelly's phone about six weeks ago. Their calls and texts grow more frequent from then on. Of course, we don't have any content for phone calls, but recent messages are telling." Todd jabbed a finger at his laptop. "But, on Sunday, there are six unanswered calls from Kelly to Troy. He phoned her back that evening, and they had a call that lasted just over six minutes. Afterward, Kelly texts him five times that evening and twice Monday morning. Troy doesn't answer any of her texts."

"What do her messages say?" Matt asked.

"Of the seven, four are nonspecific apologies. The other two are *please call me*. The final text is *How could you do this to me?*"

"Was he ghosting her?" Bree mused.

"Maybe they had a fight, or he broke up with her," Todd suggested.

"Inquiring minds need to know." Bree motioned to the board. "Troy Ryder is next on our interview list. Do we have an address?"

"We do." Todd read off a rural route number. "He doesn't have a criminal record, and he's lived at the same address for seven years. He does have one social media account, which he uses sporadically. There is one selfie of him with Kelly from a few weeks ago outside a café. He didn't tag her, though, because her only social media account has been deactivated since last summer. You can't even see her account unless you're signed into it." He turned the laptop around to show them a photo of Troy with Kelly. They were both wearing knit hats and holding take-out cups.

"So, she didn't have any other male connections via social media," Matt said.

"Correct," Todd confirmed.

"Did Kelly communicate with any other people on the dating app?" Bree asked.

"Not beyond quick, in-app introductions. Troy is the only person she gave her actual phone number to."

"Then let's go talk to Troy Ryder and Virginia Hobbs." Bree stood and stretched.

"Let's not forget Marina Maxwell either." Matt capped his marker. "Troy first?"

"Definitely," Bree said.

On the drive, Matt looked up Troy's motor vehicle records. "Three vehicles are registered in Troy's name: a Rivian SUV, a Porsche 911 GT3, and an Audi A8. Considering the fancy sports car, his driving record isn't too bad. Two speeding tickets in the last two years."

When the GPS announced they were approaching their destination, Bree slowed the vehicle.

A long driveway spilled onto the road just ahead. Matt pointed. "There it is."

She rolled closer, then stopped the vehicle. The morning sun reflected off the house windows. Matt squinted through the windshield at a contemporary two-story home built in front of a thick patch of woods. The place looked gorgeous and expensive, with a three-car garage, tons of windows, and a partial stone facade. "Looks like Troy has some money."

"How many acres?" Bree asked, tapping on the wheel.

Matt checked the real estate record. "Twelve."

The sound of an engine broke the quiet. Matt followed the noise to the house, where one of the overhead garage doors rolled up. A blue Porsche 911 GT3 rumbled out. The door rolled closed, and the Porsche zipped down the driveway toward them.

"Oh, good. We caught him before he left," Bree said.

Sunlight bounced off the windshield, obscuring Matt's view of the driver. "I see a shape behind the wheel. The driver looks tall."

But the driver couldn't *not* see the sheriff's vehicle. Matt expected the car to stop and wait to see what they wanted.

It did not.

Bree turned on the lights and gave the siren a quick blast to notify the driver to stop, but the Porsche kept coming.

"What is he doing?" Bree asked.

"Not stopping," Matt said.

"We'll see about that." With a huff, Bree turned into the driveway, blocking the vehicle's exit. But the Porsche didn't slow. The engine revved. The sleek blue car swerved around them, cutting a swath through the wet grass. The rear end kicked out on the slick surface. Chunks of frozen earth flew from the tires. But the driver whipped the front tires back into line, and the car veered back onto the pavement. The vehicle shimmied with a quick fishtail before accelerating again. Tires squealed as the small car turned onto the main road, in the opposite direction from which Matt and Bree had come.

"He's making a run for it!" Matt checked the map on his phone. "He's headed toward the state forest." He grabbed the chicken strap and held on.

Bree slammed the SUV into reverse, backed onto the road, and shifted into drive. She stomped onto the gas pedal, reached for the radio mic, and called in the chase to dispatch, hoping other surrounding law enforcement officers would aid in the pursuit.

Releasing the mic trigger, she asked Matt, "Do you have the plate number?"

Matt took the mic and relayed the information. Unfortunately, they were in Grey's Hollow, which had no local PD, and there weren't any patrol deputies close enough to cut off the Porsche's escape should it evade Bree.

Which looked likely. The car was already barely a blue speck in the distance. A sheriff's car had extra horsepower and could outrun most standard vehicles, but the 911 GT3 was a racing model. It was as quick and agile as a thoroughbred. The SUV felt like a plow horse in comparison.

Over the next half mile, the speed limit dropped as the road narrowed, trees closing in on both sides. Patches of black ice shimmered where the light broke through the canopy.

"He'd better slow down," Bree said as a wicked curve forced her to ease off the gas pedal.

Far ahead, the Porsche disappeared around another curve in the road.

"I'm not going to catch him." Bree's knuckles whitened as she steadied the wheel.

"That car doesn't exactly blend." Matt tightened his own grip as the SUV slowed, then leaned into the curve. "He can't get far. The troopers will pick him up when he hits the interstate."

"Let's hope." Bree straightened out the SUV and accelerated. The SUV leaped forward toward the next wicked curve. She steered through the dogleg.

Matt squinted. About a quarter mile in front of them, the road took a sharp left. Matt spotted long black skid marks on the blacktop. He tracked their trajectory beyond the hairpin turn, to something blue in the trees. Sunlight glinted on metal. "Hold up!"

Bree slowed as they reached the bend. "He crashed!"

The Porsche had overshot the turn, skidded off the road, and slid down the embankment. The car was wedged at the base of a huge pine tree. A tree trunk pinned the passenger door closed. The driver's-side door stood open. The collision had buckled the hood, but the impact didn't appear to be devastating.

Bree called it in as she steered onto the shoulder, stopped the SUV, and shifted into park. Matt reached into the back seat for his body armor. He'd been caught unprotected in the past. Never again. He had too much to live for—his days of taking chances were over.

Bree exited the SUV. Matt did the same. While he fastened the Velcro straps of his body armor around his torso, Bree rounded the vehicle and removed the AR-15 from the back. She handed it to him and drew her own sidearm. He had no confidence in his aim with a handgun, but he could shoot a long gun just fine. Hefting the rifle, Matt scanned the sports car. His line of sight didn't allow him to see inside. He pointed to his left. Bree nodded, drawing her weapon as they approached the Porsche. Matt walked in a wide arc to get a view of the driver's seat. Empty. The vehicle cockpit was so small, there was nowhere for a person to hide.

"It's clear." He turned his attention to the woods, then dropped his gaze to the ground, which was still spongy in the low-lying area. Footprints led into the woods.

"I see them." Bree touched her lapel mic and updated dispatch. The closest deputy was nine minutes out. They couldn't wait. Troy would get away.

Matt led the way into the trees. Within a few yards, the ground rose and dried out. Pine needles covered the forest floor, and the footprint trail disappeared. "There's no more trail."

Matt stopped and listened. Wind rustled through branches overhead. A small animal scurried in nearby underbrush. The trees were spread out with plenty of open space. Troy Ryder could have gone in any direction.

"This is pointless. We need help."

"We need a K-9," Matt said. In search situations, a dog was worth a hundred men. Matt had personally selected the Randolph County K-9, and Greta was a truly skilled animal. If there was a scent to find, Greta would be on it.

"Definitely." Bree used her radio to summon the K-9 unit and to put out a BOLO alert for Troy Ryder.

Matt spent the time scouting the surrounding area for any sign that a human had run through the trees, but he found nothing. Crouching, he examined and then photographed the footprints, using an evidence marker to provide scale.

"Deputy Collins is on the way with Greta," Bree said.

Matt straightened. "The snow is too wet for the footprints to be useful. No detail. No point in trying to cast them. Can't even determine the exact size. They'll be gone entirely in another half hour."

They made their way back to the Porsche. Matt bent over to survey the cramped cockpit. A deflated airbag draped across the steering wheel. "I don't see any blood."

A piece of cloth lay bunched up on the passenger floor. Something brown poked out. Matt pulled gloves from his pocket and tugged them on. He snapped a photo. Then he crawled in and began unwrapping the bundle.

Bree crouched, leaning into the car. "What did you find?"

"Not sure." Matt lifted a corner of fabric, which looked to be a long-sleeve T-shirt. A dark-red substance stained the heather-gray material. Matt didn't need a rapid stain kit to know the substance was blood.

He carefully unfolded another layer, making sure to not touch the actual item inside, revealing an orange box cutter. A dark-red crust coated the razor-sharp edge and streaked the handle.

"Possibly—probably—the one used to kill Kelly Gibson," Bree said.

"Yeah. My bet is that he was driving out to the wilderness to dispose of the murder weapon."

Chapter Seven

Fifteen minutes later, two patrol vehicles and the K-9 unit rolled up. With pride, Matt watched Deputy Laurie Collins unload the black German shepherd. Matt had found Greta through his sister's canine rescue. Intelligent, driven, and highly energetic, she'd been returned to the rescue for being too difficult to manage. Luckily, the same qualities that made her a poor choice for a house pet also made her an excellent working K-9.

Greta loved nothing more than going to work.

Bree circled up with the team. "I've requested a warrant to search Troy Ryder's residence. Hoping to have that in hand shortly." A deputy had been sent to babysit the house while they waited for a judge to sign off on the electronic form. Bree assigned another deputy to record the Porsche and its accident scene with both photographs and video. "The vehicle will be flat-bedded to the county garage, where forensics will take charge of it. We found a box cutter that we believe was used to kill Kelly Gibson in the vehicle. This accident is a secondary crime scene. Treat it as such. Let's get an image of Troy Ryder out. I want every LEO in the state looking for him."

Matt sincerely hoped the rich dude couldn't buy his way out of the country.

Bree issued a few more instructions while Collins outfitted Greta in her working harness. Once harnessed, the dog's posture changed instantly, becoming hyperaware, excited even. Collins let the dog sniff the inside of the vehicle. Greta picked up the scent immediately, shooting off into the woods. Collins ran behind her, trying to keep up. Matt and Bree jogged after them, giving the dog enough space to work unimpeded.

Greta passed right through the spot where the footprints disappeared. She veered right, away from the road, deeper into the woods. The air turned colder. A thin coating of snow remained in areas the sun's warmth never reached. Matt checked the GPS on his phone. They'd already covered at least a mile. Nearly thirty minutes had passed since the Porsche had crashed. Matt could cover a couple of miles of wooded, flat terrain in that time. He expanded a blue splotch shaped like a potato on the map. "Blackbird Lake is ahead."

"Maybe he'll get boxed in," Bree said in a hopeful voice.

The dog kept up a steady pace. The trees opened up onto the weedy banks of a lake. Matt emerged from the darkness. Shielding his eyes, he scanned the water. The wind rippled the surface and stirred up tiny whitecaps. Sunlight glittered on the chop like diamonds.

Bree stepped up next to him. Hunching against the blustery wind, she said, "There's not much development or activity on this lake."

"It's one of the smaller ones," Matt agreed. "Full of stumps too. It's fishable from a canoe or kayak. Not good for power boating."

Trees grew within a few feet of the lake. Matt turned to survey the shoreline. The ground was spongy at the water's edge. The half-frozen mud sucked at his boots. A thin sheet of ice cracked as he moved onto drier ground.

Greta paused to sniff in a circle, then followed the scent along the edge of the trees. The suspect was clearly trying to stay out of sight and not leave footprints. The shoreline turned back toward the woods. A short, rickety dock jutted fifteen feet onto the water like an arthritic pinkie finger. Greta sniffed her way onto the wood and stopped. She lifted her nose into the air and inhaled deeply. Then she moved to the edge of the dock, sat, and turned to give Collins an eerily intelligent stare followed by a thin whine.

"The trail ends here." Collins pulled a stuffed hedgehog from the cargo pocket of her pants. "Good girl." She tossed the toy into the air.

Greta caught it half-heartedly. She'd done her job, but the dog preferred to find the person she was trailing.

"Maybe he stole a boat or canoe or something," Collins suggested. Greta bit down on the hedgehog, making it emit a long, disappointed squeak that seemed to express how they all felt.

"That's the most likely explanation. We'll talk to the owner of this dock," Bree said.

Matt glanced over his shoulder. The woods were winter-bare, and he could see the outline of a dark-brown cabin through the trees. Smoke curled into the sky from the chimney. Someone was home.

Bree propped both fists on her duty belt and stared out over the lake. "I don't see anyone."

Matt scanned the visible shoreline but saw nothing. "Me either, but he has a thirty-minute lead on us."

"How far can a person paddle in thirty minutes?" Bree asked.

"Depends on the person." Matt squinted, looking south. The shoreline curved, forming little coves. In places, the trees grew right up to the bank. "Plenty of places to drag a canoe or kayak ashore and hide it. We're not far from the state forest. Also, the interstate is ahead. He could call someone for a ride."

"He could be anywhere." Bree drew out her phone and studied the map app. "The lake is too big to walk around the entire thing. Time to let technology do some work for us."

"The drone?" Matt asked.

"Yep." She put the phone to her ear. "I'll put Juarez on it. He loves the toys."

So did Matt, but he admitted that the young deputy had mad drone-flying skills. Matt studied the lake's wind-whipped surface. "Have him start downwind."

Bree nodded. "That's the way I'd go if I wanted to get as far away as possible."

◆ ◆ ◆

Two hours later, Matt, Bree, Todd, and Deputy Zucco gathered in front of Troy Ryder's house with a signed search warrant. Matt held the battering ram. Juarez was still searching the lakeshore with the drone, but so far, he'd found no sign of Ryder or a small vessel. The cabin owner, a man in his early seventies, had confirmed his kayak had been on the dock earlier that morning and now it was gone.

The K-9 unit had remained at the lake in case they were needed to follow a trail.

"With the discovery of the box cutter in his vehicle, Troy Ryder became our prime suspect." Bree pointed to the house. "And this is an additional crime scene."

The house was newish, with a partial stone front and tons of windows. The sun's reflection on the glass blocked any view inside.

"I don't see any people moving inside," Bree said. "Do we know if anyone else lives here with Troy?"

"No one else is on the mortgage or deed," Todd said.

"We couldn't see the driver, so we aren't a hundred percent positive it was Troy behind the wheel." Bree circled a finger in the air. "Todd, you and Zucco go around back just in case someone tries to exit. Check all doors and windows for signs of forced entry."

"Are you thinking it wasn't him in the Porsche?" Todd asked.

"All indicators point toward Ryder, but we need to be thorough and not assume anything," Bree said.

Todd and Zucco headed for the corner of the house. After giving them a few minutes to get into place, Bree and Matt walked to the front door and flanked the doorway. Bree pressed the doorbell. Inside, a loud chime sounded. Matt spotted a security camera discreetly mounted under the eave.

When no one answered, Bree knocked loudly. Facing the camera, she called out, "Sheriff's department. Please answer the door."

Nothing.

"We have a warrant to search the premises," Bree shouted.

The house remained silent.

"We're going in." Bree reached for her lapel mic and updated dispatch and the deputies watching the back of the house.

Matt swung the battering ram, hitting the door next to the dead bolt. The door popped open. No one shot at them.

Bree signaled for Collins to move in with the dog. Matt set down the battering ram and swung his AR-15 into position. His heart did a slow roll in his chest. Then he and Bree moved into the house as a team, exactly the way they'd drilled dozens of times.

Not that he was expecting to find the killer in the house. Ryder was probably deep in the state forest on the other side of Blackbird Lake. Matt slung the rifle strap across his chest anyway. He'd been shot before, and he had no desire to repeat the experience. Better to be prepared for the unlikely worst-case scenario than be caught unprepared.

A library and sitting room flanked the foyer. No clutter and minimal furniture made the rooms easy to clear. Neither looked like anyone ever used them. A hallway led to a huge great room. A white leather sectional faced a linear gas fireplace. No one was hiding under the couch or behind the matching chair.

From the great room, they moved into a modern kitchen. Matt skirted the stainless-steel island. Opening a door, he aimed his rifle into a walk-in pantry. Expensive small appliances and clear containers of cooking staples were lined up in neat rows on the shelves like British soldiers during the Revolutionary War.

They made quick work of the home office and a book-lined study. The attached garage held a black Audi. "No workbench, no tools. I've never seen a garage this clean." He tested the rubbery floor with his boot.

A row of cabinetry spanned the far wall. None of the cabinets were large enough to hold a human being.

"It's freaky, isn't it? Our kitchen isn't this neat." Bree leaned over to peer inside the Audi sedan.

Matt itched to search every nook and cranny, and they'd get to that stage of the search after the property was cleared.

They returned to the house and went up a fancy, open staircase. The primary bedroom was pristine, as were the three guest bedrooms on the second floor. Matt checked the walk-in closet, which had a freaking granite island in the middle. "Troy Ryder isn't home."

Bree holstered her weapon. "But I would kill for this closet." She sighed. "Not kill, but there are *things* that I would do."

Matt snorted. "It's bigger than our bedroom."

Bree said, "I don't have enough clothes to warrant this gorgeous space. My uniforms would just look sad in here."

"Efficient, not sad." Matt pictured his wardrobe of jeans and T-shirts, plus a row of identical tactical cargo pants and sheriff logo polos. He owned a couple of suits and a tux. What else did he need?

They left the bedroom and headed downstairs.

"Nothing is out of place. It's creepy." *Like living in a museum.* Even when Matt had lived alone, he'd had tufts of dog fur tumbleweeding down the hallways and random, slobbery KONG toys scattered on the furniture. Now, in Bree's crowded house, the kids left their mark everywhere. And they weren't just regular kids—they were farm kids. Most of their clothing was covered in dirt, hay, and/or horse hair. The dogs were in and out, running through the barn and pasture, and back inside. The floors were muddy. The furniture was covered in fur. Big dogs sprawled everywhere.

Their house would never be clean, and Matt wouldn't have had it any other way. Dirt was healthy, right? He hoped so.

He and Bree entered the great room.

"I don't see an alarm panel," Matt said. "Or cameras or motion detectors inside."

Bree paused to examine a window. "No alarm contacts."

She led the way out of the patio door. Todd and Zucco were emerging from the monster shed.

Todd jerked a thumb over his shoulder. "Clear."

Bree turned to scan the rear exterior of the house. "He had a camera on the front door, but we didn't see an alarm system, and I don't see any surveillance out here either."

They returned to the front of the house. In the driveway, Bree checked her phone screen. "We need to start searching the premises for any evidence that Troy killed Kelly. Whoever killed her didn't walk away completely clean."

A soft whirring sound drew their attention to the driveway. A large, utilitarian gray SUV cruised toward them, an electric vehicle from the sound of the engine. The vehicle drew closer. It was a Rivian.

"That's Troy's vehicle." Matt started toward it.

The SUV parked next to the sheriff's vehicle. A tall man with a long, trimmed beard and short cropped hair stepped out. Matt recognized Troy from his driver's license photo. He wore a black down jacket, a gray T-shirt, and faded jeans. The tailored clothes fit like he was walking a runway. But his shirt was wrinkled, as if he'd slept in it. Blood oozed through a bandage on his forehead. Around the white bandage, the skin was darkening into the beginnings of a bruise. Matt pictured the crime scene. Had Kelly swung something at him when he slashed her throat? He didn't remember seeing anything Kelly could have used to defend herself. Maybe Troy took it with him?

Troy reached into his jacket chest pocket.

Bree drew her gun. "Stop right there. Let me see your hands."

Troy froze. His head tilted in confusion. "What?"

"Let me see your hands!" Bree moved closer.

Matt circled to the left to surround Troy.

"This is my house!" Despite his protest, Troy did as instructed. He slowly removed his hand from his pocket to show a cell phone. Then he raised both hands in front of his body in a surrender position.

Nodding at Matt, Bree kept her weapon trained on Troy.

Matt stepped forward and patted down Troy's pockets. He found a wallet and a key fob. "He's clean."

Bree slid her gun into its holster.

"What is going on?" Troy lowered his hands but didn't move otherwise.

Bree introduced herself and Matt. "We need to take you to the station to answer some questions."

But Troy didn't budge. "What is this about?"

"Kelly Gibson," Bree said.

Troy tilted his head. "What about her?"

Bree tried to brush off his question. "Let's finish the task at hand, then we'll have a discussion."

But he was not having it. "No. I want to know now."

Bree's chin dipped in a curt nod. "How well do you know Kelly?"

Troy's face went blank until it was devoid of emotion. "We've dated," he said vaguely. "Why? Has she done something?"

"Why would you automatically think she did something wrong?" Bree asked. Why wouldn't he assume something had happened *to* her?

Troy drew his chin inward, clearly regretting his words. But he didn't bite on Bree's response. "What is this about?"

Bree hesitated. Matt wondered if she would just say it or continue to evade giving Troy the reason for their visit. There was a tricky line to walk when interviewing suspects. You wanted them to be open. So you needed to appear to be honest as well. But the news of Kelly's murder might make Troy less likely to share information. Technically, it was legal for cops to lie to suspects, but it wasn't always the best idea to do so. On the other hand, if Bree continued to press him and simultaneously withhold the knowledge of Kelly's death, Troy could be resentful and extra wary when he discovered she'd been willfully holding back that information. He might feel like they'd been lying to him in an effort to set him up.

With a man like Troy, who was clearly smart, Matt would be up front. Wealthy, successful people weren't intimidated by the law. Annoying a man like Troy could result in him shutting down this interview and calling his attorney. And face it, this guy could afford the best. He could hire an army of lawyers.

Bree must have read him the same way, because she said, "Kelly was murdered."

"What?" Troy's entire body stiffened. He shook his head a single time, as if clearing it.

"Her body was found yesterday," Bree added without giving too many details.

Still confused, Troy lowered his brows into a solid, disbelieving line. "That doesn't seem possible."

"There's no mistake." Matt broke into the conversation. "She's dead."

Troy took a minute to absorb the information, but he didn't seem sad at the news that the woman he'd been dating was dead. In fact, shock was the only emotion he'd exhibited. Maybe he would be upset when he'd had a chance to process her death?

"When did you see her last?" Bree asked.

"Last week." He scrolled on his phone and opened a calendar app. "I had dinner with her last Thursday night. We went to Café Aldi's in Scarlet Falls."

"Did you go back to her place afterward?" Matt asked.

Troy didn't answer. Was he too smart? Or did he have something to hide? He appeared oddly cool and composed, but Matt sensed there was a lot going on beneath the surface. Troy returned his phone to his pocket without responding to Matt's question.

"Did you communicate with Kelly since your date?" Bree asked.

"Yes," Troy said after only a slight pause. "We talked on the phone Sunday."

Bree pushed. "What was the nature of the call?"

Troy scanned her face, then turned to search Matt's. Did he suspect they already knew? "I'm not going to answer any more questions without an attorney."

And that was that.

Chapter Eight

Defense attorney Morgan Dane brushed a coffee cake crumb off the skirt of her navy-blue suit. Her husband, private investigator Lance Kruger, appeared in the doorway of her office. "Busy?"

He had blue eyes, blond hair, and the body of a Hollywood action star. He looked a little like Brad Pitt but bigger and buffer. How did he end up with her? Morgan was as athletic as a newborn giraffe.

She waved a hand over her legal pad full of notes. "Not drastically. The prosecutor received his continuance on the Johnson case."

"Good." Lance walked into her office. "Because I need a favor."

She smiled. "Anything."

He rounded her desk and planted a kiss on her mouth, one of the perks of working in the same building. She rented an office from Lincoln Sharp, Lance's PI boss. Since she often required PI services, the situation was ideal. Plus, she loved having her husband close all day. She considered herself to be a very lucky woman. Not just because Lance was a total hottie, but because she'd found true love twice in her life. Most people never found it once. She'd been widowed years before, her soldier husband dying overseas and leaving her with three little girls to raise on her own. She'd trudged through a deep depression before coming out on this side. Then Lance came into her life. Now she intended to make the most of every moment of her second chance at happiness.

"Did you see the news about that woman who was murdered in her home the other night?" Lance didn't sit. "I just got a call from a guy on the hockey team, Troy Ryder. He's at the sheriff's office. They want to question him about her murder." Lance played in an adult hockey league and coached in a youth hockey league for underprivileged kids. "He needs a lawyer."

"Right now?"

"Yes."

Morgan rose, swept her notes into her drawer, and locked it. "Does he know not to answer any questions until I get there?"

Lance nodded. "I told him not to say a word to anyone."

"Good." Morgan changed the flats she wore in her office for a pair of heels. After donning her suit jacket, she grabbed her giant tote bag, shoved her flats inside, and headed for the door. "Let's go. You can tell me the rest in the car."

Lance grabbed his jacket and her black overcoat from the closet. Since his boss was out of the office, Lance locked up on their way out.

He drove while she touched up her makeup. Her attention to her looks wasn't *pure* vanity. She'd learned long ago that the way she presented herself mattered. A put-together appearance was interpreted as successful and confident, which translated to competence in the public eye. Her suits were tailored. She wore classic jewelry: a single strand of pearls and tiny gold hoop earrings. She checked her hair. Since she'd been to court that morning, it was bound in a smooth and elegant chignon. Not that Sheriff Taggert—Bree—would be impressed by Morgan's accessories. Morgan knew the sheriff professionally and personally. Bree's niece was the same age as Morgan's oldest daughter.

As a sheriff, Bree was all business. Morgan would always remain wary—a defense attorney and a law enforcement officer were in an adversarial relationship by design—but she respected the sheriff for her integrity and intelligence. Bree wasn't driven by arrogance or ego. She would be tough but fair.

But the media would most likely be pursuing the latest development in the murder case, and Morgan always wanted to show the press her cool, competent, kick-ass defense attorney persona.

"There's not much to tell." Lance headed out of Scarlet Falls toward the neighboring town of Grey's Hollow, where the sheriff's office was located. "It didn't seem like Troy knew all that much about the case, other than the woman he's been dating for about six weeks was found murdered and he feels like he is the prime suspect."

"Did the sheriff say that?"

"I don't know."

Morgan doubted it. Bree would be careful with her words. "That doesn't necessarily mean they have evidence against Troy. The spouse or boyfriend is always on the primary suspect list when a woman is killed." With good reason. Statistically, more than half of female murder victims were killed by an intimate partner. Men were more likely to be killed by strangers.

Lance continued. "The call was quick, but he sounded worried, which is not like Troy at all. His nickname on the team is Iceman."

"That's a *Top Gun* reference, right?"

"It is."

Morgan considered the movie. "Is he as arrogant as the character?"

"No, he's more introverted than arrogant. But he's able to keep his cool to an annoying degree."

"So not impulsive or violent?"

"He didn't lose his cool if we lost or anything, but he wouldn't hesitate to deliver a hard body check either."

She zipped her makeup bag and stuffed it back into her tote just as Lance turned into the sheriff's station parking lot. "How well do you know him?"

"We play hockey together, go for beers occasionally with the team, but we aren't best bros." Lance paused. "Troy can be aloof when you first meet him. He's awkward in social situations and with new people. Once you get to know him, he warms up."

"I'm assuming he's single if he's dating," Morgan said. "Do you know if he has ex-wives or ex-girlfriends?" If an ex would vouch for him . . .

"I don't know."

"What do you talk about when you hang out?"

Lance lifted a shoulder. "Mostly sports."

"If I had drinks with a group of women, we would know all about each other's families within an hour."

As Morgan expected, media vans clogged the parking lot at the sheriff's station. She slipped out of the passenger seat and into her role. She strode across the asphalt, her strides long, her head high, her game face firmly into position.

The reporters swarmed her before she reached the door. She stopped as microphones were shoved at her face.

"Ms. Dane, is Troy Ryder your client?"

They already know Troy's name.

"Yes." Morgan turned to face the press. "You'll have to give me some time. I haven't met with my client yet today. I'll give you a statement after I do." With that, she turned toward the sheriff's station. Lance stuck close, always prepared to clear a path for her, but the reporters gave her room.

The sheriff's staff recognized her, and she was quickly ushered into an interview room. Lance paced while Morgan removed her coat, took a legal pad and pen from her tote, and sat patiently. A few minutes later, a deputy escorted a tall, bearded man into the room.

"The sheriff will be in shortly." The deputy withdrew.

Morgan sized up her client. His clothes were understated but pricy. He was not handcuffed, and he carried a bottle of water in one hand. He did not appear to be under arrest. But then, forensics and autopsy reports wouldn't be completed yet. It would take time for the physical evidence to be processed.

Lance shook hands with him and introduced him to Morgan. Troy didn't look worried. Instead, his face was blank—no, detached. He rested his folded hands on the table like they were in a stock portfolio meeting. "I didn't do anything to Kelly." His eyes narrowed, his voice remained low and level.

Wishing her client were showing some sadness or shock at the death of the woman he'd been dating, Morgan glanced at the camera in the corner of the ceiling. The light was red. Off. Not that she thought the sheriff would intrude on her client meeting. But it paid to be careful.

He stared at her, the directness in his gaze almost disconcerting. "You're going to get me out of here today, right? I can't stay in jail. I have money. I can pay."

Money always helped, but her new client needed a dose of reality. "If the sheriff had enough evidence to arrest you, she would have. But don't get cocky. She's going to ask you questions. If I don't want you to answer, I'll stop you. Keep your answers short and to the point. Don't elaborate. Do not offer any additional information."

Troy didn't move, but he was clearly thinking.

"Tell me what happened today," Morgan said.

"There's nothing to tell." He shifted backward, resting his hands lightly in his lap, as if he were in a board meeting instead of a police interview. "I was out at my cabin at Blackbird Lake. When I drove home, the sheriff was at my house."

"You don't know why?" Morgan asked.

"She said the woman I've been dating, Kelly Gibson, was murdered."

"You didn't know about it before she told you?" Morgan asked.

"No."

A knock sounded, the door opened, and Bree walked in. Morgan switched positions to sit at Troy's side, and the sheriff dropped into the chair facing him, setting a notepad on the table in front of her. Lance retreated to lean on the back wall. Taggert read Troy his Miranda rights, had him sign an acknowledgment, and listed interview attendees' names for the record.

Instead of waiting for the sheriff to initiate the interview, Morgan took the offensive. "Why is my client here?"

Bree began. "The body of Kelly Gibson was found yesterday at approximately ten thirty a.m. At the scene, the medical examiner determined the time of death to be between noon and six p.m. on Monday."

Morgan took notes. "Cause of death?"

"The autopsy is currently underway," the sheriff said. "But her throat was cut."

Troy made a choking sound.

"The autopsy isn't complete?" Morgan's pen stopped moving. She lifted her brows. "Again, why is my client in the sheriff's station when you don't even have a solid cause of death? Did the ME even confirm the death is a homicide?"

Though throat cutting was a rare method of suicide, it wasn't impossible.

Bree said, "Dr. Jones agrees that Kelly Gibson was murdered. If you saw the pictures, so would you."

Morgan didn't react, but she knew from the tone of the sheriff's voice that the death had been particularly terrible.

Bree continued. "Troy has exchanged calls and text messages with Kelly for the past six weeks, and he confirmed that he was in a romantic relationship with her."

Before he realized he should call an attorney.

Bree consulted her notepad. "On Sunday morning, Kelly's phone shows six unanswered calls from Kelly to Troy. He phoned her that evening and they engaged in a six-minute conversation. Later, Kelly sent text messages that Troy did not answer."

Troy sat completely still. "I turned off my phone."

Morgan brushed his arm, a silent *shh* as she responded to the sheriff. "And what do those messages say?"

"Four apologies, two requests for a call back." Taggert glanced down at her notes again. "The last message Kelly sent Troy reads, *How could you do this to me?*"

Morgan didn't comment. The messages suggested an altercation of some sort between Kelly and Troy, but she wouldn't put ideas in Bree's head. "And how did we get from a few text messages to my client being detained?"

"We went to your client's home to conduct an interview," Bree said. "A Porsche 911 GT3 registered to Mr. Ryder drove out of the garage and refused to stop when signaled to do so." She described the pursuit and finding the crashed vehicle. "Inside the Porsche, we also found a box cutter with a dried, dark-red substance on the blade. Footprints showed where the driver ran into the woods. Our K-9 followed the trail to Blackbird Lake but lost the scent on a dock. The owner of the dock confirmed his kayak was missing. We searched with a drone, but we haven't found the missing vessel."

Blackbird Lake. Where Troy owned a cabin. *Not good.*

"No one saw the person steal the kayak?" Morgan confirmed.

"Correct."

Morgan appreciated that Bree provided the facts without added drama or conjecture. "Did you see the driver of the Porsche?"

"No," Bree admitted.

Two points to Morgan.

Except this wasn't a courtroom, and Bree was immune to subtle theatrics. Morgan knew from experience that the sheriff played the long game. This interview was a scouting maneuver.

Morgan needed to throw real doubt on Bree's arguments. "Then how do you know it was my client?"

"Who else would it be?" Bree asked Troy.

"Whoever stole my car," he said.

"Your house doesn't show any signs of a break-in," Bree responded.

Morgan interrupted. "It isn't my client's job to prove his car was stolen. He was driving his other vehicle at the time. How could he have driven away from his house in his Porsche, then returned to it in a different vehicle?"

Bree stared at her for a few seconds.

"And if he was running from the police, why would he return to his own residence?" Morgan asked.

"That's a question for your client." Bree turned her focus toward him.

Troy remained completely still. "Because I wasn't running from anything. I was just going home."

"Where were you Monday and Tuesday?" the sheriff asked.

"I own a cabin on Blackbird Lake. I go there for at least twenty-four hours every month. Sometimes I manage a couple of days. Once every summer, I take a solid week off."

When Troy told Bree about his cabin on Blackbird Lake, her eyes lit up in a way that Morgan didn't like at all. Yes. It was conceivable that Troy had escaped the crash of his Porsche, run to his cabin, and—unwilling to run away from his very nice life—returned to his primary residence later in the day ready to lie his head off.

"What's the address of your cabin?" Bree asked.

Troy supplied the house number and street.

Bree and Matt Flynn exchanged a look, and Matt left the room. Morgan guessed he was going to request a warrant to search the cabin.

The sheriff leaned her body a hair forward, focusing on Troy again. "Do you have any proof you were at this cabin?"

"Proof? Why do I need to prove where I was?" Troy's voice held no inflection.

"A strong alibi would clear you." Bree waved a hand. "Make all this inconvenience go away."

Troy's tone shifted slightly as he enunciated words with extra clarity. "I go to my cabin to be alone and unplug."

"Unplug?" Sheriff Taggert asked. "As in get away from your electronics?"

"Yes." Troy nodded. "No phone. No computer. No Wi-Fi."

"You do this every month?" she asked.

"Not always on the same days, but yes." He lifted his chin. "I make maintaining my mental health a priority the same way I exercise my body daily. I schedule the downtime on my calendar."

"What if one of your clients needs you?" Bree asked.

"They can wait a day," Troy said. "I require solitude. It's just the way I'm wired. In my business, I'm connected all the time. It's important to clear my mind. Like a battery, it won't perform optimally unless properly recharged."

Bree arched a single, skeptical brow. "And you didn't encounter anyone at your cabin? A neighbor, a delivery driver, another person walking in the woods?"

Troy stared back. "I saw a woman when I was out trail running."

"Can you describe her?" the sheriff asked.

He closed his eyes. "About thirty. Blond. Ponytail. She was wearing black tights and jogging on the trail around the lake."

Bree made a note. "You don't know her name or where she lives?"

"No," he said. "I've never seen her before."

"Do you usually run that trail?" Taggert asked.

"Yes," Troy said. "It's a three-mile loop. I run it every day when I'm at the cabin."

Bree tapped on her notepad with the pen. "Do you know any of your other neighbors at the cabin?"

He shrugged. "I would recognize their faces, but I don't know their names. I go there to get away, not to talk to people."

Bree tilted her head. "Where do you work?"

"I'm self-employed as a cybersecurity consultant." Troy's posture straightened almost imperceptibly. "I have an office in my home. Because of that, I need to leave it to truly have time off."

Morgan wanted to object and to stop the interview, not because his answers were damning but because he was almost robotic. He had the emotional control—or suppression—of a monk, but underneath that rigid facade, Morgan sensed a lot was happening, that his almost disconcerting lack of emotional response was a mask.

Bree nodded. "So, you were at your cabin, with no communication. Kelly called you on Sunday?"

"Yes."

"Why did she call you?" Bree asked patiently.

He blinked twice, the first sign of any real discomfort. "She said she was pregnant."

But Bree didn't pause. She probed. "Did she take a test?"

He paused for a few seconds, not moving, just staring. "I don't know. That's all she said."

"You had sex with her?" Bree confirmed.

Again, Troy hesitated before replying. Was he thinking about his answer? "Yes."

"How long ago?" Bree asked.

"The first time was about four weeks ago. Then again last Thursday night."

Four weeks would be just barely long enough for a pregnancy test to be positive.

"If she's pregnant, it isn't mine," Troy added.

Bree raised a brow. "And you know this because . . ."

"I had a vasectomy fifteen years ago," he said.

Morgan had not seen that coming. Clearly, neither had the sheriff, because silence ticked off a few heartbeats.

Troy looked away. His face remained blank, but Morgan could see the sorrow buried deep under his facade. "I was married. My wife had a congenital heart defect that made pregnancy very dangerous. So I had a vasectomy." His gaze dropped to his folded hands. "We were going to adopt, but, uh"—he paused with a sound that was half cough, half choke—"her heart gave out."

"I'm sorry for your loss," Bree said.

Without lifting his gaze from his own hands, Troy nodded. He wasn't completely a robot.

Bree cleared her throat. "So what did you say to Kelly?"

"I told her I can't have children." Troy's animatronic voice returned. When he raised his gaze, he'd regained his composure. "Then I went to my cabin as planned."

"You left?" Bree asked.

"Yes." He looked confused. "I needed to process what she'd told me—what her claiming to be pregnant meant. She was either lying or she'd been with someone else. Given that we haven't been dating very long, I'd hope that occurred before we met, but who knows? It's not like I've never been cheated on before." He said this in the same disconcerting monotone.

Morgan nudged him to stop elaborating.

But Bree picked up on the jealousy motive immediately. "Did you feel betrayed?"

"No." Troy swallowed, then seemed to brace himself before continuing. "Of course I was hurt. She lied to me. But we didn't have a long-term relationship, and we didn't have fireworks or incredible chemistry. I doubt the relationship would have lasted much longer."

Except for the moments when he'd talked about his late wife, Troy's lack of emotion made him hard to read. But to a stranger—or a jurist—his flat personality suggested he could be a good liar. Or a sociopath.

Morgan ended the line of questioning. "The autopsy will tell us if she was pregnant. If she is, DNA will determine who the father is. Speculating is fruitless."

Bree now has potential jealousy or betrayal as a motive.

Bree acknowledged her point with a nod, then turned back to Troy. "Did you read the messages she sent you while you were at the cabin?"

Troy shrugged. "No. I always lock my phone in my truck. I told her I wouldn't be available until Tuesday. I don't know why she kept messaging me."

"Your getaway cabin is awfully close to your home," Bree commented.

"It's convenient," Troy said.

"What do you do there?" the sheriff asked.

Troy said, "Fish, chop wood, run the trails, read. I have a stand-up paddleboard for summer."

"I don't see where that's relevant," Morgan said.

Bree gestured toward Troy's bandage. "How did you injure your forehead?"

"I ran into a low-hanging branch," he said.

Taggert looked doubtful. "You didn't see it?"

"No." Troy flushed. "I was watching that blond woman."

Bree switched gears. "Were you driving your Porsche earlier today?"

Troy said, "No."

"Where do you keep the vehicle?"

"In my garage."

"Does anyone else have a key to your house?"

"No."

"There was a keypad on your garage door. Does anyone have the code?" Bree asked.

"No one," Troy said in a firm voice. "And I change the code every week or two."

Bree tilted her head. "Do you have house cleaners?"

"Yes, but they don't enter my house unless I'm there, and I don't leave them unattended."

"Do you watch them every moment they're in the house?" Bree asked.

The question seemed to throw Troy off his game. "I don't follow them around, if that's what you're asking."

Bree made a notation, then tapped her pen on the pad. "So who else could have been driving your Porsche?"

"I don't know." He shrugged. "I guess someone broke in and stole it."

"There was no sign of a break-in," Bree pointed out again. "And you don't have a security system."

Morgan held up a hand to stop Troy from responding. The interview had already covered the basics. This was a rehash. "We're not speculating. My client has told you where he was and explained Sunday's phone calls and texts with Kelly. He has nothing to add at this time." Morgan shoved her legal pad into her tote.

The door opened, and Matt Flynn returned. He whispered in Bree's ear. She looked up. "We have a search warrant for the cabin. If you provide a key, we won't have to damage your door."

Morgan had known it was coming, but *damn*.

Troy stammered, "You can't—"

Morgan silenced him. "They can. Do you have a key?"

He couldn't stop the search. Bree might not have enough evidence to arrest him at this time, but she could show probable cause for a warrant. There was no point in protesting.

Reluctantly, Troy pulled a key ring from his pocket. He selected a key, worked it off the ring, and handed it across the table.

"Thank you." Bree accepted it.

If Troy was telling the truth, then the cabin wouldn't hold any incriminating evidence. But the case already suggested that someone had broken into his full-time residence, stolen his car, and planted the murder weapon in it. Had someone been in his cabin as well?

Even if the box cutter found in Troy's vehicle *was* the murder weapon, the official autopsy and forensic reports would take time. Time that Morgan would use to conduct her own investigation. Bree would be pursuing all evidence to solve the murder. Morgan could concentrate on leads that concerned Troy.

Everyone rose. Bree tucked her notepad under her arm. "Thank you for your cooperation."

She was always a professional, which was refreshing. Morgan wouldn't have to worry about Bree pulling something underhanded. But if she thought Troy was guilty, she would go all in to prove it.

Morgan said nothing else to Troy until they were in the parking lot. The media clogged the sidewalk. Morgan let Lance part the sea of reporters.

A short woman slipped under his arm. "Are you a suspect, Mr. Ryder?"

With some clients, Morgan would allow them to make a quick declarative statement of innocence, acting indignant at the suggestion that they were guilty. But Troy's aloof attitude might not play well. She stepped in front of him and leaned closer to a mic. "Everyone in the life of a murder victim is naturally questioned. I wouldn't respect an investigator who didn't talk to all of the people currently close to Ms. Gibson. My client is fully cooperating with the sheriff's department. Mr. Ryder wants nothing more than justice for Kelly. Our thoughts and prayers are with the Gibson family as they grieve."

With that, she herded Troy away from the microphones, tucking an arm around his shoulders as if he too were grieving and needed support. When they were out of range, she leaned close to his ear. "Did you drive here or did the sheriff escort you?"

He nodded toward an SUV at the rear of the lot. "I drove."

Good for him for not letting the sheriff intimidate him into a patrol car. The optics were better if he came and left under his own power. One photo of Troy in the back of a cop car would imprint his guilt in the minds of the public—all potential members of a jury.

She said, "Don't talk to anyone about the case. No one at all. Not your mother, your best friend, or your trusted mechanic. All questions are to be deflected with 'My thoughts are with Kelly's family. I hope the sheriff's office finds her killer and brings them to justice.' Do you understand?"

"Yes." But his jaw tightened as he said it, indicating he didn't like her instructions. Or perhaps he didn't like being told what to do. "I didn't do anything wrong, but it feels like I'm already on the defense."

"That's because you are," Lance said. "But Morgan is the best, so do what she says."

"It doesn't seem right." Troy shook his head. "What now?"

"You come to the office. We'll take care of paperwork, my retainer, et cetera, and review more details while the sheriff's office finishes searching your house."

He opened his mouth to complain, but Morgan shut him down. "I'll examine the warrant itself in case there's any cause to have evidence thrown out." But Morgan doubted that would happen. Sheriff Taggert was thorough with paperwork and very good at her job. "But you need to stay out of their way. After they're finished, you go home. Lay low. No press. No social media, and as I said before, no talking to anyone about the case. That includes emails and messages. I don't want you running around town, where people will ask you questions."

"But I didn't do anything wrong," he protested. His voice rang with disbelief.

"I know, but contrary to what the Constitution says, we need to prove that you're innocent. Otherwise, you might avoid prison, but Kelly's death will follow you for the rest of your life."

His face paled and he nodded. "I'll stay at home. I won't talk to anyone. It's mostly what I do anyway."

"I'm sorry about your wife," Lance said.

Troy folded his arms across his chest. "I'm not good with people, but she didn't care." For a few seconds, his grief played across his face. Then he wiped it away. "I have to go."

They climbed into their vehicles, and Troy drove off.

Morgan fastened her seat belt. "You didn't know about his wife?"

Lance kept one eye on the rearview mirror. "No. Look, he's amazing with computers, but social skills are not his strength. He's not a people person, but he gives a ton of money to the youth foundation. He practically supports the youth hockey team."

"I get it." Morgan toed off her heels. "But I hope we don't go to trial, because an inability to elicit empathy from a jury could sink him."

Chapter Nine

Bree parked in front of Troy's cabin on Blackbird Lake. "It really is a cabin. I don't know what I expected, but this isn't it."

Matt snorted. "Same. His other house is swanky. This is . . . not."

Usually, when someone with a ton of money owned a cabin, the home turned out to be a mansion made of cedar or logs. But this was a small, squat house built of actual logs. A wooden rocking chair sat on the long, covered porch that spanned the front of the building. Wood chips surrounded a tree stump. Next to it, split logs were stacked waist high. They walked behind the cabin, where a rear deck overlooked the lake. A paddleboard was lashed to the back deck.

"How many houses are in the area?" she asked.

Matt pulled out his phone and opened his map app. "Maybe four or five within two square miles."

"A neighborhood canvass seems ridiculous, but I'm going to send a deputy to those houses and see if anyone saw Troy."

"The blond woman?" Matt asked.

"Or anyone else. Just because Troy didn't see anyone doesn't mean no one else noticed him." Bree called Juarez and assigned him the task.

Matt went to the window. Cupping his hands over his eyes, he peered inside. "This is basic. There's a wood fireplace and lots of books. No TV. He really does rough it out here."

They returned to the front door and used the key to unlock it. Both donned gloves as they stepped across the threshold. The cabin was one big, open space, except for a rustic bathroom. A well-worn recliner sat next to a packed bookshelf. The kitchen was as basic as basic got: fridge, stove, and an old-fashioned percolator coffee maker. A king-size bed occupied the far corner. A single chest of drawers next to it served as both nightstand and dresser. She lifted the lid of a small clothes hamper. Empty.

Bree slid open a drawer. Black crew socks and boxer briefs. Jeans, athletic pants, and sweaters filled the rest of the drawers. The bathroom held a few towels, deodorant, and a single pump dispenser of a combination body wash, shampoo, and conditioner. A stackable washer and dryer had been stuffed into the back corner. The lid of the washer stood open. Bree peered inside. Empty.

She left the room. "That's basic."

"Same out here." Matt leaned into the open fridge. "Stocked with condiments. No perishables."

Bree turned to the short row of kitchen cabinets. She found cleaning supplies under the sink. A small closet held a few jackets and a vacuum cleaner. "This place is spotless."

"Do you think he cleans it?" Matt asked.

"We'll have to ask him." But Bree suspected Troy didn't want strangers in his retreat space.

Through the window, Bree saw the forensics van park. They watched the techs suit up and enter the cabin.

"This won't take long," one said.

"We'll let you get to work."

With such a small area, Bree and Matt would only get in the way. If there was any evidence to be found, it would likely be trace or microscopic anyway. The techs split up.

"Ma'am?" one called from the bathroom before Bree made it to the door. She crossed the wood floor and peered into the bath. The tech was under the sink, looking in a small trash can. A few balled-up paper towels lay in the bottom of the can, stained with blotches of dark red.

"Could be where he cleaned up the cut on his forehead," Matt said.

"Could be," agreed Bree. "Or this is where he cleaned up after the murder. Make sure you check the washer and dryer and drains for more blood." Laundering bloody clothes left residue that was very difficult to completely eliminate.

A half hour later, Bree led the way into the Pilates studio owned by Kelly's BFF, Virginia Hobbs. The machines looked like medieval torture devices. There wasn't a class in session. A lean woman with a rag and spray bottle looked up as they entered.

Bree introduced herself and Matt. "Thanks for talking with us."

Virginia's long, lithe body was showcased in black workout tights and a loose tank. She was in her midforties and had the body of a person who worked hard to stay in shape. She sprayed liquid on the machine and wiped it down. "I don't have another class until this evening, and I'll do anything to catch the bastard who killed Kelly."

"How long have you been friends?" Matt asked.

"Decades." She set down the bottle and rag and folded her arms across her chest. "We met when our kids were in kindergarten."

"Did Kelly express any unusual concerns lately? Was she afraid of anyone?" Bree asked.

Virginia angrily swiped a tear from her cheek. "Just Harrison. He's been harassing the hell out of her."

Bree rested a forearm on her duty belt. "What about?"

"He wanted the house sold ASAP. He couldn't move out of his mother's place and continue to keep the mortgage current."

"But the place is in mid-reno," Matt said.

"Yes, and that's all Harrison's fault. After he left, Kelly was forced to do most of the work herself. He stopped putting money in their joint account and refused to give her any. She wanted to recoup the maximum profit from the sale. Unlike Harrison, she didn't have other income. He wanted money now. She needed the sale price of the house to be as high as possible."

"She never worked outside the home?" Bree asked.

Virginia's nostrils flared. "No. Harrison liked her as a stay-at-home mom. She liked being at home too, but the reality of the situation is that after she devoted their whole marriage to caring for him, their children, and their home, he dumped her for a younger version as soon as she wasn't young anymore. Such a cliché. She thought he would always look after her. I kept my mouth shut because it was none of my business. But I never liked the way he treated her."

"Why not?"

"Because he was very controlling. The whole time they were married, she had to account for every nickel she spent. I don't mean asking if they could afford a major expenditure like a car or a vacation, I mean she had to submit an itemized accounting each month, complete with receipts, for every purchase from milk to prescription copays."

"Was she a big spender?" Bree asked.

"Hell no!" Virginia's eyes brightened. "She was the most frugal person I've ever met. If couponing was an Olympic sport, Kelly would have won the gold medal."

"You said she was doing the renovation work herself?" Matt clarified. "Did she have the skills for that?"

"Yes." Virginia nodded emphatically. "Kelly's dad was a contractor. She hired people when she had to for specialty work like tile and granite or anything that required a license—like electrical. But she could do basic carpentry and plumbing herself. Harrison doesn't know a saw from a screwdriver." She punctuated her anger with a forefinger stab in the air. "She didn't have a paying job outside the home, but Kelly always worked her ass off."

"Are her parents still alive?" Matt asked.

"No, her dad had a heart attack a few years ago, and her mom passed within six months of his death." Virginia looked sad. "It was hard on Kelly. Plus, if her dad was still alive, he would have helped her. She wouldn't have been so desperate for cash."

Money was a definite motive, thought Bree. "Harrison mentioned her strict diet. He said she wasn't fun anymore."

"Ass," Virginia muttered, rolling her eyes. "Kelly knew her marriage was falling apart. Harrison was working late too much and acting disinterested in her. He would make remarks about her 'letting herself go.' She was scared. She didn't have the means to support herself. She was convinced he was cheating and going to dump her. Around the same time, she was depressed and drinking too much. At her annual physical, her doctor told her she was headed for a major health issue. Her cholesterol, blood pressure, and sugar were all too high. So, Kelly—being a woman of action—decided to do something about that. She came to me for help." Virginia gestured around her studio. "She started taking Pilates classes. I helped her come up with an eating plan. She quit drinking completely. The weight began to come off, but more importantly, she started to feel better. Her next round of bloodwork showed improvement. She got a new haircut. She started getting dressed in real clothes every day. She looked amazing. It wasn't the physical changes as much as the confidence. You'd think Harrison would be happy, right? His wife was healthier and happier."

"Right," Bree said.

"I'm guessing he wasn't," Matt added.

Virginia pointed at him. "Bingo. Instead of complaining about her weight and negative attitude, he started bitching because she wasn't *fun*. He gave her a hard time about not drinking. Like, who does that? I mean, Kelly knew she'd been using alcohol as a crutch and that it would be so easy to slide right back into her old habits. She told me she wasn't able to have just one glass. Not ever. For her, booze was a trigger. His lack of support in improving her health really hurt her, even more than the suspected cheating. He made her medical issues about himself. For years, she blamed his lack of sexual attraction on her appearance." She exhaled in an angry puff. "Then after she transformed herself, he found other ways to find fault with her. In my opinion, he was abusive, not physically, but emotionally. He put her down continually. In the past, she accepted his criticism and blamed herself, but when she stopped drinking, she realized what was happening. She wanted to leave him at that point, but she didn't have any income. She was looking for a job when he left her."

"How did she react?" Bree asked.

"Who wants to be left? And even though she saw the end of her marriage coming like a subway train, she was still depressed about it. *But,* after he was out of the house, she realized how much happier and relaxed she was without him." Virginia's eyes misted. She sniffed and wiped a palm across her face. "She called me one day. She'd just been to the doctor. Her blood pressure had dropped like, twenty points. Even with the emotional turmoil of the breakup and her financial worries, her stress levels were still lower. She said she used to crave alcohol every night, just before he usually came home from work. That his impending arrival elevated her stress. And now, that was gone too. She started talking about house flipping after the current house was done and sold. She thought she had a knack for it. She was starting to live her best life." Virginia's voice broke. "I'm sorry. It's just that she'd been through so much, and her life was just getting on a good track."

"It's OK. We understand." Bree gave her a few seconds to recover. Once she'd composed herself, Bree resumed her questions. "When did she start dating?"

"She spent the first few months happily alone. Then she got on one of the match apps just for fun. Took her a couple of months to get up the nerve to go on a date."

"Did she date men other than Troy?" Matt asked.

"No, he was the first and only one that I know of. They haven't been seeing each other that long." Muscles rippled as Virginia lifted a shoulder. "She liked him, but she wasn't enamored, if you know what I mean."

Bree nodded.

Virginia continued. "He was her rebound relationship. I don't think it would have lasted."

Which is what Troy said.

Bree asked, "Did she say anything to you about being pregnant?"

"What?" Virginia's arms dropped to her sides.

"So, that's a no?" Bree asked.

"That's a definite no." Virginia toyed with a lock of hair. "But now that you mention it, she was out of sorts over the weekend. She didn't come to class. Said she had a headache. I texted her to ask how she was feeling, and she didn't respond. That wasn't like her. I assumed it was because of what Harrison had done earlier in the week and that maybe she just needed a little time to decompress, but I should have checked in with her again." Regret filled her eyes. "I had a flat tire on Saturday. It took half the day to get a new one. Threw off my whole weekend." Tears overflowed her eyes. "I should have made time for her. I knew something was off. I should have stopped to see her."

"What did Harrison do earlier in the week?" Bree asked.

"He was waiting for her in the parking lot when she finished class."

"You saw him?" Matt asked.

Virginia pointed through the glass front of the studio. "Right out there. He'd parked next to Kelly's minivan."

"You're sure it was him?" Matt asked.

"I'm sure. I know that smug face." She rolled her eyes. "Plus, that midlife crisis on wheels is hard to miss."

"Did they argue?"

"I don't know. He looked mad. I opened the door and yelled to Kelly, asked if she needed help." Virginia shrugged. "She waved me off and said it was OK. But I stood there at the window where he could see me until he left."

"How long did they talk?" Bree asked.

"Just a couple of minutes." Virginia chewed on her lip. "Kelly looked more annoyed than upset, but I should have called the cops. He wasn't supposed to bother her."

"We didn't see a restraining order," Bree said.

Virginia shook her head. "She didn't think it was necessary. But I feel like I let her down. It's my fault she's dead." She stifled a sob by pressing a fist to her lips.

"If she didn't have a restraining order and you had called the police," Bree said, "they wouldn't have been about to do anything except tell him to move along. He didn't break the law."

Virginia sniffed.

"The only person responsible for Kelly's death is the person who killed her," Matt said.

But Virginia didn't look convinced.

"Do you have surveillance cameras in the parking lot?" Matt asked.

"Yes. Do you want me to copy the video for you?"

"Please." Bree remembered the neighbor, Jeff, saying he'd seen Kelly and Harrison argue. "Did they have any specific arguments recently?"

"Yes. A little while ago, she changed the locks on the house, and he was so, so mad." Virginia lifted her chin. "I was proud of Kelly for finally shutting him out. Why should he have the keys to a house he didn't live in anymore?"

Why indeed?

They went into the back office, where Virginia found the parking lot surveillance video showing Harrison confronting Kelly in the parking lot the previous Tuesday. The video didn't include sound, but it confirmed her story—and his lie.

Back in the SUV, Bree asked Matt, "What do you think?"

"I think we have two very strong suspects."

"Same."

Chapter Ten

Marina Maxwell lived in the smallest single-family home Bree had ever seen, but she had to give Harrison's new girlfriend credit: The place was immaculate and cozy. A wooden reindeer and a light-up snowman occupied a front lawn the size of a basketball court.

Bree parked at the curb and looked over at Matt. Rain pattered on the windshield. "What do we know about her?"

Matt checked his notes. "Marina is thirty. No tickets. No record. She's the assistant manager at a women's clothing boutique in Scarlet Falls. Drives a minivan."

They climbed out of the SUV. The wind kicked up, and Bree turned up her collar against the wet chill. The house had no garage or driveway, just a narrow brick path that led to the front porch. Bree and Matt flanked the front door. A frosted wreath hung on the door, and a WELCOME TO OUR HOME doormat adorned the concrete front stoop. Bree rapped on the door with an old-fashioned brass knocker.

The woman who creaked open the door looked absurdly like a younger version of Kelly. She was petite with dark hair and brown eyes. She wore a sweaterdress, knee-high boots, and a full face of makeup, including false eyelashes. She stared at Bree through the six-inch gap for a few seconds. She didn't look surprised. "I don't have to talk to you."

"No, you don't," agreed Bree. "If you don't want to confirm Harrison's alibi, that's fine with me."

Marina's confidence faltered. She stepped back and opened the door wider. "Come in."

Bree stepped directly into a tiny living room, grateful for the warmth that enveloped her. The cramped space was ruthlessly organized. Cubbies near the door held shoes and backpacks. Jackets hung on pegs.

Matt joined her in the foyer, and Bree introduced them both.

Marina shot her an annoyed glance. "I'm making dinner, so you'll have to ask your questions while I work." She led the way into an equally small kitchen, where a cutting board sat next to a slow cooker. "You have fifteen minutes. Then the boys will be home, and I'll need to take them to karate class."

Bree didn't waste time. "Harrison took your boys on Monday afternoon?"

"Yes." She chopped two carrots with the rapid-fire knife action of a cooking show chef and transferred them to the slow cooker with one smooth motion of her thick-bladed knife. "He picked them up at school and took them to the trampoline park. It was a big help to me. I was supposed to be off, but an employee called in sick. It's hard to get a sitter at the last minute."

"What time did Harrison bring them home?" Bree asked.

"I don't remember exactly." Marina kept her head down, moving a small onion to the center of the block. Without raising her head, she said, "Around five?" She kept her gaze on her work, slicing the onion into perfectly even segments.

"What time did he leave?" Bree asked.

"Probably around six. It was a school night. The boys had homework to do." She scraped the sliced onion into the pot and waved her knife in a circle to indicate the kitchen. "My house is small. There isn't room to entertain." Her eyes met Bree's for a split second before skittering away. Was she nervous about speaking with the sheriff? Or was her discomfort caused by lying? Most people weren't very good at it.

"It might be small, but you've done a great job making it feel like a home," Matt said.

She smiled at him, her gaze softening. "Thank you. It's hard to do the homemaking and work full-time."

"Does the boys' father help out at all?" Matt asked.

Since Kelly seemed to like him better—many women did, for obvious reasons—Bree let him cozy up to her. He could be very persuasive and was a masterful interviewer.

Kelly's eyes welled with unshed tears. Her reaction felt genuine, unlike her confirmation of Harrison's alibi. "My husband died three years ago in a car accident. Before that, I was a stay-at-home mom. I loved it. That's all I really want to do. But no one expects their husband to die so young. We weren't prepared. We didn't have enough life insurance. And without Wyatt, we suddenly didn't have health insurance either. I was one health emergency away from bankruptcy. Even with insurance, it's hard to cover copayments, deductibles, and coinsurance. Last month, Brandon fell off the swing, cut his hand, and needed stitches. My deductible is five thousand dollars. Harrison paid the bill for me. I don't think most people have that kind of money just laying around." She took a heaving breath to compose herself. "Anyway, you don't realize how much money you're going to need when your spouse dies. I had to start working again, sell our house, and downsize considerably to make ends meet. I'd been out of the workforce for years, and my pay reflects that."

"You must work nonstop," Matt said. "Yet you still obviously make time to exercise."

Marina flushed. Her long eyelashes fluttered like caterpillar legs. "I do my best."

Matt was really pouring it on, and Marina was reeled right in. He made a sympathetic noise. "How old are your boys?"

"Six and nine." Kelly went to the fridge and retrieved a package of chicken thighs. She opened it and dumped them onto the cutting board.

"Great ages. Losing their dad must have been rough," Matt said.

"It was." She deboned the thighs like a pro, then cut the meat into smaller pieces. "Which is why I appreciate when Harrison spends time with them. They need a good man in their life."

"They like him?" Matt asked.

"Yes." Kelly put the chicken in the pot and added a carton of broth. Then she set the lid into place and turned the appliance on high. "He's great with them. He really misses his own kids since they went to college."

"Sounds like you two are a great match. Think you'll marry him someday?"

"Oh, yes. We have a lot in common—he's a real family man."

Bree restrained her eyeballs, which wanted to roll right into the back of her skull. Harrison had cheated on and dumped his first wife. Did Marina not think that could happen to her as well? Or was she betting that by the time she hit forty-five, he'd be sixty and too old to replace her with a younger model? Bree prescribed to the *once a cheater, always a cheater* philosophy, but it wasn't her life.

Matt lowered his voice. "Did you ever meet his ex?"

"Once, by accident." Marina cleaned the counter with disinfectant. "We were in the grocery store and she walked right up to us."

"That must have been awkward."

"I don't like to speak ill of the dead, but she was awful." She paused, her paper towel in midsweep. "I don't know how he stayed with her that long."

"What did she say?" Matt's tone turned conspiratorial.

Marina's lips pursed like she'd bitten down on an unripe berry. "She looked right at me and said, 'No returns. You took him. Now you have to keep him.'"

The corner of Bree's mouth twitched. *No laughing.* But damn, that was a good comeback.

Matt was better at playing a role. "That *is* awful."

"And she refused to sell their house. She strung him along for months and months." Once Marina started whining, she couldn't stop, like a car rolling down a steep, icy hill. "He had to pay the mortgage even though he didn't live there anymore."

Matt tsked and shook his head. "So unfair."

"Right?" She returned the spray cleaner to the cabinet. "Harrison was so patient. The man is a saint."

Matt's eyes narrowed. Bree knew that look. He was done playing.

"So you don't think he killed her?" he asked. "I mean, her death solves a lot of his financial problems."

"Oh, no!" Marina froze, her eyes wide as dinner plates. "He would never hurt anyone. She's the mother of his children."

Matt lifted both palms. "Oh, wait! Kelly was killed between noon and six on Monday. Harrison was at the trampoline park and then he was here, right? He couldn't have done it."

Marina sputtered. "Right." But was that a hint of doubt in her voice?

"Anyway. Thanks so much for speaking with us. Your alibi is really helpful." Matt smiled. "Do you want to come to the station to sign your statement, or would you prefer if a deputy brings it to you?"

A quick flash of panic crossed her face. "I have to sign something?"

"Well, yes," Matt said. "We need it to be official and legal."

Marina didn't respond. She just stared at him, her mouth slightly open. A chime sounded on her phone, startling her. "I—I have to get the boys at the bus stop." She headed for the door, pulling a jacket off a wall peg. Then she took an umbrella from a stand.

Bree and Matt walked to the SUV.

The cold drizzle pelted Bree's face. As she slid behind the wheel, her phone buzzed. She glanced at the screen. "The ME says to drop by. The autopsy is finished."

She started the engine. Waiting for the heat to kick on, she watched Marina step off the porch, open the umbrella, and head toward the corner, where a yellow school bus rumbled to a stop. Two little boys emerged, jackets hanging open, backpacks trailing on the wet ground. The smaller boy dropped his backpack and jumped with both feet into a puddle. Water splashed onto Marina. Her jacket didn't fully cover her dress, and water splashed the front. She lunged at the little boy, grabbing him by the jacket shoulder and pulling him close to her. She spoke in his ear, her face contorted in anger. The boy began to cry. The older boy stood on the sidewalk and watched. Were those tears or raindrops on his face?

Anger welled in Bree.

Marina straightened, her face shifting into perfect mommy mode once again as she led the boys home. They followed in her wake like sad, subdued ducklings.

"Guess she isn't perfect after all." Bree shifted into drive. She didn't want to watch anymore. There wasn't anything she could do. Marina wasn't abusing her child. She was just being a bitch. No law against that.

"Nothing says *doting mother* like dimming your kids' joy over a puddle," Matt said, clearly disgusted. "What did you think of Harrison's alibi?"

Shivering, Bree thought about Marina's obvious discomfort. "She seemed uncomfortable verifying the times. I think we definitely need that surveillance tape from the trampoline park."

"Marina is looking for a ring. She's playing the pretty traditional woman role, hoping to reel in Harrison's paycheck."

Bree adjusted the dashboard vents, so the heat blew in her face. "He's hardly Mr. Innocent. I'm sure he knows what's what."

Matt pointed the vents in front of him toward her as well. He was never cold. "Do you think she realizes that providing someone with a fake alibi could mean keeping a murderer out on the street—and in her life?"

Chapter Eleven

"I hate autopsies." Matt shivered. The sterile and clinical nature of the procedures always seemed like an additional insult to the body of a person already victimized once. But it was necessary in order to bring a killer to justice. Every gain had a cost.

"No one likes them." Bree turned into the lot. "We can check in with forensics while we're here."

The medical examiner's office shared a building with the forensics lab in the county municipal complex. The rain continued as they parked and hustled across the lot to the front door. Matt stamped his feet in the lobby and shook water off his jacket. Cold rain wasn't his favorite weather, but nature's mood felt like a good precursor to a brutal autopsy.

Bree checked in with the receptionist, who sent them back to the autopsy suite. Since the procedure was complete, they didn't fully suit up before pushing through the door. The sting of formalin hit his nostrils. Bright side: the body was relatively fresh, without the overwhelming smell of decomposition. Today, the room smelled more like a cross between a meat locker and a science lab.

Dr. Jones stood in front of a rolling cart equipped with a laptop. She still wore her gown over her scrubs but had removed her face shield and gloves.

The body lay on a stainless-steel table. The ME's assistant was closing the Y-incision. Except for the autopsy cuts and the neck slash, the rest of the body looked perfect.

Dr. Jones greeted them with a lift of her chin. "You want the CliffsNotes?"

"Yes, please," Bree responded.

Dr. Jones began. "Victim was a healthy forty-five-year-old female with no obvious conditions that would have contributed to her death. Autopsy results confirm the postmortem interval determined at the scene. She died between noon and six p.m. on Monday. You can read the details on wound biomechanics in my report. I'll summarize by saying the victim died by exsanguination, caused by the cut to the neck. The blade on the box cutter is consistent with the neck wound. The debris in the wounds looks like cardboard, but the lab will confirm." She cleared her throat. "Measurements confirm she was attacked from behind by a right-handed assailant."

Matt said, "Which is ninety percent of the population, including both of our suspects."

"The neighbor is also right-handed," Bree added.

Dr. Jones scrolled. "She ate chicken and lettuce shortly before she died. If you can determine what time she ate, you might be able to narrow down the time of death window. Tox screens are pending. That's about it for significant findings."

"Was she pregnant?" Bree asked.

"Pregnant?" Dr. Jones tilted her head. "No. Did you expect her to be?"

"The man she'd been dating said she told him she was," Bree said.

"She was not," Dr. Jones confirmed.

"So she was lying," Bree said.

"Not necessarily." Dr. Jones contemplated the body. "At her age, she might have confused perimenopausal symptoms with pregnancy.

Dramatic fluctuations in hormones can cause similar mood swings and shifts in the menstrual cycle."

"Her claim could have been completely innocent?" Bree asked.

"Definitely. In layman's terms, when a woman approaches menopause, things get weird." Dr. Jones turned back to her computer. "I'll send the preliminary report in a day or two and lab results as they come in."

"Thank you," Bree said.

Matt gratefully led the way out of the autopsy suite. Even though they hadn't touched anything, both Matt and Bree washed their hands before heading for the forensics lab.

Bree's phone buzzed in the hallway. She answered the call. "Juarez."

"Ma'am. I went to all five properties near the Ryder cabin on Blackbird Lake. Two of the places have clearly been unoccupied for some time. The other three homeowners all said they know who Mr. Ryder is but haven't seen him lately. He's known for being reclusive."

"That'll be all. Thanks, Juarez." Bree slid the phone back into her pocket. "Dead end there. I hope Rory has something for us."

The door was open. Matt knocked on the frame. Rory MacIniss looked up from his computer. "I was just typing an email to you."

"You have news?" Bree asked.

"More of an update." He gestured toward his laptop. "I was sending you the list of evidence collected at the crime scene. Nothing popped out as unusual to me, but you might find something of interest." He tapped on the keyboard. "Secondly, the red substance on the box cutter is human blood. A sample of the blood on the box cutter and the T-shirt it was wrapped in have been sent for DNA analysis. The blood type matches the victim, but she was O positive. So that would be more meaningful if it didn't match."

Thirty-eight percent of the population was O positive.

Rory continued. "We found no usable fingerprints, but the handle was swabbed for touch DNA."

"The killer probably wore gloves," Matt said.

"But they usually make a mistake somewhere." Rory was thorough. If the killer got sloppy, he would find the error.

Bree leaned a hip on the stainless-steel table. "Dr. Jones mentioned that the victim ate chicken and lettuce shortly before she died. Would you check her phone for a food order on Monday?"

"Of course. We found a Styrofoam food container in the trash, so we know she ordered takeout recently. I haven't had a chance to dig into every app on her phone." Rory turned away from his computer and picked up a smartphone in a pink skin that sat next to a laptop.

Bree pointed. "Is that Kelly's computer?"

"Yes. We broke the passcode, but again, accessing everything on it might take a few days." There were other techs to handle evidence collection, but Rory was the digital whiz.

"You're only one person." Matt always wanted Rory to handle the tech.

"Better to be right than fast," Bree agreed.

Rory nodded. "And we're down a tech. I should be able to devote all day tomorrow to Kelly's digital life." He tapped on Kelly's phone screen. Everything had already been fingerprinted and swabbed for touch DNA, so gloves were no longer necessary. "She used DoorDash to order a chicken Caesar salad and a lentil soup. The food was delivered at 3:05 p.m. on Monday."

For someone on a budget, paying a delivery fee for one meal seemed expensive.

"She was probably alive at that point anyway," Matt said. "But we should verify."

"Can you send us Kelly's account data?" Bree pulled out her notepad and wrote down the restaurant information.

Matt said, "We need to talk to the driver and see if she answered the door or if he left the order."

"That's a process." Bree shoved her notepad in her pocket. "I'll put a deputy on it."

"Are the techs done going through Troy Ryder's house and cabin?" Matt asked.

Rory returned Kelly's phone to the table with the other evidence and pulled out his own device. He typed with his thumbs. "They're packing up right now." He sent another text. "There was one item of note at the house. They found a single white sock in the hamper with a spot of human blood on it. Odd thing is, all the rest of his socks are black. At the cabin, they only found the bloody paper towel you pointed out."

Discomfort pooled in Matt's empty belly like grease. "If he was on his way to ditch the box cutter and T-shirt, would he have overlooked a bloody sock?"

Bree lifted a shoulder. "He waited twenty-four hours to ditch the box cutter. Maybe he was in panic mode."

Matt pictured him in the interview room. "He didn't look like the type to panic."

"We've seen weirder things." Bree rested a hand on the radio on her duty belt.

"But we also didn't see the driver of the car." Matt couldn't picture Troy making mistakes this big. He was definitely intelligent, and they'd seen no signs of impulsive behavior.

"So someone is framing him?" Bree asked. "We need actual proof beyond *he's too smart to have made mistakes*."

"As the boyfriend, Troy is the obvious suspect. If I were going to frame someone, I'd pick him."

Chapter Twelve

At six o'clock, vehicles filled the parking area of the trampoline park. Matt scanned the exterior of the building, which looked like a giant warehouse painted in primary colors.

He sent a text. "I let the family know we'll miss dinner."

"Thanks." Bree circled the lot. "I'd still like to be there before the kids go to bed."

"Me too, and I need to go over to Cady and Todd's place."

"Worried about Cady?"

"Always," Matt said. "But I also need to work with Turbo. He's driving Cady nuts. He's too smart for his own good." When Matt's injuries had forced him to leave his job as a deputy, he'd intended to train police K-9s. He'd bought a house with acreage and built a kennel. But Cady had taken over the space with her canine rescue operation before Matt could invest in a single dog. A few months ago, Cady's rescue had taken in a Belgian Malinois that needed to be rehomed. Too many people bought purebred dogs without truly understanding what they were getting themselves into.

"How is Turbo?"

"Supercharged as ever. He might have the most potential of any dog I've ever worked with. If we can harness his powers for good, he'll be an incredible working K-9. Last week, he went over the six-foot fence like it was nothing. He also let himself and two other dogs out of their kennels. They broke into the break room and destroyed the couch."

"Parkour dog or Houdini dog?"

"Both, apparently," Matt said. "How did your request for money to hire an officer to be his handler go?"

"About as you would have expected." Bree sighed. "The county board of supervisors doesn't see the need for another K-9 or officer."

"We can raise the money for the dog's training. The public will donate for a dog."

The public does love dogs.

"Your sister was instrumental in getting those funds, but we can't ask her to commit to that task, not with her baby due any day."

"You're right," Matt agreed. "I'll take it on, but with my considerably less honed public relation skills, it's going to take more time."

"Cady raised that money with a couple of big events."

Matt's sister was creative, organized, and skilled at blasting open rich people's wallets. "After we solve this case, I'll make raising that money my primary focus."

"That would be great, but I'm still a deputy short. Either I pull Juarez from patrol, or I hire an experienced K-9 handler. Either way, I need an additional deputy and a specialized vehicle. I can't add a K-9 without the approval of the board of supervisors."

"We'll figure it out." But in the meantime, Matt would continue to work with Turbo.

As Bree turned off the engine, he scanned the light posts. "I see multiple security cameras."

"I hope they work."

They went inside. Voices and laughter echoed in the high-ceilinged space. A middle-aged man was checking in a group at a counter. He eyed Bree's uniform. "I'll be right with you, Sheriff."

Bree raised a hand in acknowledgment.

"We should bring the kids here," Matt said. "Looks like fun."

Bree laughed. "I'm sure they'd love it."

A few minutes later, they stepped up to the counter.

"What can I do for you, Sheriff?" the man asked.

"I need to speak with the manager," Bree said.

He tapped his chest. "That would be me."

Bree introduced Matt.

"I'm Robert Lenny," the manager said.

Two little girls raced by, their delighted squeals piercing Matt's eardrums in a good way.

"Is there somewhere we can talk privately?" Bree asked.

Robert's brows wrinkled with worry. "Sure. We'll go into my office. Is something wrong? We're not over capacity or anything."

Bree smiled. "You didn't do anything. We need your help."

Robert called another employee to take over the registration counter. Then he led the way down a narrow hallway, past the restrooms, to an office the size of a horse stall. A fiftyish woman sat behind a computer.

Robert gestured to her. "This is my wife, Heather."

Four people crowded the space. Bree sidled in next to the desk. Matt stood in the doorway.

"Do you recognize this man?" Matt pulled out his phone and showed them a photo of Harrison Gibson.

Robert and Heather leaned in to scrutinize the screen. Robert frowned. "I don't know. A lot of people come here."

Heather cocked her head. "He's been here, all right, and it was recently. I wish I could remember which day."

"That's OK." Matt shoved the phone into his pocket. "Do your security cameras work?"

"They do," Heather said with pride.

"We'd like to see the feeds from Monday afternoon," Matt said.

"Easy peasy." Heather tapped on the keyboard. "For what time?"

Bree pursed her lips. "Let's say noon to six p.m."

Heather's fingers hovered above the keys. "Exterior *and* interior?"

"Yes, please," said Bree.

"We have five outdoor cameras: front and back door plus three in the parking lots." Heather tapped away. "Inside, there are fifteen cameras."

"That's a lot," Matt commented.

"We cover every inch of this space. Trampolines aren't risk-free. We require everyone to sign a waiver, but we also want all activity recorded in case there's an injury." Heather paused, looked up. "I can copy all one hundred twenty hours for you. It'll take a few minutes. How do you want it?"

"Thumb drive or email," Matt suggested. "Either would be fine."

"Thumb drive will be easier, if I have one." Heather opened a desk drawer and rummaged for a USB stick. "Here we go." She scrolled and tapped. "We can look at the front door feed while we're waiting."

"Thanks," Bree said.

"It's about the murder, right?" Heather lowered her voice. "Did the killer come here?"

"Heather!" Her husband looked appalled. "I apologize for my wife. She's a true crime junkie."

"What?" Heather protested. "I'm helping."

"I'm afraid I can't comment on any of our active investigations," Bree said.

Heather opened a window on her computer. "Here's the registration desk feed for Monday."

Matt and Bree crowded behind her.

"Let me see that picture of the guy again," Heather said.

Matt held his phone over her shoulder. She squinted at it, then turned back to her computer and fast-forwarded past a dozen people entering the building. She paused the video. "Here he is."

Harrison approached registration. Barely tall enough to see, Marina's boys peered over the counter. They watched Harrison pay and sign waivers before leading the boys away.

Arrival time: check.

"Can you fast-forward to four o'clock?" Bree asked.

"Sure." Heather moved the slider at the bottom of the screen, then let the video play, forwarding from customer to customer as people checked out, until after five o'clock. "I don't see him. I'll go backward from four o'clock."

She repeated the process in reverse until Harrison appeared. "Found him!"

Matt checked the time. "Three thirty-two."

A full hour before he'd said he left.

"The download is done." Heather plucked the drive from the USB slot. "You'll be able to find him on more than one feed, I'm sure. Can we do anything else for you?"

"No, thank you for your cooperation." Bree accepted the USB drive and slid it into her pocket. "Thank you both."

Matt led the way out of the office. They didn't speak until they were back in the SUV.

"Are we calling Harrison in for another interview tomorrow?" Matt asked.

"Yes." Bree started the engine. Then she just stared out the windshield for a few seconds. "Why did he lie about the time he left the trampoline park?"

"People usually lie to us because they have something to hide."

Chapter Thirteen

Bree turned into her driveway and parked next to her brother's vehicle. Lights glowed from inside the barn. She needed to hug her horse.

"I'd better hurry or I'll miss my book club meeting with Kayla." Matt reached for the door handle. "We just finished *Matilda*. I believe she has talking points."

Kayla had heard about book clubs and decided they were the best thing ever. Now she and Matt read books and discussed them.

"What's the next book?" Bree asked.

"It's my turn to pick. I already bought two copies." He sounded excited.

They climbed out of the SUV. The sky had cleared, but the air was still cold and damp. Bree turned up her collar against the chill.

"You're welcome to join our club." Matt rounded the SUV and kissed her lightly on the lips.

"That's OK. She and I have 4-H. This is your thing."

Bree kissed him back, grateful for the billionth time that he'd come into her life. Before him, she'd never had a significant other. She'd never met a man she didn't want to live without. Their relationship went beyond physical attraction and common interests. They had a true partnership. "Have I thanked you for everything you do yet today?"

The corner of his mouth turned up. "Not today."

"Well, thank you."

"Back atcha."

"I can't help but think you give more than you get." Bree relied on him every single day to help with the kids and farmwork.

"Not from my perspective. You gave me purpose. You gave me a family. I was floundering before I met you." He put a hand on each of her shoulders. "Because of you, my dad has stopped asking me when I'm going to give him grandkids. You can't minimize that level of peace."

She laughed. "Thank you anyway."

With another quick kiss, they headed for the house. The kitchen smelled like pot roast.

Dana was in the family room, curled on the couch with a book and her evening cup of tea. "Leftovers are in the fridge. Luke is upstairs studying. Kayla is putting on her pajamas."

"Then I'll make the cocoa." Matt backtracked to the kitchen.

Bree jogged upstairs to change into yoga pants and a big hooded sweatshirt. She washed her face and took down her hair. Then she said hi to Luke and left him to finish his calculus homework. She returned to the kitchen, where Matt was rummaging in the fridge. Steam wisped from the teakettle's spout.

"Hungry?" He pulled a container of pot roast from the fridge.

"I'll get some later. I want to talk to Adam before he leaves." She grabbed a few carrots from the vegetable drawer, put on her coat and boots, and went outside. The damp air smelled farm fresh. She inhaled it deep into her lungs. How had she lived in Philadelphia all those years, breathing exhaust fumes instead of country air? The wet ground sucked at her boots as she crossed the backyard to the barn.

Her brother, Adam, was grooming his horse, Bullseye, in the aisle. Beneath the hem of his winter jacket, paint spotted his jeans and boots.

She walked into the aisle and closed the door behind her to block out the wind. "Hey."

Adam looked up. The corners of his hazel eyes crinkled. "Hey yourself."

Bree scratched under the horse's forelock. Bullseye stood placidly, his head low, one rear leg cocked. As a former Amish buggy horse, he was enjoying the spoiled life. "Not seeing Zucco tonight?"

"She's tied up." Adam had been dating Bree's deputy for a few months.

"Did you ride?" Bree asked.

"Yeah." Adam swept his brush across his horse's side. "I took a short ride out to the tree. Sometimes I just want to say hello to her."

He didn't need to specify. Bree knew he was referring to their sister, Erin. They'd scattered her ashes under a tree on the hill overlooking the farm so that she would always be near them.

"I do that too sometimes." Bree stroked the placid horse's soft neck. His eyelids drooped. "I've been thinking about Mom lately."

"Really?" Adam tossed the brush into his grooming tote and faced her. He'd been a baby when their parents had died. He didn't remember anything about their family or the trauma that had left them orphans.

"Do you want to hear about it?"

"I do."

Always the attention hog, Matt's Percheron, Beast, nickered like a gigantic baby. Luke's horse, Riot, kicked his stall door.

"OK, already. I'm coming." She took a minute to distribute carrots to the other horses. It wasn't cold enough for blankets yet, but she gave each horse the evening once-over. She checked water buckets. No ice. She saved her own horse, Cowboy, for last. Opening the door, she slipped into the stall with the paint gelding. He'd been Erin's, and just being with him gave Bree the same sense of peace Adam had sought at the tree. She leaned on Cowboy's neck. It was like holding on to a little bit of her sister. With the dusty smell of horse as her anchor, she told Adam about the memory she'd had at the library. When she lifted her head, Adam was resting his forearms on the half door.

"Thanks for telling me," he said. "I know you don't like to talk about her."

"In the past, I only had bad memories. Now it seems I have good ones too. I don't mind sharing those at all." She recognized the words as truth as she spoke them. "I like knowing she loved us."

"You doubted that?"

"I don't know. Maybe?" Bree searched herself. "No. The truth is that I blamed her. Not in the same way I blamed him. I guess I always thought of her as an enabler. That somehow she allowed it to happen."

Adam said nothing. He was seven years younger than her, but he had old-soul eyes—artist eyes—that saw beneath the surface. He was able to scrape off her tough exterior like a spackle knife.

"I know that's not right." The self-analysis sent guilt coursing through her. "Victim blaming is horrible, and I know better. She was trapped by money and fear. He never allowed her to work. She couldn't support herself, let alone three children. He terrified and threatened her. He used us as leverage, and she had nowhere to go. Family and friends were too afraid of him to help her. Most importantly, she knew he'd never let her go." Bree patted her own chest. "But I also knew that she loved him. As self-destructive as that love was, it was very real."

"You were a child," he said in a soft voice.

"That's why these memories are so disorienting. It's like I'm two people. I can still feel my child emotions and reactions, but simultaneously, I also see the situation from my current adult perspective."

"You *are* messing with the space-time continuum."

Bree snorted. "That sums it up nicely."

"Are you OK?"

"I am. Thank you for asking."

"Do you think that memory was real?"

Bree sighed. "I think it happened, but I can only guess as to when. And I don't know how accurate my recollection is." Memories were always clouded by the time that had passed and the experiences one had lived. Disorienting. All of it.

"Makes sense," Adam agreed. "How old was the woman Mom was talking to?"

Bree straightened. "Older than her. Maybe around forty? It's hard to say. Kids think everyone over thirty is ancient."

"She could still be alive and living here," Adam pointed out. "Plenty of people don't leave Grey's Hollow. Look at us, born here. I never left." He nodded to her. "You came back."

Bree's head spun. "Why didn't I think of that?" Perhaps she hadn't been ready to face the memory in a concrete sense. "But what if I'm not picturing her right? My imagination could be filling in gaps in my memory."

"What if you are seeing her?"

"I suppose there's a chance I'm getting some of it right."

"I could try to draw her for you." Adam had helped several witnesses draw memories in past cases. He had an uncanny ability to listen and understand what people said underneath their words. "Who do you think she was?"

"I don't know. I haven't thought about that." But Bree concentrated on the memory now. The woman's face was clear. She'd looked tired, frustrated, and resigned. Her hand had rested on a closed manila file. "Maybe a social worker? Maybe someone had finally reported Dad."

"If so, it's possible the county was trying to take us away," Adam finished.

"They usually go to the house to check out the situation."

"Maybe they already did, and you didn't know."

Another disconcerting wave passed through Bree as she realized, again, that there were gaps in her knowledge of her parents' lives—and deaths. Did she want to know more? The flashbacks suggested she did.

Bree gave Cowboy a final pat and ducked under his neck. "How do you feel about doing that sketch?"

"Right now?" Adam pushed off the stall door and stepped back.

Bree opened the door and walked into the aisle. She was suddenly starving. "Yep. I don't want the memory to fade. I'm going to heat up some leftover pot roast."

"Do you think there might be some extra?" Hope lifted Adam's voice.

"Dana always makes extra."

"She's the best." Adam reached for the cross-tie clips on Bullseye's halter. "Then I'm in a drawing mood."

He put his horse away, and they headed for the house.

Matt and Kayla sat at the table, their copies of *Matilda* open in front of them. Matt was working on a huge bowl of leftovers.

Kayla dunked a cookie into her hot chocolate. "It's your turn to pick next."

"I know." He reached over to the sideboard and opened the drawer. "Here we go." He handed Kayla a book.

"*Big Red.*" She flipped it over to read the back. "Ooh. It's about a dog. Yay."

"It was one of my favorite books when I was your age," Matt said.

"I'm going to start it right now." Kayla bounced out of her chair.

"Bedtime in thirty minutes," Bree reminded her.

"I know." Kayla spun and raced out of the kitchen.

"Does she ever walk anywhere?" Adam asked.

"Nope." Matt set down his fork. "She'll probably finish that book tomorrow."

"No doubt I'll find her reading under the covers with a flashlight." But there were far worse things than a kid who read too late.

Matt squinted at Bree, then Adam. "You look like something's up."

"Adam is going to try to sketch the woman I saw in that flashback of my mom," Bree explained.

"Good idea." He stood. "I'll be in the office. I'm going to write and review reports."

Bree warmed up two bowls of food while Adam fished a notepad and pencil from a drawer. Then Bree and her brother ate while she described the woman in the library. Adam sketched at a leisurely pace, asking questions and making adjustments to his drawing between forkfuls of tender meat and vegetables.

Adam pushed the notepad across the table. "How's this?"

Stunned, Bree stared.

It's her.

"Really good." Bree touched the edge of the paper, as if needing to ground herself to the image. "Thank you. You're incredible."

Adam flushed. "It's just a sketch."

"Nothing you do is *just* anything," Bree said. "Your talent blows me away."

Adam was hot in the art world. His paintings commanded hefty price tags, and he'd recently had a showing at a trendy gallery. His success and modest lifestyle were the reasons Erin had been able to pay for the farm, and Bree never had to worry about the kids losing their childhood home. He'd already set aside enough money for both Luke and Kayla to go to college. Yet, with all the fame and fortune, Adam had no ego. He didn't understand why anyone paid money for his work. Bree didn't know anything about the art world, but there was something special about his paintings—and the raw emotion they evoked.

"Is there anything else I can do?" he asked.

Bree shook her head. "No. You made the drawing. Now it's my job to find her."

"Keep me posted, OK?"

"I will." But what was the chance that a woman who had met with her mom decades ago was still alive, still in Grey's Hollow, and remembered? And that was assuming she *was* a social worker. Bree could be completely wrong. The woman could have been anyone.

Chapter Fourteen

Morgan studied Kelly Gibson's street through the windshield of her minivan. The neighborhood was quiet. At eight thirty in the morning, kids would be in school.

"What's the plan?" Lance asked from the driver's seat.

Morgan reached for her tote bag. "Knock on doors. See who will talk to us and might have noticed activity at Kelly's house Monday afternoon."

Lance opened his car door. Morgan fished two clipboards out of her bag, then zipped it and shoved it under the passenger seat. Not that anyone would want to break into her vehicle. Empty reusable bottles, animal crackers, and pretzel crumbs littered the carpets, like a convenience store had exploded inside. Every square inch of faux leather was covered with scratches, dog fur, kid safety seats, and shiny blotches one instinctively knew were sticky without touching them.

She joined Lance on the sidewalk. Normally, she dressed as a high-powered attorney. Today, she'd chosen a suburban-mom vibe: jeans, ankle boots, and a powder-blue parka. She wanted to look approachable. She glanced at Lance, who couldn't help but look intimidating. But his Hollywood looks would open more doors than one might think.

She handed him a clipboard. "I'll take this side of the block."

Lance nodded and walked south.

Morgan headed for the houses across from Kelly's. No one answered at the first three homes, though she could feel someone inside at house number three. Four doors down the street, a man of about thirty answered her knock. Disheveled and dressed in sweatpants, he held a tiny infant on one shoulder.

She introduced herself. "My name is Morgan Dane. I'm an attorney working on a case."

"I'm Steve Dixon." His eyes opened wide. "It's about my neighbor Kelly, isn't it?"

"Yes," Morgan admitted. "Do you know her?"

"Not well. I mean, I wave when I see her."

"Did you notice anything unusual Monday afternoon?"

"There was a car parked outside her house." He lifted a hand off the baby's back and pointed to its head. "She cries nonstop, and my wife just started back to work last week. The days have been long."

"How old?" Morgan asked.

"Three months. Heidi took the first twelve weeks off, and now I'm taking my family leave."

"That's good planning."

He laughed. "Well, it seemed like a good idea when we arranged it. Now it's week two, and I'm going to lose my mind."

"It'll get better. I promise. Is this your first?"

"Yes. She might be an only child." Despite his exhaustion, humor filled his words.

The chill penetrated Morgan's jeans. "Do you want to close the door?"

"No. This is the first time she's stopped screaming all day. I'm just going to stand right here while it lasts."

"Tell me about the car you saw in Kelly's driveway?"

"It was a sports car. A two-seater. Black. I'm not a car guy, so I can't help you with specifics."

"Did you see anyone go in or out of the house?"

"No, but I was looking out the window. I didn't go outside."

"What time was this?"

He shook his head. "I really can't say. After lunch, before dinner is the best I can do."

"I might need you to sign a statement or talk to the sheriff. Is that OK?"

"Sure," he said.

Morgan wrote his contact information on her clipboard. "Thank you so much."

She retreated to the sidewalk. She could see Lance at the other end of the block, striding up a walkway toward a blue Colonial. Morgan walked in the other direction, energy livening her steps. Someone had been at Kelly's house Monday afternoon. *Does the sheriff know?*

She heard voices and turned. Three women were walking toward her down the center of the street. They wore athletic tights, bright sneakers, puffy jackets, and knit hats. Smiling, Morgan stepped into the street. "Hi. May I ask you a couple of questions?" She introduced herself. "I'm working on Kelly Gibson's case." She left it up to the women to decide which side of the case she was on.

The women stopped and started chatting nervously.

"What an awful thing to happen."

"I hope they catch her killer."

The first woman said, "We usually walk together, but sometimes I go alone. Not anymore."

"It's frightening." Morgan nodded. "Did you know Kelly?"

"Oh, yes," Woman Number Two said. "I used to see her all the time. Our kids went to school together. I haven't seen her lately, though. Once my youngest left for college, I went back to work part-time."

"I haven't seen her recently either," Woman Number One added. "She withdrew from everyone when her husband left her."

Woman Number Three said, "I saw her at the grocery store a month ago. She said hello but didn't have time to talk."

Morgan nodded. "Did any of you notice any activity on Monday afternoon? Did you see anyone at Kelly's house?"

"Monday afternoon?" Woman Number One asked. "I thought she died Tuesday. That's when the police cars were here."

"She was killed on Monday," Morgan explained. "She was found on Tuesday."

The three women went silent, as if processing the information.

"Oh." The third woman pressed a gloved hand to the base of her throat. "I saw her ex at her door on Monday."

"Her ex?" Morgan asked.

"I'm sorry. Harrison," the woman clarified. "I don't know if they're divorced yet or not."

"Do you know what time this was?" Morgan asked.

She looked at the sky. "Late afternoon. Wait. I can check my fitness app. It logs all my exercise." She pulled a phone from her pocket, tugged off a glove, and scrolled. "Here. On Monday afternoon, I walked from 4:06 to 4:55. I lapped the neighborhood several times, so I can't say which lap I was on."

Morgan wrote down the time. "You're sure it was Harrison?"

"Yes. I've known the Gibsons for years."

"Did you see a vehicle?" Morgan asked.

"I did." The woman closed her eyes. "That little black two-seater he bought after he dumped Kelly. It was late Monday afternoon, he was banging on the door and shouting, 'Come on, Kelly. Don't be such a bitch. Let me in.'"

Morgan poised her pen over her paper. "Would you be willing to sign a statement or speak with the sheriff? I know Sheriff Taggert is looking for witnesses."

"I guess." The woman looked unsure. She glanced at her friends. "You don't think it would be dangerous, do you? He won't come after me? He knows where I live."

Her two friends didn't respond, but they both shifted their weight as if uncomfortable.

Morgan reasoned, "We don't know that he's responsible, but the safest way to protect everyone in the neighborhood is to help the sheriff solve the crime. Otherwise, there's a killer at large."

All three women paled.

"When you put it that way, of course I'll help." The witness recited her name, address, and phone number.

"Thank you." Morgan tucked the notepad under her arm and handed the woman her business card. "You'll be hearing from me or the sheriff."

The woman nodded. Her friends patted her shoulders and huddled close as they walked away. Morgan returned to her minivan and waved for Lance. He jogged back, and she filled him in.

"Did you show her any pictures?"

Morgan settled in the passenger seat. "No. I didn't want to taint her statement, but she knew him by name. No doubt the sheriff will have her look at a photo array." Morgan was always thinking about how evidence would be presented in a potential trial.

"What now?"

"Now we find out what vehicle Harrison Gibson drives and call the sheriff." Morgan couldn't wait to present Bree with her new witness statements. She pulled out her cell and punched in the sheriff's number. The call went to voicemail. Morgan tried the main number for the sheriff's office. Marge answered the phone.

"This is Morgan Dane. I need to speak with the sheriff."

"She's in a meeting," Marge said. "I expect she'll be tied up for at least another hour or so."

"I'll try back." Morgan ended the call. She drummed her fingers on the armrest. "Let's go to Troy's cabin."

"Let me guess. You want to find the blond jogger."

"We have some time. The sheriff doesn't have the resources to wander around the lake for days in hopes of seeing this mysterious woman. We do."

"Let's do it." Lance drove toward Blackbird Lake. A short time later, the minivan bounced down a narrow road riddled with potholes. "We should have brought my Jeep."

"That's it." Morgan pointed toward a gap in the woods.

Lance turned onto a dirt driveway, which ended in a tiny clearing. "This is rustic."

Morgan traded her heels for a pair of flats, then changed her mind and reached for the gym bag on the floor behind the driver's seat. She pulled it into the front seat and took out a pair of barely worn gym shoes.

"Good thing I always intend to go to the gym, even if I never actually go there." To Morgan, the gym was more of a goal than a reality. "Glad I wore pants today."

They got out of the car.

"We don't have a key," Lance said.

Morgan zipped her jacket to her chin and pulled out her gloves. "We don't need to go inside."

Lance led the way behind the cabin. "He said he saw her on the trail that goes around the lake, right?"

Morgan picked her way across the grass. A cold wind whipped off the lake, and she shivered.

"Do you want to walk the path?" Lance asked.

Not really. "Yes."

"If you want, I could run it. You could wait in the car," Lance offered. "No offense, but it would be much faster without you."

"No offense taken. We both know I'm a slow and reluctant runner." But Morgan thought running the whole trail seemed like a waste of time. "What are the chances the same woman would be running right now?"

"Not very good."

Morgan watched tiny whitecaps churn on the surface. "Troy said he knew most of his other neighbors on sight, but he'd never seen this one before. Is there any public parking on Blackbird Lake?"

Lance shook his head. "Not that I know of." He pulled out his phone. "Let me double-check." He tapped and scrolled. "There doesn't seem to be any park areas here at all. The closest is the public boat ramp for Scarlet Lake." He lowered the phone. "Maybe she's visiting someone."

"Maybe," Morgan agreed.

Lance circled a forefinger in the air. "Troy said the trail around the lake was three miles. If it's flat, I'll be back soon." He turned and set off on the trail at a brisk jog.

She stared out over the lake. The chances that the blond woman was running again right now were slim, especially if she had just been visiting someone on the lake. If she did live here, and Troy said he knew most of his neighbors' faces, how could he not know her? She could live a bit farther away and simply be trying a new route. Or she could have just moved here.

Morgan pulled out her phone and called Lance's mom, who was the computer expert used by Sharp Investigations. "Could you check recent real estate transactions for a property near Blackbird Lake that might have changed ownership?"

"Sure," Lance's mom said.

Morgan heard the clacking of her keyboard over the line.

A few minutes later, Lance's mom said, "Seventeen Gulph Run sold in November to Gerald Lindo. Two weeks ago, 120 Sagemore Court sold to Susan Duffy. Number twelve Loon Lane was purchased by A. A. Kulmann on October fifteenth."

"Can you text me that info?" Morgan asked.

"I'll do it right now," Lance's mom said.

Morgan's phone beeped almost immediately. "Thanks so much."

"You're very welcome. I'm always glad when I can help."

Morgan said goodbye and ended the call. She walked to Troy's back deck and sat on the steps. The house blocked some of the wind. She started with an internet search for Gerald Lindo and found him quickly. He was an engineer who worked out of a firm in Albany. Morgan switched to his social media site and viewed photos of him currently working on a job in Puerto Rico. She scrolled through his photos. No blond women. No runners.

She moved on to the next name: Susan Duffy. With a more common name, the local Susan took a few more minutes to locate. She was a physician's assistant with a local practice. About sixty years old, Susan had short gray hair. A current photo on social media showed her on crutches with one foot in a boot. There were no younger blond women or runners in any of her recent photos.

One left.

Mentally crossing her fingers, Morgan google-searched the name A. A. Kulmann, but the search results didn't appear relevant. This was her only lead. Morgan needed to find this blond runner.

She opened a social media app and typed the name into the search bar. Thirty-six A. Kulmanns appeared. Morgan began checking their profiles one by one, beginning with Aaron Kulmann. The blond woman could be AA Kulmann, or she could live with A. A. Kulmann. She spent the next twenty minutes scrolling through profiles. Well down the list, she clicked on Annette Kulmann. The photo was of a blond woman in her midthirties. Morgan scrolled to the ABOUT section. Annette didn't give much personal information. Morgan clicked on PHOTOS. Yes! She found photos of Annette with two other women. All three of them were dressed in running tights. The caption read: the Disney half marathon with Paula and Jeanine.

Hopeful, Morgan continued to scroll and found a check-in for Annette at a bakery in Scarlet Falls. *This must be her.*

Footfalls pulled her away from her phone screen. Lance jogged toward her. He wasn't breathing hard and had barely broken a sweat on his three-mile run. He stopped next to her and stretched a calf. "No luck."

"I found her." Morgan shook her phone, then explained how she'd tracked down Annette Kulmann digitally.

"And you did it without running three miles." He laughed, then kissed her. "You're brilliant. I love you."

"I love you too."

"Even if I'm more brawn than brain?" he joked.

"That's hardly true, but my answer would be the same regardless."

"Why don't I text her photo to Troy? He can tell us if it's her or not."

"Good idea." Morgan forwarded the social media page. "In case it isn't her, don't send her personal information. Just the photo."

"OK." Lance tapped on his phone. It vibrated in a few seconds. "Troy says yes. That's her."

"Great."

He opened the door to the minivan. "Let's go see her."

Twelve Loon Lane was on the other side of the lake. Though only a short distance as the crow flew, the drive took nearly thirty minutes of bouncing along winding dirt roads. Lance parked in front of a cedar-and-glass A-frame. A silver Prius sat in the driveway. Behind the house, a lush lawn led to a dock that extended over the lake.

"Hope she's home." Morgan climbed out of the minivan.

They walked to the front door and knocked, but no one answered.

"Damn." Morgan stepped back, scanning the front of the house.

"We know where she lives now. We can come back."

But Morgan wanted her statement now. The clock was ticking on Troy. Bree would have that DNA from the box cutter expedited. If the results came back positive for Kelly's blood, she could arrest him. Morgan could make a jury doubt that Troy had been driving the Porsche. Verifying at least part of his story would help.

But it appeared that Annette wasn't here.

"We'll get her phone number and call her to explain," Lance said.

"Explain what?" a woman's voice called out.

Morgan spun. A woman walked up the lawn from the lake. She wore black running tights, a base-layer long-sleeve shirt, and a puffy vest. Her blond ponytail popped out above a blue fleece ear warmer. Thin black gloves covered her hands. "Ms. Kulmann?"

"Who are you?" the woman asked warily.

Morgan introduced herself and Lance, then produced a business card.

Annette read the card. "You're an attorney? Who are you representing?"

"Troy Ryder," Morgan said.

Annette didn't show any recognition. "I don't know him." She extended the card back toward Morgan, as if handing it back.

"I know." Ignoring the card, Morgan pointed to the lake. "He lives on the other side of the lake."

"And?"

"And he says he saw you on Monday afternoon while he was out running." Morgan turned to Lance. "Do you have a photo of Troy?"

"Probably." Lance pulled out his phone. "I do." He extended the phone toward Annette. Morgan peered at the screen. Troy was dressed in hockey gear but the picture had been taken off the ice, and his helmet was off.

Recognition lit Annette's eyes. "I remember him. Yeah." She snorted. "We passed each other on the lake trail a few days ago. He was staring back at me so hard, he ran right into a tree branch." She sobered. "He didn't die of a weird head injury or something, did he?"

"No," Lance said. "Nothing like that."

"Whew. I didn't stop to help him or anything, but a woman alone on an empty trail just doesn't do that. You know?"

"Yes," Morgan agreed. "I wouldn't have stopped either."

"But you definitely remember him," Lance said.

"Yes." She blushed. "I saw him hit the tree because I turned back to get a second look at him too. He's fit."

"He is." Morgan smiled. "Do you remember what time you saw him?"

Annette pulled her phone out of a flat pocket on the side of her leggings. "Let's see. I ran seven miles on Monday between 11:30 and 12:19. I would have seen him around the halfway point, so close to noon. I can't be exact, though."

"That's good enough," Morgan said.

"Seven miles is impressive," Lance said.

"Meh. It was an easy day for me." Annette adjusted her ponytail.

"Would you be willing to tell the sheriff this story?" Morgan asked.

Annette pulled back. "Why would I need to do that?"

"Because Troy is being accused of a crime."

"So, I'm like, his alibi?" She didn't sound happy about that. "I really don't want to be involved with a crime."

"What about keeping an innocent man out of prison?" Lance asked.

Annette's eyes opened wider. "Prison? What did he do?"

Morgan steered the conversation away from crimes and prisons. "All you need to do is say you saw him on the day and time you did. That's all. Just tell the truth."

Annette bit her lower lip. "I don't know."

Morgan could subpoena her, but she'd rather Annette be cooperative. Hostile witnesses weren't the best. "Troy deserves for the truth to come out. So does the victim."

Annette scraped the toe of a sneaker in the dirt. "What is the crime?"

Morgan couldn't avoid the truth either. "Murder."

"What?"

Morgan held up a hand. "Evidence will solve the crime, and your statement will be part of that evidence."

Annette pressed a palm to her forehead. "This is about that woman who was killed over in Grey's Hollow, isn't it?"

"Yes," Morgan said. "The most important thing is for the sheriff to catch the real killer. Don't you agree?"

Annette hesitated, then nodded. "Yes. You're right. I'll do it."

The interaction between Annette and Troy didn't cover the entire period that comprised her time of death, but it would allow Morgan to poke the first holes in the sheriff's case.

Chapter Fifteen

Matt went directly to the conference room Thursday morning and spent an hour updating the whiteboard while Bree was tied up with staffing issues and roll call. He pulled Troy's late wife's death certificate and spoke with the medical examiner's office.

Todd walked in with his laptop and a short stack of folders.

"How's Cady?" Matt asked.

He set his laptop on the table. "Good. Uncomfortable. Nervous. Excited. Ready. Not ready."

"And how are you?" Matt asked as Bree walked into the room.

"I'm definitely not ready." Todd laughed. "I'm terrified for the birth and everything that comes after it. How do you take care of a newborn? They're so tiny and helpless."

Matt had never cared for a newborn, but he was sure his sister and Todd would be the best parents. "It's a learn-by-doing activity. You and Cady will figure it out, and my dad is always around." Having a father who was a semiretired family doctor had plenty of perks.

"And I'm grateful."

Bree took a seat at the table, her eyes full of grief.

"Is something wrong?" Matt asked.

"No. I just talked to Kelly's kids."

"Ugh," Matt commiserated. Even though the kids had been notified by their father, the conversation would still have been emotional. "I'm sorry."

"Yeah. It was rough. They're both coming home this evening."

"Any insights into Kelly's life?" Matt asked.

"Not really." Bree sighed. "Kelly didn't talk to them about the man she'd been dating. They only knew because *Harrison* told them, something both kids seemed irked about. Both kids are still mad at him for leaving their mom. They both mentioned how much they dislike Marina, and they rarely talk to Harrison." Bree settled at the table. "The son called Kelly every Friday. Kelly and her daughter texted a few times a week, but they both wanted to stay out of the divorce. Neither kid has been home since summer break, not even for Thanksgiving."

"Ouch."

"Yeah. Kelly spent the holiday alone, so they both feel guilty for that."

"That's rough. I get it, though. Even as young adults, they didn't want to be in the middle."

"No one would," Bree agreed. "Do we have any new information?"

Matt began, "I confirmed that Troy's first wife died of a congenital heart issue. The ME says there's no question."

"Todd?" Bree asked.

"Yes," Todd said. "Deputy Juarez got Kelly's order information from the food delivery app. He spoke with the driver, who recognized her photo and said she opened the door to receive her order. He didn't see anyone else inside, but he just shoved the bag at her and left. He didn't remember if there was a car in the driveway or not."

"We now know that Kelly was alive at 3:05 p.m. on Monday." Matt changed the time of death on the board to between three and six p.m.

"Where do we stand on the neighborhood canvass?" Bree asked.

Todd consulted his notes. "We've spoken with eighty percent of households on Kelly's street. So far, no one saw anything."

"Keep trying. Send a deputy over there between three and five in the afternoon. Look for parents and kids coming home from school bus stops. They might live a couple of streets away, but they might have seen something."

Todd made a note. "Good idea."

"Let's take it suspect by suspect, starting with our lead contender, Troy Ryder." Matt tapped the board with his marker. "Troy."

"Currently involved in a relationship with the victim," said Bree. "He says she claimed to be pregnant. We now know that wasn't true. Did she make the claim as an honest mistake, as Dr. Jones suggested was possible? Or did Kelly have a secret agenda?"

"Like what?" Todd asked.

Bree considered the possibilities. "Maybe she felt like he was pulling away. He's loaded. She's broke. Maybe she just wanted to hang on to him."

Matt capped his marker. "Even if he could have kids, he'd learn she wasn't pregnant pretty quick."

Todd shrugged. "She could string him along for a couple of months, then claim to have a miscarriage. You couldn't tell Cady was pregnant until she was four or five months into her pregnancy."

"Other evidence against Troy?" Bree asked.

Matt turned to the board and tapped next to each bullet point. "The calls and texts between Troy and Kelly on Sunday, the box cutter found in his Porsche after that weird pursuit, the bloody sock forensics found in his hamper."

"Let's double-check with forensics and see if we can expedite the DNA tests on the box cutter and sock," Bree said.

"I'll text Rory," Todd volunteered. He picked up his phone and typed.

"Seems like it's a pretty good bet that the box cutter will come back positive for Kelly's DNA." Bree leaned both elbows on the table and stared at the board. "But Morgan Dane will argue someone stole his car."

Matt underlined the items on the list. "We found no evidence of forced entry."

"We also didn't see the driver of the vehicle," Bree reminded him. "Forensics found a sock with a spot of human blood on it in his hamper, but that won't mean anything until the DNA results come back."

"If they're going to claim someone broke into his house, then the sock could be tainted evidence as well," Matt said.

"Rory responded to my text about the DNA." Todd scrolled on his phone. "He wants us to call him."

"Let's do it," Bree said.

Todd picked up his cell phone and made the call. "Hey, Rory. I'm putting you on speaker. The sheriff and Matt Flynn are also in the room." He pressed a button on his screen and set down the phone.

"Cool," Rory said. "First, the DNA report isn't in yet. But I have something else for you. I just sent you the preliminary forensics evidence list from the crime scene. You're going to see animal fur found on the kitchen floor listed, along with unknown types of fibers, hairs, and dirt. The victim did not appear to own a pet, so the fur evidence could be important. The fur is dark brown or blackish. The lab should be able to give us more information."

"If we find the specific animal, can the DNA be matched to the hair?" Bree asked.

Matt went to look over Todd's shoulder as the chief deputy opened the report on his laptop. As Todd scrolled, Matt scanned the list of trace evidence. As usual, forensics had collected a long list of trace materials, all of which would need further optical and chemical analysis. Unless such trace evidence seemed out of place—like the animal fur in a home with no pet—it would be logged and stored until further analysis was deemed necessary. If the victim was found on a dark-gray carpet, then dark-gray fibers would be expected.

"That depends. Shed fur doesn't typically contain a root, so there's very little DNA to work with," Rory said. "Most cat lineages aren't distinguishable from one another, but there's always the chance that we'll find a more unusual variant. If it's a dog hair, then the lab might be able to determine the breed."

"So all we know right now is that dark animal fur was at the scene," Bree said.

"Pretty much," Rory said. "Sorry."

"Thanks, Rory." Todd signed off the call. "The fur doesn't sound too helpful."

"We could get lucky." Matt thought back to the scene. "Kelly didn't have a cat or a dog."

Bree flattened a palm on the table. "Jeff Burke has a black cat. I saw it in the window of his house. Let's bring him in for a formal interview. We want him to verify it was Troy Ryder that he saw at Kelly's house and not someone else. We'll set up a photo array. Jeff Burke gave off stalker vibes when he talked about Kelly. He's impulsive and quick tempered as well."

Matt noted the animal fur in the evidence column and wrote *interview Jeff Burke* on the to-do list.

Bree leaned back and scrubbed her hands down her face. "Who's next?"

Matt stepped sideways to point at the next column on the board. "Harrison Gibson."

"There were barn cats on the farm," Bree said.

"Harrison also lied about the time he left the trampoline park. Was he mistaken, or was the lie intentional to give him a more solid alibi?"

"I'd bet on the lie." Matt felt it in his bones. "But can we prove it? I remember him using vague words like *around four thirty* and *sixish*."

"Hedging in case we caught him?" Bree asked.

"Yep," Matt said. "And he probably lied about when he started seeing Marina. We know he left Kelly last spring, but Marina posted a photo of them together on social media before that."

Bree turned to Todd. "Do we have any financial information on the Gibsons?"

"We do." He read from his screen. "Neither of them have much money in the bank. No unusual recent withdrawals, deposits, or charges. The mortgage for their house eats up a significant portion of Harrison's paycheck. Kelly had no income of her own. We found life insurance policies in her home office. They had two term policies of five hundred thousand each, payable to the surviving spouse. I called the insurance company. The policies are still valid."

Bree drummed her fingers on the table. "That seems like a reasonable amount, considering the amount of the home mortgage and the tuition at the kids' colleges."

Matt turned to the whiteboard, where he'd added the interview with Kelly's best friend. "According to Virginia Hobbs, Harrison wanted Kelly to be a stay-at-home mom, until he dumped her for a younger woman. Virginia said he wanted the house sold so he could get his own place with Marina. Kelly's murder solves all his problems."

Bree added, "He also lied about when he last spoke with her. He conveniently forgot about ambushing Kelly in the parking lot of the Pilates studio last week."

"Is that all?" Todd asked.

"I think so? It's a lot," Bree said. "We're going to need a spreadsheet to keep track of Harrison's lies."

Todd nodded. "To summarize: We're calling Jeff Burke in to pick out Kelly's new boyfriend from a photo array, and to give us more details about the last fight between Kelly and Harrison."

Bree added, "Ask him nicely if he'd be willing to help with Kelly's investigation. Treating him as an ally might resonate with him. He seemed like he wanted to help."

Which felt suspicious to Matt. "He wouldn't be the first killer to try to help with an investigation."

"True," Bree agreed.

"OK," Todd said. "We're also calling Harrison Gibson in for a second formal interview to confront him about his lies regarding the last time he saw Kelly and the time he left the trampoline park."

"I'll call Harrison," Bree said. "His ego will want the attention of the sheriff."

Marge poked her head into the conference room. "Morgan Dane and Lance Kruger are here. Ms. Dane says she has important information for you. Do you want me to put them in an interview room?"

"Yes," Bree said. "Matt and I will talk to them in a minute." She dismissed Todd and motioned to Matt. "Let's go."

Matt set down his marker. "This should be interesting."

What did the defense attorney know? Matt liked and respected both Morgan and her husband, Lance. They might usually be on the opposite side of a case, but they both had integrity.

Matt locked the conference room on their way out. Integrity didn't mean neither Morgan nor Lance would be curious, and the murder board was for law enforcement eyes only.

In the interview room, Morgan didn't waste any time. "I have two witnesses who can put Harrison Gibson at Kelly's house between four and five p.m. on Monday, and we found the blond woman who ran into Troy on the lake trail Monday afternoon."

Chapter Sixteen

Bree was still processing Morgan's information, but she had other responsibilities beyond the investigation. She spent a few hours in her office reviewing paperwork and emails with a fresh cup of coffee.

Matt walked in. "You missed lunch."

"Probably." She tapped her phone to check the time. Two o'clock. "I'll eat when we're done with the Gibson interview. Did you get the statements from Morgan's witnesses?"

"I did." Matt read from his notes. "The witnesses confirmed everything Morgan said. Harrison was seen at Kelly's house between four and five on Monday afternoon. *And* the blond woman saw Troy hit his head on a branch around noon on the lake trail."

"He still had time to kill Kelly," Bree said. "But at least her statement verifies that he was at his cabin that day and how he injured his head." She paused. "Harrison should be here shortly. I sent a deputy to collect him, but he insisted on driving himself."

"Where's Todd?" Matt pulled a protein bar from his pocket and tossed it to her.

"Tied up with a multivehicle accident." She caught the bar, opened the wrapper, and tried a bite. "Tastes like a candy bar." She smoothed the wrapper and squinted at the ingredients. "Are you sure this is better for me?"

"No." Matt laughed. "But it's better than nothing."

"I like it." She ate the bar in four bites. "Unfortunately, I want to eat a whole bag of them."

"I'm getting coffee. Want some?" Matt asked.

"Nah, I'm good." Bree drained her mug. "I'm already overcaffeinated."

"Then none for you," Matt called as he left her office.

A few minutes later, someone knocked on the doorframe, and Marge walked in. "Harrison Gibson is here. He brought an attorney. I put them in room one."

"Damn." Bree had known that he would secure legal counsel, that common sense would eventually overshadow the man's bravado, and he'd realize he was in deep trouble. But she wished she could have had one more crack at him before he lawyered up. "We're also expecting Jeff Burke to come in this afternoon."

"Want him in room two?"

"Yes, thank you," Bree said. "Oh, Marge. I have something else for you. It's not part of the case. It's not official business at all, but you know everyone who's worked for the county for the last few decades."

"*Almost* everyone," Marge qualified with a chuckle.

Bree pulled Adam's sketch from her messenger bag and placed it on her desk in front of her admin. "Do you recognize her?"

Marge lifted her reading glasses from the chain around her neck and set them on her nose. Leaning over, she studied the drawing. "Maybe? She looks a little familiar, but I can't place her."

Bree shifted against the back of her chair. "She would be older now."

"How much older?"

"Could be as long as thirty years."

Marge removed the glasses from her nose. "Is this a cold case?"

"No."

"Can you give me some context? Why do you need to find her?"

Bree sighed. "I think she knew my mother."

"Oh." Marge replaced her glasses and assessed the sketch again. "Can I make a copy?"

"Yes."

Sketch in hand, Marge stared at it while she turned toward the door. "Do you have any idea who she might be?"

"I don't want to influence your memory."

"But it might help narrow down who I'm looking for. Thirty years is a long time."

"OK. Maybe a social worker or something like that?" Bree suggested. "I think they met, and just knowing my mother's situation, I'm making assumptions that might not be valid."

"But they make sense. Is it all right if I show this to other people?"

"Yes."

"OK, then." Marge considered the drawing again. "Give me a few days."

"Thank you."

"Anytime, and I mean that." Marge gave the paper a shake. "I'll copy this and leave the original on your desk."

"Thanks again. I'll be in the interview room with Harrison Gibson." Marge had worked for the county for as long as Bree had been alive. Marge had more contacts than the governor. If anyone could find the woman who'd met with Bree's mother—if she existed and if Bree's memory was remotely accurate—then it would be Marge.

Feeling like she'd done what she could, Bree set the distraction aside and headed for the interview room. She stopped at the conference room and collected Matt on the way.

A tall man in a nice suit—the attorney, she assumed—sat at the interview table. Harrison paced the floor behind him.

Bree slid into the seat opposite the empty chair, with Matt facing the lawyer. Harrison reluctantly sat across from her.

"This interview is being recorded." Bree did the introductions, read the Miranda sheet, and slid the acknowledgment across the table.

Harrison signed it and sat back, folding his arms over his chest. He was obviously trying to look confident, but Bree could see his apprehension in the twitchiness of his fingers and shifting of his weight on the chair.

The attorney rested his forearms on the table. "My client is here to cooperate with your investigation in the death of his wife. He wants nothing more than to help catch her killer."

Bree leaned forward. "Then why did he lie to me?"

Harrison opened his mouth. The attorney stopped him from speaking with a hand on his forearm. "You'll have to elaborate."

"Number one," Bree began. "When we asked Harrison when he'd last seen Kelly, he said at the attorney's office a few weeks ago. But that's not true, is it?"

Harrison squirmed.

Bree continued. "You went to the Pilates studio she attended last week. You waited outside in the parking lot to ambush her, didn't you?"

Harrison's face reddened. "I—"

His attorney cut him off. "Don't answer that."

"We have the altercation on video." Bree woke her laptop and turned it to face Harrison and his lawyer. She leaned over the machine and tapped "Play." The video feed from the Pilates studio parking lot camera rolled. "As you can see, this recording is date- and time-stamped."

All color drained from Harrison's face as he watched. At the end, Bree tapped the pause button.

The attorney's face pinched into a sour expression. "Where did you get this video?"

"The Pilates studio," Bree said.

Harrison leaned close to his lawyer's ear. "It's owned by Kelly's friend. She hates me."

Despite his whisper, Bree heard every word.

The attorney made a note on his legal pad. "But the studio is owned by someone biased against my client. The date could have been altered. It won't be difficult to refute."

"The studio owner witnessed the entire incident," Bree said.

The attorney scowled. "I'd like a copy."

"I will forward a copy when and if it becomes appropriate." Discovery rules for evidence didn't apply until a suspect was formally charged and their attorney submitted a written request. Bree didn't want details and evidence from the case leaked before the investigation was complete. For now, all evidence would remain under wraps. "Why didn't you tell us about this?" Bree pointed to the computer screen, where the paused video showed him looming over Kelly. His face was frozen in an angry scowl.

Bree expected the attorney to object to the question, considering he wanted to dispute the validity of the evidence, but he didn't.

Harrison sat back. His shoulders slumped. He shifted on his chair and stared at the table's edge for a few seconds.

Bree waited, letting the silence play out and hoping Harrison would be compelled to fill it.

He looked away, then brushed a knuckle across his nose. "I'm going on a ski trip next weekend, and my gear is still at the house. I just wanted to pick it up. That's all. I couldn't contact her directly because she blocked my number."

Matt picked up the thread. "You weren't supposed to contact her at all, were you?"

"No," Harrison admitted.

"Why did she block your number?" Matt leaned forward, resting his forearms on the table, using his body to pressure Harrison's personal bubble.

"Because she wanted to make everything difficult," he snapped.

The attorney touched his arm. Harrison flashed an irritated glance at him.

Matt kept pushing. "So you didn't call or text her excessively?"

"Don't answer that," the attorney warned. "It's subjective."

Bree made a mental note to check Kelly's historical phone records for excessive calls and texts from Harrison. "How were you supposed to contact Kelly?"

"Through our lawyers." Harrison straightened his spine and belligerence lifted his chin. "But I didn't want to pay hundreds of bucks to arrange to pick up my boots and shit."

Some people think rules don't apply to them.

"There was no restraining order against my client," the attorney pointed out. "While he was *encouraged* to communicate through their mutual legal counsel, there was no penalty for not doing so. My client didn't do anything illegal."

"But it did turn out to be a bad decision," Matt said.

Harrison mashed his lips flat but didn't respond.

"Did you pick up your stuff?" Bree asked.

"No." Harrison folded his arms across his chest. "Is that it?"

Not by a long shot.

Bree folded her hands on the table. "That's not all, and frankly, it's not the biggest issue. Let's talk about the day Kelly was murdered."

The attorney frowned. Harrison's gaze darted from Bree to Matt and back again. Was that a flash of panic in his eyes?

Bree continued. "You claimed you left the trampoline park at four thirty on Monday. But that's not true, is it?"

Harrison seemed to shrink. "I said *around* four thirty, not exactly."

His attorney hushed him with a look, then asked Bree, "What time do you think he left?"

"You're clearly shown on the surveillance video of the trampoline park leaving at three thirty-two."

The attorney cut in. "My client used the word *around* precisely because he was unsure of the exact time. He didn't lie. He was mistaken."

"Really?" Bree paused, letting Harrison sweat for a few seconds. "We also know you didn't leave Marina's house at six o'clock, as you previously claimed. We have two witnesses that put you on Kelly's porch between 4:06 and 4:55 p.m.—during the time window in which she was killed."

Harrison looked like he was going to pass out. Could a man get any paler? The attorney's face froze.

"Did you drop off the boys at Marina's first, or did you take them to Kelly's house with you?" Bree asked.

"I dropped them at home," Harrison squeaked, as if his throat were tight.

"Did you ask Marina to lie for you about the times?" Bree watched his eyes for signs of guilt. Would he feel bad for involving his girlfriend? Instead of guilty, he looked caught.

His attorney saved him. "Did either Mr. Gibson or Ms. Maxwell state that they knew the times precisely, or did they use words like *around* or *about* to imply they weren't sure about the exact time?"

Bree stalled a knee-jerk retort. "They weren't off by a few minutes. An hour is a long time."

The attorney looked nonplussed. He waved a hand. "Busy people managing two young children lose track of time."

Bree addressed Harrison. "You didn't tell me you went to Kelly's house on Monday."

"Did you specifically ask him if he had been at the house on Monday?" the attorney asked.

Before Bree could respond, Harrison chimed in. "She asked me when I last saw Kelly. I didn't see her on Monday, so I didn't lie." He looked proud of himself.

"As my client clarified, the issue was with the phrasing of your question," the lawyer said. "Not his answer."

"Feels like a telling omission to me. Why did you really go to Kelly's house that day, Harrison?" Bree waited.

Harrison's swagger didn't last. Sweat broke out on his forehead, but he didn't blurt out a response as Bree had hoped he would.

"Did you kill her?" Matt pressed. "Did you kill Kelly?"

"No!" Harrison leaped to his feet, sending the chair skittering backward, its metal feet scraping the tile.

Bree rose slowly and uttered one word. "Sit."

Without breaking eye contact, Harrison eased himself downward, reaching back and tugging the chair under his ass.

"You'll need to provide copies of those witness statements." The attorney's face had gone blank.

His courtroom face, Bree assumed.

"You'll get everything on schedule," she said vaguely. She would not allow the witnesses' names to be outed any earlier than necessary. She read the quote from her notes. "Harrison was banging on Kelly's door between four and five p.m. on Monday, yelling, 'Come on, Kelly. Don't be such a bitch. Let me in.'" As she finished, she looked up and watched the hint of remaining color drain from Harrison's face.

"I didn't— I—" Harrison stammered.

"That wasn't a question," the lawyer said. "Therefore, you don't need to answer."

"What did you do?" Bree leaned forward, pressing the question with her physical movement. "Did you keep knocking until she gave in?"

"No. I left." But Harrison's voice was shaky. "I went to the liquor store and bought a six-pack."

"Did you use a credit card or get a receipt?" Bree asked. If a liquor store clerk and/or surveillance camera verified that he went to the store and his shoes weren't covered in Kelly's blood, that would be a factor in Harrison's favor.

"Maybe." He looked panicked. "I was only at her door for like, five minutes."

"Stop talking," the attorney said.

But Harrison couldn't. "She was supposed to give me my ski gear. That's it! And she either went out or wouldn't open her goddamned door!"

The room went silent except for Harrison's ragged breathing. Bree didn't move as he wheezed, the truth sinking into his thick skull. His mouth dropped open, and he inhaled, preparing to speak again.

His attorney cut him off. "Shut. Up."

But Harrison was clearly beyond following instructions. Horror shone from his eyes. "She *was* inside, wasn't she?"

Bree didn't answer. If Harrison didn't kill her, she could have been bleeding to death while he threw a temper tantrum over his ski gear on her porch. Kelly could very likely have already been dead. Was the killer still inside the house at that time?

Harrison's gaze turned inward. Was he reliving the moment, picturing Kelly dead or dying?

The attorney stared at Bree as he addressed his client. "Do not say a word."

"We know you were seeing Marina before you left Kelly," Matt said. "How long was your affair going on with her?"

"Do not answer that," the lawyer said.

"Can you really blame him?" Matt asked, sarcasm dripping from his words. "Kelly was your partner for a couple of decades, but the years affected her, right? She wasn't the hot young thing you married anymore. She aged. She looked like a normal middle-aged woman. How fair is that?"

"That's not how it was." Harrison's pale face flushed an unhealthy color of red.

Bree wanted to think he was ashamed, but she doubted it. He was mad that they were calling him on his bullshit. "Then she expected you to keep paying for a house you weren't living in. Again, totally unfair."

Harrison couldn't hold it in. "She could have at least gotten a job."

"Quiet!" the lawyer admonished. "Do you have any more actual questions, Sheriff? Or just conjecture?"

"Oh, I have questions." Bree leaned forward. "How badly did you want to get out from under paying the mortgage, Harrison? Did you think you could collect Kelly's life insurance, sell the house, then set up house with your new girlfriend?"

Harrison's eyes slowly lifted to meet Bree's. "I didn't kill her."

"And yet her death makes your life easier, doesn't it?" Matt said, his voice heavy with disgust. "You're free to do as you please now."

"Really?" Harrison shouted.

The lawyer tried to intervene. "Stop!"

But Harrison's anger drove him to respond. "How am I supposed to sell a house that someone was murdered in? I bet you didn't think of that."

His point wasn't the flex he thought it was.

"Are you going to arrest my client?" The lawyer looked like he wanted to duct-tape his client's mouth closed.

"Not at this time," Bree said, wishing she could have said yes.

"Then this interview is over." The lawyer stood. "We're leaving. Don't call my client again unless you have an arrest warrant."

Bree didn't have enough evidence to arrest Harrison. Opportunity and proximity weren't sufficient, not even with his omissions and lies. Physical evidence would add relevance to Harrison's false statements. If only she worked on the TV set of *CSI* or *Bones*, where an obscure piece of sand found on the body would unequivocally tie Harrison to his wife's murder, but reality was never as simple as Hollywood crime. She'd yet to solve a case in thirty minutes.

She stood and pressed both palms on the table. "If you did kill Kelly, I will prove it, and you *will* go to prison."

Chapter Seventeen

Matt exited the interview room last. "I'll see them out."

"Thanks," Bree said, and turned into the break room.

Still contemplating the interview, Matt directed Harrison and his attorney down the hallway toward the lobby. Kelly's husband was a garbage human, but had he killed her?

Opportunity wasn't proof. But his answers didn't sit well with Matt.

Guilty people lie.

A few feet down the corridor, Harrison halted.

Juarez was walking toward them with another man in his midfifties. Matt recognized Jeff Burke from his photo, and knew he was scheduled to come in for an interview that afternoon. Jeff was huge, taller than Matt and just as broad.

Harrison froze suddenly. Matt nearly walked into him. He took a step to the side to avoid the collision.

Jeff stopped cold. Anger narrowed his eyes. "Harrison."

"Jeff." Harrison's voice was just as hostile.

No love between those two.

With no warning, Jeff launched himself at Harrison. The attorney executed a deft, graceful spin and sidestepped through the break room doorway, like a running back evading a tackle. Harrison wasn't as quick. Jeff caught him around the midsection, his shoulder plowing into

Harrison's gut, his greater weight and momentum driving the smaller man backward.

Matt let them go by. He couldn't stop the fight if he was on the bottom of the dogpile. The two men went flying. Harrison hit the floor flat on his back, and the wind left his lungs with an audible *whoosh*. Jeff landed on top and used his larger size to pin Harrison to the floor. He scrambled onto his knees, straddling Harrison.

"Did you fucking kill her?" Jeff leaned right into Harrison's face and shouted.

Harrison didn't seem to have enough oxygen to answer. Wheezing and purple-faced, he gasped and shook his head.

Juarez and Matt waded into the fray.

"Can't. Breathe," croaked Harrison.

Jeff straightened, cocked back a fist, and prepared to punch Harrison in the face. Matt grabbed his arm, preventing the blow, but he was unable to unseat the big man. Juarez snagged Jeff around the chest. Juarez wasn't tall, but he was stocky and had the strength of youth on his side. Still, he and Matt together couldn't budge Jeff Burke. The guy was strong as a bull and just as focused.

Frustrated, Matt strained, throwing his weight backward. But his position didn't give him leverage, and there was no room to maneuver in the narrow hallway.

"Get up!" Matt shouted in Jeff's ear.

But Jeff was beyond hearing him. A vein on his temple pulsed, and his eyes bulged with rage. "You killed her!"

Over Jeff's shoulder, Matt saw Harrison still shaking his head, his eyes rolling backward.

"Let go!" Matt snaked his forearm across Jeff's throat. Technically, choke holds weren't legal, but what could he do? Harrison couldn't breathe. Jeff was going to kill him. Still Matt took care not to compress Jeff's windpipe. He braced his body and pulled, but Jeff still didn't move.

Juarez had his baton out, but he didn't have room to swing it.

Something cracked. Jeff seized. His body convulsed hard, then went limp and collapsed on Harrison's chest.

Harrison wheezed, "Help."

Juarez shoved Jeff off Harrison's body and into the wall. Harrison rolled away, his hand on the center of his chest, just breathing and gagging.

Matt looked up. Bree stood a few feet away, shaking her head, Taser in hand. She pointed to Jeff, twitching on the floor, and snapped out an order to Juarez. "Cuff him."

Juarez scrambled to obey, his expression sheepish. Once he had the cuffs secure, Juarez checked Jeff's pulse. "He's OK."

The attorney magically reappeared, poking his head out of the break room. "How did you two not get shocked? You were touching him."

Bree holstered her Taser. "Because the current travels between the two probes in the shortest path possible."

From the other side of the altercation, she'd had a direct shot at Jeff's chest. One prong had struck the front of his shoulder. The other had hit him in the ribs.

Now that the scuffle was over, the attorney helped Harrison to scramble a few feet away and sit up with his back against the wall.

The lawyer speared Bree with his gaze. "Is this how you run your sheriff's department?"

Bree said nothing, and kept her expression carefully guarded.

"I'll be taking my client to the emergency room," the lawyer huffed. "He could have broken bones or other hidden injuries. We demand you bring assault charges."

"Mr. Burke is looking at charges," Bree affirmed.

"And we're going to sue you, your department, and the county too." He pointed at Bree. "This shouldn't have happened. A person should be safe in the sheriff's department of all places."

With the giant man no longer on top of him, Harrison looked fine. Matt doubted he'd suffered more than a couple of bruises. His ego would be more damaged than his body. Hell, Matt's ego had taken a hit. He guessed that Jeff Burke had some sort of grappling experience. He knew how to position his body to utilize maximum leverage.

The lawyer heaved Harrison to his feet and made a show of assisting him down the hallway. Matt followed them to the lobby, then returned to Bree.

She propped a hand on her duty belt. "Never a dull moment."

Jeff Burke still lay on the floor, an occasional twitch running through his entire body.

Bree crouched. "You OK, Jeff?"

Jeff nodded.

"Give it a couple of minutes." She didn't move, clearly intending to stay with him until she was sure he was all right.

"I'm OK now. Sorry about that." His jaw clenched and released. "Sometimes, my temper gets the better of me."

"You should work on that," Bree said. "You're under arrest for assault. Do you need medical assistance?"

Jeff lifted his head, almost experimentally, then did the same with his legs. "No. I'm good."

Bree rose. "Can you stand?"

Jeff nodded. Matt and Juarez heaved him upright. He weighed a ton.

"Put him in the holding cell," she said to Juarez. "We'll talk when you feel better."

"I'm OK," Jeff insisted. "I'm sorry for going off on Harrison, but I want to help you prove he killed Kelly."

Or did Jeff kill Kelly and want to poke his nose into the case to throw off the investigation?

Bree shrugged. "Interview room two."

Juarez started down the hall. The jolt seemed to have brought Jeff back to his senses. Bree and Matt followed. Matt was curious about what Jeff was going to say.

Matt glanced at Bree. She looked annoyed at the entire situation. He couldn't blame her. But no one had a Magic 8 Ball. They couldn't have foreseen Jeff's explosion. "Harrison's lawyer is going to use this against us," he said.

Bree lifted a palm. "I don't blame him. He's just doing his job."

Matt still didn't like it.

"He's right, though. It shouldn't have happened." Bree frowned.

Ahead, Juarez marched Jeff into the interview room. The knuckles on Jeff's hand looked red. Bruises? He hadn't landed a single punch.

They entered the interview room. Matt usually liked to remove handcuffs before asking questions. People tended to be more open when they weren't restrained. But given Jeff's strength and volatility, freeing him wasn't a good idea. Cuffs would limit the amount of damage he could do and make him much easier to control if necessary.

Juarez guided Jeff into a chair, and Bree sat across from him. Jeff seemed calm. Matt stayed on alert in case the guy flipped out again, but Bree seemed to have a power over him that Matt didn't.

Juarez took a step back, then hesitated. "Do you want me to stay, ma'am?"

Bree shook her head. "No. Jeff isn't going to give me any trouble, are you, Jeff?"

"No, ma'am." Jeff was downright subdued.

Was it the Taser shock or something else? The psychology of interrogation fascinated Matt. He'd seen combative criminals turn meek when confronted by a female authority figure. The next suspect might despise women and refuse to speak to one at all. The key was using whatever worked. So, in this case, Matt sat back so Bree could take the lead. She would do the same if the subject responded better to Matt.

She started the video recording, made the usual disclaimers, and read Jeff his rights. Then she started with easy questions. "What do you do for a living, Jeff?"

"I have a podcast." Jeff squeezed his eyes shut and opened them, as if they were sticky or something. "I teach people how to stay off the government radar."

"Does that pay enough to live on?"

"I do OK," said Jeff. "I bought my house a long time ago. It was cheaper then. I couldn't afford to buy it at today's prices, though."

"How long have you lived across the street from Kelly and Harrison Gibson?"

"I lived here when they moved in." His tone turned wistful. "She was so beautiful."

Bree was right. Jeff did sound like a long-term stalker. Had he been enamored with his neighbor's wife for decades? Did he finally snap when her husband left her, and she still didn't want him?

"Did they appear to have a good marriage back then?" Bree asked.

"Yeah, it was good enough, I guess," he admitted in a grudging tone.

"When did their problems seem to start?"

Jeff contemplated her question, staring at the ceiling for a few seconds. "I don't remember a sudden start. Maybe a slow disintegration over the last ten years." He rolled his eyes. "Anyway, a few years ago, at a neighborhood block party, I heard him criticize her for gaining a few pounds."

"Do you remember when this happened?"

"Summer, three or four years ago, maybe Memorial Day or the Fourth of July?" He shook his head. "That's the best I can do."

"What did Harrison say to her?"

"Somebody had set up a folding table for food. Everyone brings a dish to these things. Kelly was putting a brownie on her plate, and Harrison asked her if she thought she should be eating it." Jeff's mouth flattened in disapproval. "Sure, she'd gained a few pounds over the years. Who doesn't change after a couple of decades? Harrison doesn't exactly look the same. Neither do I. Kelly was a beautiful woman. I thought she was aging just fine."

"What did Kelly say?"

"Nothing. But she looked like she was going to cry. Then she pulled herself together and threw out her whole plate. I could tell what he said really hurt her." He blew air out of his nostrils like an angry horse. "I should have hit him, but I thought that might make things worse for her. Now it feels like I picked the wrong time to exercise some self-control. I should've punched him in the face. Maybe he would have thought twice about killing her if he knew he had to answer to me."

Matt didn't even try to make sense out of that argument.

Bree followed up. "Why do you think he killed her?"

"He wanted a younger wife, and he already has one in the queue. But Kelly was making the divorce hard. She was pissed off—and rightly so. Plus, she didn't have any way to support herself. She raised his kids, and he didn't think he owed her anything."

"Was she dragging out the renovation to get even?"

"No." He drew his head back, as if that idea were unfathomable. "Kelly wasn't like that. But she wanted a fair settlement."

Bree asked, "How do you know this?"

"They had a fight a few weeks ago, right out in the driveway 'cause she refused to let him inside. I was in my garage. I heard every word." He sounded proud of his eavesdropping. "Harrison didn't think she was entitled to any money. He kept saying he earned it all. It should be his. Kelly was mad—which was better than sad, right? She refused to sign divorce papers until the settlement was even.

"He was angry. Got in her face and yelled. I almost went over there, but Kelly handled him." Pride oozed from his words. "She stood her ground, and he backed off." His face hardened again. "So I think he killed her to get her out of the way and so that he didn't have to split the assets with her. With Kelly gone, Harrison can sell the house. He doesn't have to worry about paying any alimony either."

"Did he threaten her?"

Jeff waggled his head back and forth. "Not exactly. He said stuff like, 'My lawyer will get you out of this house.'" His imitation of Harrison's voice was decent. Jeff brightened. "At the end, he did say she'd be sorry."

Weak, but better than nothing.

"Tell me about the other man you saw at Kelly's house recently," Bree said.

The question seemed to knock the air out of Jeff. His whole body slumped. "Drove a fancy car. Dressed in fancy clothes." A sigh shook him. "I never expected Kelly to latch on to a rich guy. I know she was tight on money, but I still didn't expect her to look for money in a man. But then, maybe she was just . . . tired."

Bree spread six photographs on the table. All of the men fit Troy Ryder's basic physical description.

Jeff didn't hesitate. "Third from the left. My left."

Bingo. Troy.

Bree asked a few more questions, but Jeff didn't seem to know anything.

"What's going to happen to me now?" he asked.

"Deputy Juarez will take you to the jail for processing. You'll be arraigned. If you can't afford a lawyer, one will be appointed free of charge."

Jeff scoffed. "My cousin is a lawyer."

"Don't give my deputies any more trouble," Bree warned.

"I won't," Jeff promised. But Matt didn't have much faith in his self-control.

Now that Bree had gotten all the information she could out of Jeff, Matt asked his one question. "How did you get the bruises on your knuckles?"

Jeff's expression switched from cooperative to raw rage when he turned his gaze from Bree to Matt.

If looks could kill...

Jeff's voice was cold enough to freeze rain. "I hit them on the concrete when the sheriff knocked me down."

"They look less recent than that," Matt pointed out.

"They're not," Jeff snapped. He turned back to Bree, his face compliant again.

After Jeff was led away, Matt and Bree walked to the conference room.

"What do you think?" she asked.

"Moody as hell."

"Yes," she agreed.

"He was definitely too focused on Kelly."

"Stalkerish, right?"

"Yep."

"But that doesn't mean he's guilty."

"Nope," Matt said. "Except for the animal fur found at the scene, the physical evidence suggests Troy is more likely the killer."

"Harrison lives with cats on his mother's farm," Bree added. "For that matter, Kelly could have picked up that fur anywhere and brought it home with her. The fur could be meaningless."

As was the case with all trace evidence. Anytime there was contact between two objects, trace evidence could be transferred. Kelly could have stopped to pet a stray cat outside the grocery store. Their job in an investigation was to sift through the facts and know which ones mattered.

"Jeff will be out of jail fast," Bree mused. "And Troy and Harrison are free to do as they please."

The brutality of Kelly's murder would haunt Matt forever. "Whoever did that to Kelly Gibson should never see the outside of a prison cell again."

"Agreed."

Matt turned to the murder board. "Then we'd better get cracking."

Before he could even update the board, his phone buzzed. Hoping it was forensics, Matt dug his phone from his pocket. Cady's picture stared back at him and nerves curled in his belly as he pressed "Answer." "Tell me you're OK."

Chapter Eighteen

"I'm OK," Cady said.

Matt breathed in relief. "Are you in labor? Do you need Todd?" The chief deputy was still handling the accident investigation, but Matt was sure Bree would relieve him if Cady was in labor.

"No." She sounded grumpy. "This is the first time I have ever uttered these words, but I cannot handle this dog. I need you to come and get him." She didn't need to say the name *Turbo*. Matt knew.

"What's going on?"

"He got out. Again. I can't contain him. I don't even know how he does it. He's too smart, too athletic, too . . . everything." She ended the last word with a sob. "Since the last time he got loose, Todd put a GPS tracker on him. This morning, I trekked all the way out to the pond to get him."

Matt smoothed his beard, guilt ripping through him. Cady never complained and rarely cried. She poured her heart into saving dogs. But his sister was nine months pregnant. She didn't need any additional stress, and she certainly didn't need to be trekking across acres of meadow to fetch an errant dog. "I'll come and get him right now."

Cady sniffed. "OK."

Matt pictured the Malinois he'd watched in K-9 training. Belgian Mals were nicknamed "Maligators" for a reason. When they latched on to a bite sleeve—or a suspect—they held on.

"Has he snapped or shown aggression at anyone?" Matt asked.

"No. He's boisterous, not vicious. But he has superpowers."

"That's the breed." Ironically, Turbo's lack of aggression now worried Matt. Was Turbo too friendly? Too soon to say. He'd worried about the same thing with Greta, but she'd been successfully trained to bite. Now she thought pursuing and taking down a suspect was a great game. Hopefully, Turbo would also respond to K-9 training.

"Yeah," Cady agreed. "If only people who wanted them knew that."

"I'll be right there." Matt ended the call.

Bree was watching him, her eyes sharp with concern. "Is Cady OK?"

Matt relayed the conversation.

"Go!" She waved toward the door. "We'll catch up later."

Matt drove to Cady's place. His sister and Todd lived in his old house. She'd based her canine rescue there for years, so when Matt moved in with Bree, it made sense for Cady and Todd to take over the property.

He parked near the kennels. Cady was standing in the grass, staring up, one hand braced on the small of her back. Instead of greeting him, she pointed to the roof of the kennel. Matt squinted into the setting sun. Silhouetted against the orange sky, Turbo stood on the one-story roof, tail wagging, tongue lolling.

"How did he get up there?"

"That's my guess." Cady pointed to the trash cans lined up next to the building.

Matt held back a laugh. "The dog needs a job."

"Or three." Cady arched backward, stretching.

"You feeling OK?"

"No. Everything hurts, my bladder has been squashed to the size of a thimble, and I have vicious heartburn. Forget about eating." She patted her solar plexus. "There's no room."

"It won't be for much longer."

Cady rubbed her stomach in slow circles. "I want to be done with this part, but I'm also terrified of what comes next."

"You're going to be a great mom." Matt wrapped an arm around her shoulders. "Can I help? Other than taking this knucklehead off your hands."

"That'll do it for now." She rested her head on his shoulder. "I have the rest of the dogs covered by volunteers, but that"—she jabbed a finger at Turbo, who looked like he was having the best day of his life—"is too much."

"I'll handle him."

"How are you going to get him down?"

Matt fished a tennis ball out of his pocket, turned, and threw it into the adjoining field. The ball was still in the air when Turbo bounded after it. Using a trash can as a jumping pad, the dog bounced to the ground and shot off after the ball without breaking stride like Super Mario.

Cady handed Matt a leash. Turbo raced back to Matt, dropped the ball at his feet, and barked. Matt scooped up the ball and threw it as far as he could. The dog shot off across the grass. When he returned the second time, Matt commanded him to heel in German. The dog snapped into position, his body quivering with anticipation of the next command. Intelligence and obedience were not Turbo's issues.

Matt snapped a leash onto his collar. "We're going for a ride."

Turbo vibrated.

"Where are you taking him?" Cady asked.

Matt laughed. "I don't want you to worry about him at all. I'll figure out something for him. He's got skills. They just need to be channeled." He leaned over and kissed his sister on the cheek. "It's almost dinnertime. I hope you're done out here for the day."

"I'm not hungry at all, but I'm going to put my feet up. They're so puffy. I have cankles, and I waddle." She turned and headed for the house. She did not waddle one bit. Being six feet tall and athletic, she carried the pregnancy well, but Matt kept his mouth firmly shut. Now was not the time to disagree with his sister about anything.

He loaded the dog into his Suburban. "I guess you're going back to the station with me." Luckily, Turbo was friendly, even if he was a handful.

Matt hadn't driven two miles before Turbo leaped over the seat to ride shotgun.

"Dude," Matt said. "The airbag could kill you."

Paws on the dashboard, tail wagging, Turbo didn't care.

When Matt led the dog inside the station, Marge was putting on her coat. Her purse sat on her desk. She greeted Turbo with a dog biscuit. "Who's a handsome boy?"

Turbo wagged and wiggled like a puppy. For a powerful, elite canine, he had no pride.

Marge stroked his head. "Is he yours now?"

Matt raised a hand. "This is temporary. Cady is too pregnant to deal with his energy."

"And a newborn isn't going to make her life any easier." Marge zipped her coat and slung her bag over her shoulder.

"No, it isn't." After Marge left for the day, Matt took Turbo back to the conference room, where the dog paced around the table, sniffing everything.

Bree tensed as he sniffed her boots. She extended a tentative hand, and the dog shoved his head under it with an enthusiastic wag.

"He likes you," Matt said.

Bree just nodded. Turbo snuffled away, investigating the entire room and walking laps around the table.

Two years ago, Bree had been terrified of dogs. She still carried the scars from a childhood mauling. But Brody and Ladybug had worked their way into her heart. Except for intense canines—like Greta—Bree had made great progress toward overcoming her fear. But Matt knew that Turbo was just as intense and intimidating as the department's working K-9.

"Does he ever get tired?" she asked.

"No." Matt sighed. "Todd's been running with him every morning, but it isn't enough. Also, this dog needs more than just physical exercise. He needs mental stimulation. He *needs* to work."

"What are you doing with him tonight?"

"What do you think about taking him home with us?" Matt asked hopefully.

"I don't have any other suggestions. It's a lot to ask of Brody and Ladybug, though. The last time you brought him to the house, he tormented them relentlessly."

"You're right," Matt agreed. Brody was an impeccably mannered senior and Ladybug was more couch potato than canine. "Neither of them will want to roughhouse. He can spend the night in the tack room. I'll put a bed in there. The door is too thick for him to chew through, at least in one night."

"Worth a try," Bree said. "But if he's going to be with us for any length of time, he'll need a kennel."

With a concrete base and steel fencing. High fencing. Prison fencing.

Most working K-9s lived in kennels. They weren't pets, at least not until they retired. Brody had always been different.

"I'll take him for a run. That should help a little." But it wasn't a long-term solution.

"Why don't we head home? We can have dinner with the kids, then regroup afterward. I have a stack of reports to write, and I could use a break and a change of scenery."

Matt helped her pack up the files she wanted to bring home. "What we really need are those DNA reports from forensics."

Bree held up crossed fingers. "Hoping we get those tomorrow. I have to check in with Todd before I can leave. Meet you at home."

She headed for her office.

The lean dog followed Matt outside to his vehicle. This time, he retrieved Brody's harness from the back of the vehicle and put it on Turbo. Then he tethered the harness to the seat belt in the back seat. "Stay."

Turbo's tongue lolled. The dog was quiet for the drive out to the farm. After parking, Matt opened the rear door, expecting the dog to be restrained, but Turbo vaulted from the vehicle. Matt glanced inside. The middle section of leather leash was gone. "You ate the leash."

Turbo did not look sorry. Matt called him to heel, and the dog fell into step beside him. Luke was in the barn grooming his bay horse, Riot. Turbo ran to Luke for scratches. The horse lowered his head to greet the dog. The two animals sniffed noses. Turbo barked and dropped into a play bow.

"I don't think he wants to play with you," Luke said. "Sorry, Turbo."

"I'm going to change into running clothes. Would you keep an eye on him for five minutes?" Matt asked.

"Sure." Luke returned to brushing saddle marks off his horse's back. "Just shut the door on your way out."

Matt changed and returned with an intact leash. Though he'd been working with the dog's obedience commands, Matt wasn't 100 percent sure of his off-leash recall. He snapped on the lead, and they headed out the door. Matt maintained a strong pace, but the dog kept up effortlessly. After a five-mile run, Matt was winded. Turbo was fresh as a furry daisy. They returned to find Bree's SUV parked at home.

Matt went to the barn and put the dog in the tack room with a bed and a bowl of fresh water. "I'll be back with your dinner in an hour."

In the house, he found Bree in the office and greeted her with a kiss. "Well, I tired out one of us."

"I'm guessing it wasn't the dog."

"You'd be right." Matt ran upstairs and showered. After dinner, he returned to the barn and fed Turbo. The dog seemed content lying on the floor of the tack room. Matt closed the sturdy door and fastened it on the outside with an extra carabiner clip. The door was thick enough to hold a thousand-pound animal. The dog should be fine overnight.

He went back to the office to help Bree with report writing. Sometimes it felt as if 80 percent of crime investigation were paperwork. They worked until midnight, then went to bed. It felt as if Matt had barely closed his eyes when Bree's phone rang on the nightstand.

Matt checked the time on his own phone. Just after one o'clock in the morning. If it were his phone ringing, his sister's labor would be the most likely reason. But it was never good news if the sheriff got middle-of-the-night phone calls. Stretched along the foot of the bed, Brody groaned in protest. Ladybug, who was curled into an impossibly small ball behind Bree's knees, squeezed her eyelids tighter. Neither dog was interested in getting out of bed.

Bree sat up and answered, her voice scratchy with sleep. "Sheriff Taggert." She listened for a few minutes, then said, "Text me the address. I'll be right there." She lowered her phone and ended the call.

"Someone's dead?" Matt got out of bed, adrenaline cutting through the fog of sleep.

"Yes." Bree swung her legs off the mattress and headed for the bathroom. The second she vacated the pillow, Vader claimed it. Bree emerged a minute later, still swiping deodorant under her arms. Tossing the stick onto the dresser, she grabbed a clean uniform from the closet and dressed.

"Details?" Matt stepped into a pair of cargo pants and tugged a shirt over his head.

Bree fastened her duty belt, withdrew her weapon from the gun safe, and tucked it into her holster. "Zucco says it's another bloody murder."

Chapter Nineteen

Bree pulled to the curb thirty minutes after receiving the call. The address was fifteen miles outside of town on a narrow, quiet country road.

Her belly cramped with the memory of Kelly Gibson's brutalized body. Bree took a deep breath and used a few seconds to prepare herself for another vicious crime scene. The decades of her career, finding body after body, investigating murder after murder, were taking a cumulative toll.

In the passenger seat, Matt appeared to be doing the same. He stared at the house for a few seconds, then exhaled hard through his mouth. "Ready?"

"Yes." Bree knew not to hesitate any longer. Better to rip off the Band-Aid than drag out the dread of it. They climbed out of the SUV and stood shoulder to shoulder in the street.

The house was a small cottage type, with a yard surrounded by a split rail fence in need of repairs. Fields and meadows surrounded the property. The bones of an old barn stood well behind the house. The property had likely been a farm at one time.

"The nearest neighbor is a mile down the road," Matt said.

There were no neighbors nearby to hear a scream. Though if Zucco's description of the murder was similar to the Gibson case, there wouldn't have been much screaming, since Kelly had died or been rendered unconscious quickly. Mercifully, Bree hoped this poor person hadn't suffered long either.

In winter, the front flower beds looked forlorn. A few straggly weeds pushed through the bare earth, their tendrils extending across the ground like fingers grasping the edge of a precipice. Lights glowed in most of the windows. A Toyota Camry was parked in the single-vehicle driveway. A Ford Escape sat at the curb next to the mailbox.

The porch steps creaked as they climbed onto the porch. The door gaped an inch. Zucco opened the door wider, her face locked in a grim deadpan. The hairs on the back of Bree's neck lifted as she crossed the threshold into the warmer living room.

"Do we know the identity of the victim?" Bree took in the homey space, full of worn furniture likely collected from yard sales and thrift shops. Books crammed a full wall of built-in shelves. End tables held more stacks of titles.

Zucco glanced down at her notepad. "The victim is Janet Hargrave. Identified by her roommate, Alice Miller, who found the body when she returned from a business trip."

"She was certain the victim was dead?" Matt asked.

"There's no question," Zucco said, her voice strained.

Bree could hear quiet sobbing from the back of the house. She kept her voice low. "The roommate?"

Zucco nodded. "It's brutal. She's not coping very well."

Who would?

Bree resisted the pity that filled her, but damn. Sometimes it was near impossible to remain completely objective.

"Where's the body?" Matt asked, the hoarseness in his voice clearly stemming from more than lack of sleep.

"Home office." Zucco inclined her head toward a doorway.

"Stay with the roommate," Bree said to Zucco, then headed for the doorway. She needed to talk to the woman, but first, she wanted to see the body without any preconceived ideas. The additional emotional pressure of the woman's grief wouldn't help either.

With Matt at her back, Bree stopped at the doorway and peered into the home office. She was immediately grateful for his solid presence. Even without physically touching, they supported each other through an invisible connection. She'd seen scores of dead bodies, but she would never be immune. In fact, since she'd lost her sister to murder and taken over raising Luke and Kayla, she'd softened. Death affected her more now that she knew what it was like to love and to lose. With her own grief never far behind her, she felt the survivors' pain acutely. When she'd lived alone, resisting human and familial attachments like a disease, compartmentalizing had been easier. Then again, maybe she hadn't compartmentalized her reactions as much as she'd repressed them. Now that she was in therapy, she realized those scenes had left marks she'd simply refused to confront. Her therapist said she'd probably been heading for a breakdown, but at the time, the numbness had provided its own sort of empty comfort.

The roommate's crying broke through her internal debate. A bloody and violent scene was disturbing enough to her, a seasoned law enforcement officer. To a civilian, the sight would be traumatizing on a life-altering scale. Bree blocked out the sound of grief and viewed the scene with all the detachment she could summon, which admittedly wasn't much. In the back of her mind, she wondered if a time would come when she could no longer do the job effectively—if there was a maximum amount of horror a person could process before it was simply too much.

A petite woman was sprawled out on the hardwood floor. Next to the body, a black mesh office chair lay on its side, wheels up. The throat injury was devastating. The wound gaped like a second mouth. To Bree's nonmedical eye, the slash looked deeper than Kelly's. The blood puddle beneath the victim's head was shaped like the state of Florida. Blood had also sprayed onto the desk. Dried blood matted her short blond hair. A pair of over-the-ear headphones lay a few feet from the body.

Bree had not wanted to ever see a sight as terrible as Kelly Gibson's murder scene ever again, but here she was. Bile crept up her throat. She closed her eyes, breathed deeply, and exhaled through pursed lips.

Get it together. You couldn't have prevented this. In the absence of a crystal ball, Bree had no way to predict Kelly's murderer would strike again. But the shiver of déjà vu that passed up her spine doubted the assertion.

When she opened her eyes again, she exchanged a look with Matt. His brows rose, and his mouth flattened. Without speaking, she knew he was seeing the same thing she was. Woman home alone. Killed with a slash to the throat.

Janet's murder echoed Kelly Gibson's.

With an eye on her boots, Bree took two strides into the room. She didn't want to disturb evidence or step in any bits of gore.

With equal care about his foot placement, Matt stepped up with her. He pointed to the laptop, open on the desk, where a screensaver played a slideshow of stock images. "My guess is that she was working. Someone came up behind her."

Just like Kelly.

Bree envisioned it. The desk faced the wall. "Yes. Her back would have been to the door."

Matt inhaled. "No heavy scent of decomp. She wasn't killed that long ago."

"But the blood there"—Bree pointed to the victim's head—"is dry." The death wasn't *that* fresh. "But she died recently enough that the ME should be able to give us a tight PMI."

Matt pointed to a dark bay window on the same wall as the door. The glass reflected their own images back at them. "With the lights on, she wouldn't have been able to see someone outside."

"But she would have been visible to anyone on the street," Bree added. "I'll call the ME and forensics." She turned away from the horror and left the room. Through the living room window, she spotted a news van at the curb. Someone had been monitoring their police scanner. She needed a minute but could never say so, not at the scene. If a comment suggesting the sheriff couldn't handle her job leaked to the press, Bree would never win a reelection. Especially as a woman, she couldn't show weakness. She composed her game face. She was in charge, and she'd better look capable and confident every time she donned her uniform.

"I'll check the doors for signs of forced entry." Matt backtracked out of the room.

Bree stepped outside to make her calls. The cold night air refreshed her lungs. The smell of death inside might be faint, but it lingered in the nostrils.

The house wasn't big, and Bree found her way back to the kitchen, where Zucco was babysitting Janet's roommate.

A wheelie carry-on was parked next to the kitchen island, a baby-blue puffy jacket draped over the handle. A small black purse and key fob had been tossed on the granite countertop. A woman in her late thirties sat on a stool. Hunched over, she hugged her midsection and cried. Tears streaked her face. Her blue eyes were red and devastated.

Zucco gestured. "This is Alice Miller, Janet's roommate."

Alice was tall and slim, with shoulder-length auburn hair. Her jeans, sweater, and white tennis shoes were clean, with no blood streaks or specks. Bree glanced down at Alice's hands, twisted in her lap. Also clean. No blood under the nails.

Bree sat on the stool next to her. "Hey, Alice."

Alice sniffed and looked up. She swiped a hand across one red, swollen eye and forced words out between sobs. "She was my best friend."

"I'm very sorry this happened." Bree glanced at the suitcase. "Where were you?"

"I was in Orlando for the last week. I had a business conference and stayed to visit with my brother for a couple of days." Alice shuddered. "My flight was delayed. I landed in Albany a little before midnight and drove home. I sensed something was wrong right away because the door was open, but I was so tired I brushed off the feeling."

"Was the door unlocked or open?" Bree asked.

"Unlocked and open about an inch," Alice said.

"But you went inside?"

Alice nodded. "I didn't listen to my gut. I thought maybe Janet had just put out the trash or something and the door didn't catch. The light in her office was on. She can be really focused when she's on a project."

"What did she do for a living?"

"Technical writing. She's working on a human resources manual." Alice stubbornly stuck with the present tense when talking about Janet.

"Who did she work for?"

"She freelances." Again, Alice persisted with the use of present tense, as if her brain refused to acknowledge her friend's death.

Acceptance would come with time, Bree knew. "Did she always wear headphones?"

Alice lifted both palms. "Sometimes, yeah. They help her concentrate."

She wouldn't have heard anyone sneak into the house.

"You went inside. Then what?" Bree prompted.

"I dropped my stuff." She nodded toward the suitcase. "Then I went to the office to let Janet know I was home."

"Did you go into the room?"

Alice looked horrified. "No. I stopped—froze—in the doorway. I knew she was gone, but I also couldn't believe what I was seeing." She rubbed a hand under her nose. "It's a little bit of a blur now."

Shock was a defense mechanism. The brain blocked what it couldn't handle. Bree had experienced this firsthand. "How long have you and Janet lived together?"

"Three years, but we've known each other since college. We were both tired of apartment living, but neither one of us could afford to rent a house on our own. We were both single, and it felt"—she hiccuped—"safer than living alone." Fresh tears welled in her eyes, and she pressed a fist to her mouth to stifle a sob. "I'm sorry."

"Take your time," Bree said.

Alice composed herself, straightening her posture and wiping her face with both hands. "I'm OK."

She wasn't and wouldn't be for a long time, but Bree didn't point that out. "Do you travel often?"

"Not really." Alice blew her nose. "Quarterly? Usually, I'm only gone three or four days, but this time, I thought I'd make a mini vacation out of it." She balled the tissue in her fist so tightly her knuckles went white. "But if I'd have come right home, Janet wouldn't have been alone." She broke down again.

There was no point in saying *it wasn't your fault* because Alice would probably blame herself no matter what Bree said. She let her cry for a minute, then changed the subject. "What do you do?"

"I sell insurance, mostly homeowner's and auto."

"Does Janet have family?" Bree asked.

Alice nodded. "Her mom passed a couple of years ago, but her dad lives in Scarlet Falls."

"Do you have his address?"

"His name is Barry Hargrave." Alice recited an address from memory, then went silent for a few seconds before a fresh wave of grief filled her eyes. "You have to tell him, right?"

"Yes. It's better that he finds out from me than on the news."

Alice folded her shaking hands together. "Could I go with you? He's eighty-five, and his health isn't great. I know him pretty well, and he doesn't have anyone else. Janet is—was—his only child, and they were close. They saw each other almost every day."

Bree considered the offer. Death notifications were one of the worst duties of the job, and delivering the news of a child's death to an elderly, sick man would be devastating. "Yes. That would be helpful."

"Good." Alice seemed steadier with a purpose. "I don't think he should be alone."

Neither one of you should.

"When was the last time you talked to Janet?" Bree asked.

"I texted with her yesterday, letting her know what time I'd be home today."

"Did she respond?"

Alice nodded. "Yes. I got a thumbs-up tapback." She paused. "But when I messaged her earlier today—no, yesterday—to tell her my plane was delayed, she didn't respond."

"What time was this?"

Alice reached for her purse and drew out her phone. She tapped on the screen. "I texted her at eight p.m. She hadn't texted back when I boarded at nine thirty."

So she was probably dead before eight.

"Was that odd?" Bree asked.

"No. I didn't really think about it at the time. I assumed she was working. Like I said before, she can really focus, and sometimes, she puts her phone on silent in the top drawer of her desk. She's really disciplined that way." Alice's face crumpled. "Was. She *was* disciplined." She looked away but her gaze focused inward. "I just can't believe she's gone. Just like that." She snapped shaky fingers.

"I'm so sorry for your loss." For the hundredth time, Bree lamented the inadequacy of that statement. "Do you know Janet's phone passcode?"

"Yes." Alice recited a six-digit number.

Matt entered the room. "The dead bolt wasn't in place. From the scratches on the metal, I'd guess the knob lock was picked. It's a simple lock. It wouldn't have been hard."

"Did Janet make a habit out of leaving the dead bolt unlocked?" Bree asked.

Alice drew in a shaky breath. "She always latches it before she goes to bed."

"What time was that usually?"

Alice shook her head. "She didn't keep regular hours. When she got into a groove, she often worked very late."

"Was she having any troubles lately?" Bree asked. "An argument or disagreement with anyone?"

Alice sniffed. "No."

"Did she mention any unusual incidents?"

"No."

"Would she have told you if she experienced something troubling?" Bree asked.

Alice paused, a thoughtful expression on her face. "I think so. She wasn't secretive and she didn't seem bothered or distracted by anything. She was . . . normal."

"Did she have a boyfriend?" Matt asked.

"No." Alice got up, crossed the room, and tossed her tissue in a pedal-open trash can. On her way back to the island, she took another from the box and dried her eyes gingerly, as if they hurt. "She broke up with her last one a few months ago. She said she needed to take a break from dating, which was why she was really glad for the big project she scored."

Matt's focus sharpened. "Did she date him long?"

Alice shook her head. "Three or four months? He didn't want kids and wasn't sure if he ever wanted to get married. He was also emotionally closed off and didn't like to talk about those issues. Janet said she was done with men who weren't looking for the same level of commitment she was. She didn't dislike him, but their goals weren't compatible."

Bree sensed a lead. "Was *he* angry about the breakup?"

Alice shrugged. "He called and drunk-ranted at her. She blocked his ass ASAP. He's good-looking and rich. Probably used to doing the dumping rather than being dumped. But Janet wasn't impressed by money. She wanted a deeper connection and said she'd rather be alone than settle for less than she deserved."

"Did he continue to try and contact her?"

"Not that I know of," said Alice. "That call was the last she mentioned."

"Do you remember his name?" Bree asked.

"I do because it was so ridiculous." Alice scoffed. "Like a cartoon character."

Bree knew what Alice was going to say before she opened her mouth.

"His name is Troy Ryder."

Chapter Twenty

Bree stepped away from the roommate and lowered her voice. "What are the odds that a second woman who dated Troy Ryder was murdered by someone other than Troy Ryder?"

Matt followed her back to the doorway to the home office. "That would be a huge coincidence."

Bree slipped on shoe covers. As Alice had suggested, Janet's phone was stowed in her top desk drawer. Bree picked it up with gloved hands and backed out of the room. She entered the passcode Alice had provided, and the phone unlocked. "Bingo." She opened the message app.

Matt looked over her shoulder. "There are the texts from Alice."

The second group was a message chain labeled DAD. Bree opened it and scrolled. "Looks like she texted with her father every morning at minimum."

"We need to get over there soon," Matt said.

"Yes. As soon as the medical examiner comes."

As if on cue, a voice said, "I'm here."

Bree turned to see Dr. Jones down the hall, her assistant trailing behind her. Bree stood aside as Dr. Jones stepped into the doorway and overlooked Janet Hargrave's brutalized body. The ME's sharp exhalation summed up the situation. She shook off her reaction, donned gloves, slipped booties over her rubber clogs, and picked her way carefully into the room to conduct her initial assessment of the body. She repeated the same motions as she had with Kelly's body, testing limbs for stiffness, checking the underside of the body for lividity stains, and taking the corpse's temperature.

She stepped back from examining the torso. "Rigor is peaking. Lividity is fixed. Based on those factors and body temperature, I estimate she's been dead ten to fourteen hours." She checked her watch. "It's two a.m. I'm giving a preliminary time of death between noon and four p.m. yesterday—Thursday—afternoon. Did anyone ID her?"

"Her roommate," Bree said. "But let's keep that to ourselves until the family has been notified."

Dr. Jones nodded. "I assume you want to do the death notification?"

"Yes," Bree said. "Cause of death? Do you see anything besides the obvious?"

"No," Dr. Jones said. "On initial examination, I don't see any other major injuries. Therefore, I don't think it's a stretch to say exsanguination by throat cutting, subject to confirmation on autopsy, of course."

"Defensive wounds?" Bree asked.

The ME shook her head. "I didn't find any. This cut looks deeper than Kelly Gibson's. I don't see any hesitation marks, just one quick, hard slash. She would have gone into shock almost immediately and bled out in a few minutes."

Bree lowered her voice. "I don't have to tell you how sensitive this murder is. We need to know if the murders are related ASAP."

Dr. Jones nodded. "I'll shuffle some cases and move this autopsy to the top of the list." She summoned her assistant into the room and directed him to begin photographing the body *in situ*.

Space was limited, so Bree left them to their work. She found Matt in the backyard, examining the back door.

"Anything?" she asked as she took a gulp of night air.

"Nope." He straightened. "Really, I just needed a break, and the press is already cluttering up the street out front."

Bree shoved her hands inside her pockets. "Preliminary thoughts?"

He lowered his voice. "Other than the glaring parallels?"

"Yes. We have to consider the case both as a potential follow-up to Kelly's death and as its own separate crime."

He sighed. "Time of death makes Harrison Gibson an unlikely candidate. It might be *possible*, but he was in the sheriff's station for most of the afternoon. The timeline would be very tight."

"Especially when you consider the drive out here and the necessity of personal cleanup. It's not impossible to do this clean." Bree gestured in the direction of the body. "But it's more likely they got some blood on their sleeve or hand."

"We have his time of arrival and departure at the station, so we can test the timeline. Same with Jeff Burke. The roommate says she dated Troy Ryder. We should confirm that."

"She uses the Date Smart app, just like Kelly did." Bree turned to the victim's phone again and attempted to open her dating app. "Date Smart requires a separate passcode. We'll get Rory to open it. I want to know if she met Troy through the app and who else she was dating. While we're at it, we'll request Troy's Date Smart info. We might need subpoenas." Most apps had fine print disclosures that personal information was available to law enforcement, but not all companies cooperated without warrants. From an evidence-in-a-future-trial perspective, it was always safer to have the warrant. "I'll put a deputy on that."

Matt tilted his head. "Kelly's death seemed impulsive. The weapon was on hand rather than brought along. Her door was unlocked, with no signs of being picked."

"Kelly's murder scene felt as if she knew her killer and let them in," Bree agreed.

"This murder feels more planned," Matt added.

Bree stiffened. "So, you think the killer enjoyed Kelly's and wanted to do it again?"

"I won't speculate on motivation." Matt shoved a hand through his short hair. "Hell, I don't even have proof of the premeditation. I'm just going on my gut."

Bree got the same vibe from the scene, but Dana had trained her to suppress her gut. *Follow the evidence* would be carved into her former partner's tombstone. "We also need to consider that this murder is unrelated, with throat slashing being coincidental. Possibly Kelly's killer gave this one ideas."

"And Janet just happened to have also dated Troy?" Matt's brows rose.

"Could be a copycat, but there's only one way to find out," Bree said, though it would be hard *not* to see the parallels everywhere.

They went back into the house. Through the front window, Bree studied the reporters giving sound bites. "We need to do the death notification. The ME's van is here. The media knows someone died. It won't take them long to figure out who lives here."

With that in mind, she herded Alice toward the door. "You should call your family and let them know you're all right before this hits the news. They'll show the house and everything." She turned to Matt. "I'll give the press a brief statement while you sneak Alice outside."

"Got it." Matt stepped in front of Alice. "We'll wait until Sheriff Taggert distracts them."

Reporters thronged Bree as she walked down the driveway. She went all the way to the street, where her deputies had set up sawhorses to mark the crime scene and keep out the media. The rural location meant no lookie-loo neighbors would wander over.

"Was there another murder?" A reporter jammed a microphone in Bree's face.

She gently pushed it away before it struck her chin. Sadly, she couldn't avoid the questions as easily as the mic. "Yes. We believe the victim was murdered."

"When was she killed?"

"Yesterday." Bree kept her answer intentionally vague. Holding back some details would better enable them to assess the truth of any suspects' statements.

"Who's the victim?" another reporter shouted.

"I will give you that information as soon as we have a formal identification from the medical examiner's office." Bree stalled. "All I will say at the moment is that there has been a murder. Please be patient. Out of respect to the family, I'll ask you to hold off on any speculation as to the identity of the victim." She ignored annoyed grumbling. They were under no obligation to do as she'd asked. All she could do was cross her fingers and get to Mr. Hargrave quickly so he wasn't blindsided. "I'll give a press conference this afternoon, when we have more information to share and the next of kin has been notified."

Bree also wanted to interview Troy Ryder before he learned the victim's identity. She wanted to be the one to tell him and observe his reaction. She didn't want him to have time to prepare a response. If he did it, he'd have to be a good actor to fake surprise.

Reporters yelled additional questions, which Bree waved off as she backtracked to the SUV. Matt was in the passenger seat. Alice was in her own car. She lowered the driver's-side window and wiped frost from the side mirror with her sleeve. She was on her phone, crying. "Please don't say anything to anyone just yet. OK, really, Mom. I love you too."

Bree's heart broke. Mr. Hargrave wouldn't be getting such reassurances tonight. He'd be slammed with the worst news a parent could receive. She climbed into the SUV. The seat was freezing under her butt. She started the engine and blew on her hands. When she could feel her fingers, she put the vehicle into gear and drove to Mr. Hargrave's address.

The brief interview left her bereft. The elderly man broke down immediately. His answers matched Alice's, and he provided no additional information. Janet wasn't seeing anyone, nor had she seemed particularly worried about anything, except the tight deadline for her current work project.

Bree was grateful that Alice stayed behind to comfort Janet's father. Back in the SUV, Bree slumped behind the wheel. Mr. Hargrave's grief was a physical weight crushing her shoulders.

Matt fastened his seat belt and scrubbed a hand down his face. "That was brutal."

"Yeah." Bree took a minute to compose herself, then drove back to the crime scene. The media still lingered. The ME's van was gone, and a forensics unit had parked in its place. She and Matt walked past Zucco, who noted their time of return on the scene log. Then Bree checked in with the lead forensics tech. Outfitted in full PPE, he was dusting the front doorknob for fingerprints.

"Any sign of the weapon?" Bree asked.

He shook his head. "Not yet."

"I'll have my deputies do the outside search." Bree found Zucco and issued instructions. "Have Juarez assist."

"Do you want us to do that now?"

Bree scanned the dark yard. "No. The sun will be up in two hours. May as well wait until you can see. Watch for footprints."

She went inside and stopped at the office doorway. With the body removed, it was easier to view the scene more clinically. A second forensic tech was photographing blood spatter on the wall. Yellow evidence markers dotted the space. They'd be here all night. Collection of trace evidence was a painstaking process. Everything found would be compared to the first crime scene. Unusual finds and any item collected from both scenes would be sent for analysis.

Matt spoke from behind her. "There are no neighbors to interview. No one would have seen a car coming or going. No doorbell camera or other security devices."

Because people thought they were safe in the country.

"Let's start in the bedrooms." Bree donned fresh gloves.

Matt did the same. The house was about fifteen hundred square feet and comprised three bedrooms, two full baths, and a combo living room / kitchen. Janet and Alice each had their own bedroom, with the third used as Janet's home office. Alice worked in her employer's office in town, about twenty minutes from home.

They divided their efforts. Bree veered into Janet's bedroom while Matt searched Alice's.

Janet's dresser was clear except for a row of framed photos. Bree lifted one and stared at it. Janet crouched next to her father, who sat in front of a birthday cake laden with lit candles. Bree picked up another, a wedding picture of the same man, much younger, with a woman Bree assumed was Janet's mother. The third photo was Janet and her father again, arms around each other, grinning in front of a restaurant. Bree looked closer. The photo had been folded. She carefully turned over the frame and removed the back. The photo slipped out, and Bree unfolded it.

Troy Ryder's face smiled back at her.

Bree found a pair of small stud earrings that might be diamonds and fifty-five dollars in mixed bills in a small bowl on the nightstand next to an electronic tablet. She bagged all as evidence. Janet kept the rest of her jewelry in a box in the top dresser drawer. Bree opened it to find big hoops and sparkly dangles. She was no bling expert, but all appeared to be costume. Janet didn't seem to harbor any deep, dark secrets. The most controversial item in the bedroom was a vibrator in the nightstand.

Matt appeared in the doorway. Bree looked up from Janet's sock drawer. "Find anything?"

"Nothing interesting. You?"

She lifted the evidence bag. The earrings caught the light. "Some cash and a pair of decent earrings on the nightstand."

"This wasn't a burglary," Matt concluded.

Not that either one of them had seriously thought it was. Still good to rule it out.

She showed him the folded-over picture of Troy.

"Relationship confirmed," he said.

"Find any drugs?" Bree asked.

"Over the counter only." He shook his head.

She glanced around the room, every sign pointing to the life of an ordinary woman who worked hard and hung out with her dad and roommate. "She seems so normal. So why is she dead? Because she dated Troy Ryder?"

"We'll figure that out."

"Feels a little late. I should have warned the public. I shouldn't have said Kelly's death was personal. We don't know that for certain." Guilt surged through her.

"You always say we should follow the evidence, and that's what it suggests." As usual, Matt knew what she was thinking. "Would you rather shake a Magic 8 Ball?"

"Maybe that would be more effective. Either way, I feel responsible."

"You couldn't have prevented her death."

Bree nodded, but inside she thought she might have. What if she had given the public a serious warning? What if she'd told them to be on the lookout, to be extra vigilant, instead of telling them she believed Kelly's murder was a one-time thing?

Would a warning have prompted Janet Hargrave to lock her dead bolt?

If she had, she might not be dead.

A second thought nagged at her. If she'd been willing to arrest Troy Ryder, would that have prevented Janet's death?

"Let's finish up." She moved out of Janet's bedroom and returned to the kitchen. Forensics was taking samples in the office. Bree scanned the kitchen surfaces. Her gaze landed on a knife block. She walked closer. Matching set. Empty slot. She called out, "Here's a possibility."

"What did you find?" Matt asked from the doorway.

Bree gestured to the knives. "There's an empty slot in the knife block."

She called Alice on video chat. She answered immediately, her voice shaky, her face stricken. "Yes?"

"I'm looking at a knife block in your kitchen." Bree switched the camera to front view and positioned it to show the knife block.

"Let me go outside." Alice lowered her voice. "Give me a sec." Over the line, a door creaked open and shut. "OK. I didn't want Janet's dad to overhear. He bought her that set when she moved into the house. Sometimes they cooked together."

"Are all the slots normally full?" Bree asked.

"Yes."

"Can you tell me what's missing?" Bree slid the remaining knives out, then back in one by one.

"There should be a five-inch chef's knife in that spot," Alice said.

Bree checked the dishwasher and drainboard. No knives.

Alice said, "Janet would never put her good knife in the dishwasher."

"When was the last time you saw it?" Bree asked.

"I used it the day before I left for my trip." Alice sobbed. "I even sharpened it."

"Did you return the knife to the block?"

"Positive."

Bree thanked her and ended the video call. She turned to Matt. "The weapon was on hand."

"Just like Kelly's murder."

Chapter Twenty-One

The pale gray of cloudy morning light filled the kitchen as Morgan sipped her second cup of coffee and ate the crust from her youngest daughter's peanut butter toast. She'd consumed her first cup during the usual bedlam of getting three children out of bed, fed, and dressed for school. Sitting at the table, she twirled her mug on the placemat, listening to the silence, the dogs begging at her feet. The front door opened and closed with a click.

A few seconds later, Lance walked into the kitchen. "Mission accomplished. Three children on the bus, on time, with no squabbles. Miracles *do* happen."

"Or you're pretty good at being a dad." The universe had aligned twice for Morgan in that respect, and she was immensely grateful.

Lance's joy at parenting the girls shone through his smile. He poured himself a cup of coffee, then turned to lean back against the counter.

Morgan pushed one plate aside and reached for another plate of half-gnawed leftovers from her children.

He side-eyed her breakfast. "You know we can afford for you to eat a whole slice of toast, one that hasn't already been chewed."

Morgan laughed. "I hate to waste food. Plus, it's here."

Lance shook his head. He hadn't reached the eating-your-kids'-leftovers-as-a-meal phase of parenting yet, but Morgan suspected that would come with time. She finished the toast corner and leaned back. "It's too quiet."

The house was rarely still. In addition to Morgan and Lance and the girls, Morgan's grandfather and the girls' nanny lived with them. This morning, the nanny was driving Grandpa to physical therapy.

Lance set down his coffee and crossed the room. He leaned over, brushed aside her hair, and kissed her neck. "Can we be a little late to work? Seems wrong to waste an empty house."

"Like missing a solar eclipse." Morgan angled her head to give him better access.

"That's about how often we get the place to ourselves." He chuckled against her skin.

The brush of his lips warmed her blood. She tapped her phone screen to check the time. "I don't have to be in court until eleven, but I want to get to the courthouse early." The case wasn't complicated. A drunk guy who'd gotten into a fistfight with another drunk guy in a bar. The idiots had broken a stool, overturned a table, and smashed some glassware. She anticipated the prosecutor would be amenable to a deal: community service, damages paid, and time served. A weekend in jail had sobered her client. As long as he didn't have to spend another night behind bars, he was willing to pick up all the roadside garbage in the state of New York.

"I am very efficient," Lance mumbled against her skin.

"And thorough." Morgan sighed as his mouth worked its way up to her jaw.

"Always thorough."

Her phone buzzed on the table.

"Don't answer it," Lance said.

But Morgan's gaze landed on the screen. "It's Troy."

"Shit."

"Yeah."

Lance kissed her one last time, then straightened.

Morgan pressed "Answer" and put the call on speaker. "Troy? This is Morgan. Lance is here as well."

Troy didn't bother with a greeting. "The sheriff called." His voice started flat and shifted to disbelief. "They want me to come to the station for another interview. It didn't sound optional. Do I have to answer more questions?"

"Technically, no, but doing the interview can be the best way to find out what evidence they're holding." Morgan knew the sheriff. If she had summoned Troy, then she had evidence. "You can plead the fifth or say you don't recall. If I feel like they're fishing, I'll end the interview."

"I don't have anything to hide," Troy argued. "And that makes me look guilty."

"At this point, it's the sheriff's job to prove you committed a crime. It isn't your job to prove you didn't. Nor are you required to help them build a case against you."

"What could they have?" Troy protested. "I didn't kill Kelly."

"The most critical outstanding pieces of evidence are the DNA results from the box cutter and the bloody sock found in your hamper." Morgan hoped the sheriff hadn't turned up anything unexpected.

"Someone must have been in my home, but I can't prove that." Troy's voice rose in alarm. "I didn't kill her."

"We'll go to the station. You don't say anything unless I approve it. You listen and let me do the talking. We do need to know what's going on. We'll pick you up."

"No, I'll meet you there." Troy sounded reluctant and stubborn. "I don't need an escort."

Morgan stood and headed for the bedroom. "OK. Don't talk to anyone. Lance and I will be at the station in thirty minutes. Don't even get out of your vehicle until I'm with you."

"Fine."

"I mean it, Troy," Morgan said.

But the line had gone dead.

Lance cleared their coffee cups and placed them in the sink. "Troy isn't patient."

"Agreed." On her way down the hall, Morgan called over her shoulder, "We should be there in twenty. I don't want him at the station alone."

"Good point." Lance was right behind her. They were both already dressed. Morgan brushed her teeth and stepped into the navy-blue heels that matched her suit. They were out the door in three minutes.

While Lance drove, Morgan donned tiny hoop earrings, applied lipstick, and smoothed a few flyaway hairs.

"What the hell?" Lance muttered as he slowed the car.

Morgan flipped up the visor and mirror. News vans and crews overflowed the sheriff's station parking lot. A prickle of unease spread across her skin. "Something happened. Something big."

With the frenzy of weekday mornings, she and Lance usually checked the news when they arrived at the office.

She reached for her phone and opened a social media app. She searched for a local news station account and froze on their latest post. "Oh, no."

"What?"

Morgan scanned the short article, which was scant on details. Then she clicked "Play" on a short video of Sheriff Taggert giving a quick statement outside a home in the dark. Morgan skimmed a few more posts. She lowered her phone, stunned. "A woman was murdered last night. The unconfirmed story is that someone broke into her home and slashed her throat."

"Oh." Lance eased off the gas pedal.

"Yes." Morgan suddenly wished she weren't a local quasi celebrity. The press knew she was representing Troy. Once they saw her, they'd assume he was also a suspect in this second murder. When he drove up, they'd be on him like locusts on a wheat field. "I should have insisted Troy come with us. Do you see him?"

"Not yet." Lance stopped the van before entering the parking lot. "What do you want to do?"

Morgan scanned the busy street, looking for a place to park that wasn't inundated with reporters. There wasn't one. "Turn around." She called Troy. "Where are you?"

Troy's answer was sharp, as if he sensed her alarm. "About three minutes from the station."

"Meet me at my office instead. We'll drive together."

"Why?"

"Because there was another murder. That's why you're being called in."

A few seconds of silence passed as Troy processed the news. "What does that have to do with me? I don't know anything about it."

Morgan took a breath to stop herself from snapping at him. "I don't know, but the media is all over the sheriff's station. It will be better if we arrive together." Plus, she'd be able to control his responses.

"Doesn't that make me look weak and guilty?" Troy argued.

Morgan swallowed her frustration. Why did clients resist so hard? What was the point of paying her if they were going to argue with her advice? She slipped into the soft, direct voice her kids instinctively knew not to argue with. "It will be easier for the three of us to get through the crowd than you alone. Plus, I can field media questions while Lance paves the way, which is far better for optics than you getting swarmed by reporters, not knowing what to say, and having to shove them aside."

Or worse, answering their questions without a full understanding of the consequences of recorded statements. All media attention affected a potential jury pool. Every word and response should be weighed accordingly.

They met outside the office, and Troy transferred to the back of the minivan for the drive back to Grey's Hollow.

Morgan turned in her seat and instructed him, again, not to say anything until she approved each question. "The woman's body was found around one thirty this morning. She was killed yesterday afternoon. Where were you?"

Troy brushed a hand across his scalp. "Home. The cleaners were there. I don't like to leave them alone in the house."

An alibi! Morgan jumped on it. "Your house cleaners will need to make a statement."

He made a face. "They don't speak English very well." He looked away. "I'm not even sure they're legal."

Morgan wanted to scream. "How do you pay them?"

"Cash."

Morgan rubbed her forehead. "How did you find them?"

"A friend recommended them." He threw up his hands. "How was I supposed to know I'd need an alibi for murder at some point?"

Morgan didn't have an answer to that one. But the optics of his alibi being potentially illegal immigrants he paid under the table weren't good. Even if the cleaners agreed to sign statements—which Morgan doubted they would do if they didn't have green cards—how much weight would their testimony carry? "We have to find out if they're legal. Can you give us their information?"

Troy pulled out his phone. "My contact is Maria." He read off a phone number.

Morgan made a note. "We need to know if she's legal immediately."

"If the answer is no, she might just disappear," Lance pointed out.

"She won't talk to you." Morgan eyed her husband. "You still look like a cop, and so does your boss."

Lance nodded. "You'll have to do it. Take Olivia with you. She speaks Spanish."

His boss's girlfriend, Olivia Cruz, was a former investigative journalist turned true crime writer. Her career depended on her ability to make people trust her. She was also female, petite, and not physically intimidating.

"Good idea." Morgan turned back to Troy. "Did you see anyone else yesterday afternoon? Did you get any deliveries or take a video call with anyone in your home office?"

Troy shook his head. "I spent the day looking for a code error."

Not helpful.

They arrived at the station, and Lance navigated the vehicle through the throng of news crews in the parking lot. Reporters peered into the minivan as it crawled to a parking spot.

"Don't say anything," Morgan reminded Troy. "But do hold your head up. Act like you haven't done anything wrong." She wished optics were less important than evidence.

They stepped out of the minivan into a crush of reporters. Lance moved to the front of the trio and took point. The crowd yielded to his size.

"Is your client a suspect in last night's murder?" a man yelled.

Morgan answered without stopping. "This is a routine follow-up interview. We have no reason to believe this morning's interview has anything to do with an additional crime."

A reporter tried to step between Lance and Morgan. With barely a motion, Lance body-blocked him by simply pausing his step, letting the reporter's momentum carry him directly into Lance's much larger frame.

"Oof." The reporter stumbled, then snapped, "*Excuse* me."

Morgan ignored his extended phone. She never rewarded rudeness. Instead, she addressed a woman on her other side. "We don't know anything about what happened to that poor woman yesterday, but our thoughts are with her family."

At the entrance to the station, Lance opened the glass door and held it for Morgan and Troy. Then he shut it pointedly before any reporters could follow them inside.

"If you don't need me in there," Lance said, "I'll call Olivia and get her to clear her calendar for later today. I assume you want to track down the cleaners ASAP."

"Yes. I'd appreciate that."

Lance backed away as a deputy escorted them to an interview room.

Morgan took her seat, drew out her legal pad, and set her tote at her feet. Troy had barely settled before Bree and Matt entered. Bree set a manila folder on the table and faced Troy with an intense expression. She listed the people present and time of day for the record, then went through the Miranda warning process again, crossing all the t's and dotting all the i's to ensure the interview's admissibility in a future courtroom.

Then she rested her forearms on the table, leaning closer to Troy's personal space. "Where were you yesterday afternoon between the hours of noon and four p.m.?"

The question lifted the hairs on the back of Morgan's neck. The interview request was related to yesterday's murder.

Thankfully, Troy had apparently listened to Morgan's warnings because he looked at her instead of answering.

"Don't answer that." Morgan kept her gaze on the sheriff. "Why are you asking?"

Bree, however, leveled her focus entirely on Troy. "Because another woman was killed yesterday. Someone broke into her home and cut her throat. Sound familiar?"

Morgan ignored the ending quip. "What does that have to do with my client?"

Bree blinked, her gaze darting to Morgan momentarily before returning to watch Troy as she answered. "The victim's name is Janet Hargrave."

Troy froze. The color drained from his face. *He knew her.*

"Janet?" he whispered in a hoarse voice.

Morgan touched his arm to silence him.

Bree shifted her focus to Morgan. "Mr. Ryder dated the victim."

Well, shit. Morgan had not expected that. She opened her mouth to request time alone with her client, but Troy shook his head and kept talking. "Yeah. We dated, but we broke up months ago." His tone was incredulous.

"Who broke up with whom?" the sheriff asked.

Troy shook himself, clearly trying to recover from the shock. "Janet ended the relationship, but it wasn't a long-term thing. We'd only been seeing each other for a few months."

"Why did she break up with you?" the sheriff asked.

Troy's shoulders lifted a hair and dropped again. "We weren't compatible." He paused. When he continued, it seemed like the words physically hurt him to say. "She wanted kids. I can't have any."

"Were you angry?" the sheriff asked.

He lifted a shoulder. "No. Our relationship was pretty casual."

"Did you see other people?" the sheriff asked.

"We never discussed being exclusive," Troy evaded.

"When did you last talk to her?"

Morgan interrupted the sheriff's line of questioning. "Do you have any actual evidence against my client in this case? Surely you didn't bring him in just because he casually dated the victim months ago."

"Not yet," the sheriff admitted.

"Then why are we here?" Morgan asked.

The sheriff talked directly to Troy. "The DNA test results on the box cutter found in your Porsche came back. The blood is Kelly's. If I searched your house today, would I find the blade used to kill Janet Hargrave?"

"No!" Troy leaped to his feet. Morgan touched his arm, and he eased back into the chair. He settled himself, smoothing the front of his shirt. "I had all my locks changed and a security system installed yesterday."

"That was fast," the sheriff said. "How did you get that done?"

This time, Troy didn't hesitate. "I paid a premium. Someone had clearly been in my house. Someone stole my car. I didn't want to think about that happening again. Though even with the new alarm, I don't know if I want to stay there. The idea that someone was in my house without me knowing is disconcerting."

"I'm sure it would be." But the sheriff's tone didn't suggest she believed him.

Morgan realized the sheriff hadn't given all the DNA results. Sometimes what wasn't said was just as important as what was. "What about the sock?"

The sheriff blinked. *Finally. Could this be a chink in the case?* "The blood on the sock did not belong to Kelly."

"Do you have a picture of the sock?" Morgan asked.

The sheriff drew a photograph out of her folder.

"That's not mine," Troy said. "I only wear black socks."

Morgan had to work to keep the relief from showing on her face, but if the DNA from the sock had matched Kelly Gibson's, then Troy would likely be in handcuffs at that very moment.

The sheriff slid a paper from her folder. "I have a warrant to obtain a DNA sample from your client." The sheriff rose and opened the door. A forensic tech entered with a DNA collection kit.

Morgan glanced over the warrant. Everything was in order, so there was nothing she could do except watch as the tech swabbed Troy's cheek. The process was invasive and humiliating. Being forced to open your mouth and allow someone to collect a sample of your body was intimate and humbling. Troy seemed to shrink as the tech finished up.

Morgan's mind whirled. The blood could have come from the cut on Troy's forehead, but then why didn't he just say that? If the blood wasn't Troy's, then whose was it? The actual killer's, she hoped.

"My client wasn't driving his vehicle when the box cutter was found in it."

"You say," Bree said.

"You can't prove otherwise," Morgan returned. "And without a DNA match, there's no evidence that the sock is relevant to the murder."

The sheriff's head tilted at Troy. "So, I'll ask again. Where were you yesterday between the hours of noon and four p.m.?"

"I was home, working," Troy said.

"Alone?" the sheriff asked.

"No." He paused. "My house cleaners were there."

The sheriff picked up the hesitation. Her focus tightened. "They were with you the entire time?"

"They were at my house from about twelve thirty to three thirty," he said.

"I'll need their contact information." The sheriff pulled out a notepad and pen. With a pointed stare at Troy, she clicked the pen.

Troy swallowed. His Adam's apple undulated. "There are two women. I text with Maria."

The sheriff's brow rose. "Do you know her last name?"

Troy shook his head. "No."

"The second woman?" the sheriff asked.

"I don't know her name." Troy winced. "Maria's English isn't great. I don't think the other woman speaks anything but Spanish. At least, that's what they speak when they talk to each other."

"How do you communicate with Maria?" Doubt laced the sheriff's question.

"We text. I use a translator app."

"Do you know where she lives?" the sheriff asked.

Troy shook his head. "No."

Bree asked, "What can you tell me about her? How old is she? Is she married? Kids?"

Troy's face flushed, and he looked at his hands. "Married, I think. When you have to digitally translate your conversations, you don't have many."

The sheriff deadpanned, "You let people you don't know anything about into your home?"

"That's why I don't leave them alone," Troy retorted.

The sheriff poised her pen over her notepad. "I'll need Maria's number, and we will contact her."

Morgan thought she would have a better chance of getting the cleaner to cooperate. She would do her best to make contact with Maria first, before a call from the sheriff spooked her.

Troy read the number from his phone.

"Are you arresting my client?" Morgan asked, gambling that the sheriff wasn't ready to do that. They had the bloody box cutter, but the circumstances under which they'd found it were strange. Morgan could interject reasonable doubt as to whether Troy had been the driver of the car at the time. Sheriff Taggert liked her cases tied up with a tight bow. She wasn't the sort of cop to arrest someone prematurely, only to be forced to drop the charges and release them later. Arresting people without enough evidence looked sketchy.

"No." The sheriff tapped a finger on the table, then added, "Not *yet*."

"Then this interview is concluded." Morgan rose.

The sheriff stood. "We'll be talking again soon."

"Only if you have new evidence." Morgan slid her legal pad into her tote and steered Troy from the room, not waiting for the sheriff to open the door, sending the message that they didn't need permission to leave. But theatrics aside, Morgan knew damned well that Troy's freedom could be temporary. If one piece of evidence connected him to the second murder . . .

In the hallway, Troy stammered, "I don't—"

Morgan cut him off. "Not here."

In the doorway to the lobby, Morgan passed Troy to Lance. "Take him to the car. I'll be right out."

Morgan backtracked to the ladies' room. As she washed her hands, the door opened, and Bree walked in. They made eye contact in the mirror.

Morgan chose her words carefully. "Hypothetically, if a witness is determined not to be of legal status, do they get reported if they cooperate with law enforcement?"

The sheriff sighed. "There are never any guarantees. Murder trials are public spectacles."

Morgan read between the lines. Bree wouldn't pursue Maria's legal status, but the media would certainly find out and report on it. The prosecutor would know. Politics would come into play, and the sheriff could not control the DA's office or federal agencies.

Morgan dried her hands on a paper towel and set the case aside. "How are the kids?"

"Good. Yours?"

"Also good. All of them are in school full-time this year."

"And how's that going?"

Morgan smiled. "So far, so good."

"I'm glad to hear it. It was nice to see you," Bree said.

"Same." With a nod, Morgan left the room. In the lobby, she eyed the reporters clogging the parking lot. She wasn't usually a proponent of *no comment* responses or avoiding the press, but today, she anticipated answering their questions would prove worse for Troy. She didn't have enough information on the case to make any valid points in his defense.

A deputy said, "You can use the back door if you want."

"Thank you." Morgan texted Lance to pick her up on the street behind the building. Then she followed the deputy through the station to the back door and slipped out. She slunk around the electronic arm barrier and hustled to the street. The minivan drew up to the curb, and she stepped into the passenger seat.

She turned and looked through the rear window. "I don't think anyone saw me."

"They're all waiting for you at the front door." Lance accelerated, leaving the station behind.

Morgan relaxed. She turned to Troy, who was staring out the window, his expression stunned.

"When was the last time you talked to Janet?" Morgan asked.

"A few months ago, when she broke up with me."

Morgan asked, "You didn't call or text her afterward?"

Troy looked out the window. "I drank too much vodka the next night and called her. We argued. No," he corrected himself. "I yelled, and she ended the call." He leaned back against the headrest. "I tried to call her to apologize the next day, but she'd blocked me. I wasn't angry as much as frustrated. I liked Janet. I know vasectomies are reversible, but I don't know if I can even manage a relationship, let alone be a parent. I'm not good with people, in case you haven't noticed." He hesitated. "My wife was the only person who got me. Anyway, after Janet, I changed my dating app parameters to only include women over forty who already have children. I figured I have a better chance of finding someone who doesn't want to start a new family."

At least he's being honest with me. Morgan nodded. "We can explain that call if we have to, but only if the sheriff or prosecutor mentions it. They have your phone records, but they won't have content, unless you left her a message?"

"No. No message."

"Good. Then the phone company will have a record of the call, but they won't have the content. We can explain a call or two at the time of a breakup as normal without volunteering that it was an argument." She hoped. "At some point, your backstory will need to come out."

"No," Troy said. "I won't use my wife's death to drum up pity."

"If you get charged with killing two women you dated, you can be sure your wife's death will come into play," Morgan said. Bree would undoubtedly pull Troy's late wife's death certificate. "Think about it. Three women in relationships with you have died."

"But . . . it was her heart."

"Yes, but the questions will be asked. Probably repeatedly."

Troy scrubbed both hands down his face.

Morgan changed the topic. "Now, let's talk about that sock. Could the blood have come from the cut on your forehead?"

"No. I only wear black crew socks. I don't send my laundry out, and I don't have guests. I have no idea how it ended up in my hamper. Could it have been planted, maybe by the sheriff's office? They seem to want me to be guilty."

"I've known corrupt police in the past, but I've never heard any rumors to suggest Sheriff Taggert would do that. Our best defense is to work with actual evidence."

"Well, I'm telling you that the blood on the sock can't be mine." Frustration bubbled into Troy's voice.

"Then we can hope that it could potentially be matched to the real killer."

"Oh." The idea seemed to calm Troy.

But in order for DNA to *match* the real killer, first they had to *find* the real killer.

Chapter Twenty-Two

Matt paced the space in front of the whiteboard in the conference room. "Can we arrest Troy Ryder for the murder of Kelly Gibson?"

"I'd like another piece of evidence," Bree said. "The box cutter is tainted by the weird car chase and the fact that we never saw the driver's face. But I will put a deputy on his house. I want to know where he is at all times until we catch this killer."

"What about the sock?" Todd asked.

Bree flattened her palm on the table. "If the DNA is Troy's, he can explain it away. His house. His blood. No link to Kelly's murder. If it's someone else's blood, then how did it get into his bedroom? Does that strengthen his claim that someone broke in?"

"Maybe it belongs to the cleaning ladies," Todd suggested.

"Or." Matt's mind went darker. "Is there another victim we haven't found yet?"

Bree's answering look was grim. Had that possibility already occurred to her?

"Run the phone number Troy gave for the cleaner," Bree said. "Let's get as much information about her as we can before we attempt to make contact. Then I'll have Zucco make the call, and she'll go with me for the meet."

Matt nodded. "Zucco is good with languages, and two women are less threatening."

"We'll also focus on Janet Hargrave's crime scene today," Bree said. "Review Troy's phone records again with the Hargrave murder in mind. Janet's phone also needs a deep dive. Her financials, once we get those, will need reviewing as well."

"On it." Todd typed on his laptop. "Subpoenas have been sent to the dating app service for both Janet's and Troy's dating history. Rory is working on accessing Janet's app on her phone as well."

Bree said, "Let's not assume the two murders are related or that they aren't. Today, we follow the evidence."

Her phone buzzed. "It's Dr. Jones."

"Already?" Matt asked.

"She said she was going to do the autopsy first thing this morning." Bree answered the call on speakerphone.

The medical examiner dived right in. "The time of death stands as noon to four p.m. yesterday. The cause of death is as expected, exsanguination due to throat cutting."

"Any indication as to what the murder weapon could have been?" Matt asked.

"The wound's deeper and more extensive than Kelly Gibson's," Dr. Jones said. "Possibly from a very sharp and more substantial blade."

Matt pictured Janet's knife block and its empty slot. "A five-inch chef's knife is a possibility?"

"Yes," the ME said. "We'd have to compare the actual knife to the wounds to confirm, but it's a definite possibility."

Which meant they had to find it.

The ME continued. "I'll send a preliminary report in a few days, but I know you wanted the pertinent details quickly."

Bree thanked her and ended the call.

The door opened, and Marge stepped into the room. "Madeline Jager—"

She didn't even finish her announcement before the woman in question barged in. Today, Jager wore a suit in an ice blue that matched her heart. Bree and Jager had reached a weird truce, but Matt wasn't on board. Politicians couldn't be trusted.

"What the fuck is going on?" Rather than a heated exclamation, Jager's question was delivered in a cold, angry voice.

"I'm sorry," Marge said to Bree, then shot eyeball daggers at Jager. Clearly, Marge wasn't on board the Jager train either.

"Not your fault. I'll handle it from here," Bree said.

As she withdrew from the room, Marge gave Jager a look that would have intimidated most people. But Jager didn't even notice. She was focused on the murder board. Her eyes reflected her horror at the photos, but as her gaze moved across the board, her expression tightened, shifting into anger.

As soon as the door closed, she dropped into a chair and waved at the board. "Tell me what's happening."

Matt knew Bree did not like to share information outside the department, but Jager did work for the county, and she was good at PR, something Matt wished they didn't have to worry about. They should be able to solve crimes without worrying about the press. But that wish was pure fantasy. In the real world, politicians controlled the department budget.

"We had another murder last night," Bree said.

Jager rolled a hand in the air. "Yes. That's why I'm here." Her tone was an implied *duh* that made Matt bristle.

Bree reviewed the basics. "So, the two crimes are very similar, including aspects of the cases that we didn't release to the press. For example, the fact that both women had their throats slit. We suspect both were killed with weapons found at the scene."

"And Troy Ryder dated both women?" Jager clearly had her own sources of information.

Bree nodded. "Yes, but he claims to have an alibi for Janet's murder."

"Then you'd better get to it proving he doesn't," Jager said. "We need to make an arrest for these murders before the public goes ballistic."

We?

Matt said, "We need to solve the cases."

"Arresting the wrong person would definitely not help," Bree said. "The real murderer would be free to kill again, and it would appear as if we railroaded Troy. We'd lose the public's confidence."

Matt tossed one of Jager's favorite words back at her. "The optics would be terrible."

Jager raised both hands in a surrender gesture. "Let's not argue. We're on the same side."

Sort of.

"Speaking of public confidence, we need to give a press conference ASAP." Jager rose and smoothed her skirt. "People need to know we're on top of this."

Bree snorted and uttered a rare admission. "But are we?"

Jager frowned. "We fake it until we make it."

"I hate that expression. A homicide investigation cannot and should not be faked."

"It's an expression." Jager rolled her eyes. "The public trusts you. We want to maintain that trust to avoid panic."

To avoid losing an election.

Bree opened her mouth, then closed it. Her eyes changed from doubtful to purposeful. "A press con is a good idea." What was she planning? Matt could tell from the way Bree's eyes shut down that whatever she was going to do, Jager wouldn't approve of it. "I'll have Marge set it up for this afternoon."

Jager shook her head. "No need. We need to do it sooner than that. I already made the arrangements." She checked her watch. "For eleven o'clock."

"It's ten thirty now." Bree wore her *give me strength* face. Not many people could get under her skin, but Jager had a special knack, like a human fillet knife.

"Yes, that way we only have to deal with a few reporters instead of a hundred. If you give them too much notice, this place will be a circus, and the second murder will look like much bigger news. A quick question-and-answer session with a handful of reporters makes today seem like business as usual."

"Except for two women whose throats were slashed," Matt said, his own anger rising. He hated to see Jager use her position to further her own agenda.

Jager shot him a glare. "You don't get a microphone, which is a damned shame because you are working that ruggedly handsome thing."

"I'm happy to be left out of it," he said. Bree was much better at public speaking and thinking on her feet. Matt would tell them all to go scratch.

"You stand behind the sheriff and look formidable," Jager said. "I'm going to freshen up my makeup." She squinted at Bree. "You should do the same. You always look so washed out on video."

A muscle in Bree's jaw twitched as Jager left the room.

Bree went to her office, reached into her drawer, and pulled out a little mirror. She smoothed her hair.

Matt followed, leaning in the doorway. "You don't need makeup."

"She's right. The camera makes me look like a corpse." She shoved the mirror back into her drawer. "I just don't care. And Jager is also right about the smaller press con optics, though I hate that word and everything it represents so much."

"Same."

She closed her eyes and took a few deep breaths before raising her lids again. "I'm going to use the bathroom and get a drink of water before it starts."

A few minutes later, the three of them met in the lobby.

"Damn," Jager muttered under her breath. "That's more reporters than I had anticipated."

At least forty people crammed into the lobby. Half of those were reporters, plus some cameramen.

Bree took point. Jager stood at her side. Matt stayed in the background. He had no intention of answering any questions.

Bree began with a prepared statement. "Last night, the body of Janet Hargrave was found in her home on County Line Road. The medical examiner has determined that Janet was killed on Thursday."

The press didn't let her finish before they began yelling out questions. "Was she killed the same way Kelly Gibson was killed?"

Bree leaned into the mic. "Yes."

Another reporter followed up. "Is there a serial killer in Randolph County?"

Jager's head shook slowly, anticipating Bree to answer in the negative. But Bree said, "We don't know, but it is possible."

Jager's eyes widened, and her head swiveled to stare at Bree. With her red hair and wide-open eyes, she reminded Matt of that horror-movie doll, Chucky.

Bree ignored the glare. "We're working day and night to solve these cases. Until we do, please be careful. Lock your doors. I'd like to tell you all there's nothing to worry about, but I can't do that. We just don't know what we're dealing with yet."

"Do you have suspects?" another reporter called.

"We are questioning several persons of interest," Bree said.

Jager elbowed her way to the mic. "That's where you can help. The sheriff's department has set up a tip line. If you know anything about these crimes, or you saw anyone suspicious on Oak Street on Monday late afternoon or on County Line Road Thursday afternoon, please call the number."

Again?

Jager had announced nonexistent tip lines in the past, and each time Bree was angry. Now she would need to pull a deputy from patrol or the investigation to man a phone. Then additional man-hours would be required to follow up on any tips.

"Thank you." Jager raised both hands in a *stop* gesture. "The tip line number will follow at the bottom of the screen."

Bree leaned over to speak in Jager's ear. "We don't have one set up." *Because you didn't clear this with me first* was implied.

Jager nodded and spoke into the mic again. "Ah. It seems we're having a technical issue. The tip line number will be posted shortly. For the moment, you can call any tips into the main number for the sheriff's department." She recited the phone number from memory.

She planned this.

Jager said to the cameras, "With the help of the citizens of Randolph County, this killer will be caught and brought to justice."

So much for our truce. Jager had stabbed Bree in the back yet again.

The tip line detail occupied the reporters, and Bree ended the press conference. Matt opened the door to the squad room, and Jager and Bree filed through it. He closed the door, muffling the sound of the news crews. Then he stayed out of the way.

Bree turned on Jager. "You know I don't like tip lines. They don't help us solve cases. They flood us with nonsense calls we have to waste time investigating. I guarantee we'll have at least one fake confession."

"Yes. I know you hate them." Jager leaned on the closed door. "Which is why I didn't bring it up beforehand. Better to ask forgiveness and all that."

Bree fumed, propping her hands on her duty belt. "You can't continue to make decisions that affect my cases without conferring with me."

Jager pulled a compact out of her purse and checked her lipstick. She snapped it closed and met Bree's gaze with an unflinching one of her own. "This may not help your case, but it will help your career. It's good politics. People like to feel as if they're helping. The citizens want to be on your team. A tip line helps them to do just that."

The rationale made sense in a twisted, manipulative way.

"I hate politics," Bree grumbled. "And I'll need deputies on overtime to man the phones. You'll have to approve an increase to the budget."

Jager shrugged. "That's easy to do if the public is behind you. In fact, we should hire a communications officer, someone whose job it is to deal with the public. You need to delegate, and a polished community liaison will refine your image."

That offer was insulting. Bree had requested funds for a second K-9 and deputy handler. The board had denied the budget increase. But a communications officer? *That* they would approve?

Matt pictured a slick, smarmy dude with perfect creases in his uniform and a toothpaste-commercial smile. Even as his brain recognized the benefits of such a position, his gut resisted with an uncomfortable twist. If they were in a rich suburban community with resources to spare, he could make sense of adding a media officer. But they were not. Randolph County was more rural, not wealthy. In his opinion, their very limited funds should go to protecting the community.

Bree's scowl said she didn't like the idea at all. "I don't want to delegate my image to anyone, and the board of supervisors made it clear that an additional deputy isn't in the budget."

"I can probably talk them into a media liaison, though. They all see how the department image needs to be spruced up. I mean, the public loves you." She gave Bree a condescending look. "But more polish will improve that image. I know you hate all of this." Jager shoved her compact back into her purse. "But you *are* a politician, even if you don't think you're very good at it." She gave Bree a rueful side-eye. "You wield honesty, honor, and sincerity like weapons. We can use that."

"Or maybe I'm just honest," Bree suggested in a wry tone.

Jager raised both brows. "Don't start a nasty rumor like that. Your political career will be over. No one in power wants to help someone get elected who they don't think they can blackmail or bribe. Rich people don't lift up honest citizens. They support those they think they can manipulate."

"That's not comforting."

"It's reality." Jager turned up a palm. "I'll leave you to the investigation. Please make an arrest." She didn't wait for a response before leaving the station.

Bree shook her head. "She's like a tornado. Blows in, causes chaos, and leaves us to clean up a path of destruction." She headed for her office. "I'm off to find deputies who want some overtime."

Matt followed. "What can I do?"

"Figure out who we're going to arrest?" She entered her office and dropped into her chair. "Seriously, arrange the tip line and get the number out to the media. Zucco is going to call Troy's cleaners and make an appointment for her and me to talk to them." She glanced at her phone screen. "I have an email from Harrison. He found the cash receipt for the beer purchase for Monday. We need to drive over and pick that up. Hoping it's time- and date-stamped so we can obtain the corresponding surveillance video."

"Interesting that he didn't go through his attorney."

Bree lifted a shoulder. "Either he thinks he's smart enough to handle things on his own, or he's being cheap and didn't want to pay his lawyer for an hour of his time." She typed on her keyboard and tapped send with purpose.

"You could delegate this to a deputy."

"I could, but I hate to miss an opportunity for Harrison to blab nonstop. He ignores his lawyer and is a nervous talker. Who knows what we could learn?"

"This is true." Matt's phone vibrated. He read the screen. Worry tightened his chest. "It's Luke."

"I forgot the kids were off school today for a teacher in-service day." Guilt creased Bree's face. "How could I have forgotten?"

But Matt was more concerned about the reason for the call than Bree's memory lapse. Luke normally texted. The young man acted as if he were allergic to making phone calls.

Matt punched the answer button. "What's up, Luke?"

"Turbo is gone. I'm so sorry. It's my fault. I let him out of the tack room while I groomed Riot. I thought he'd been cooped up enough. But while I was picking hooves, he opened the barn door and bolted."

"Where did he go?"

"Across the meadow." Luke sounded near tears. After all he'd been through, the young man was usually solid and stoic. But he loved animals. "I let you down. I'm so sorry."

"No. This is my fault. I should have brought him with me. I know what he's like."

Bree frowned and mouthed, "You need to find him."

"I'm coming home. His collar is GPS chipped. I can track him, but we'll never catch him on foot. Saddle up the horses, and we'll go get him. He's probably chasing rabbits." Matt hoped.

Chapter Twenty-Three

Bree drove toward the farm, her heart aching for her nephew. "Please find the dog. Luke will never forgive himself if you don't."

In the passenger seat, Matt said, "I know. I feel terrible. I shouldn't have left Turbo there." He glanced at his phone screen. "The GPS app says he's down by the creek."

"That's about two miles from the farm."

"Hopefully, he's found something not dangerous to occupy him until Luke and I get down there."

Bree parked at the house. Matt headed for the back door to grab winter outerwear. The wind would make for a cold ride.

Lowering her window, she called, "Make sure Luke is dressed warmly enough."

"Will do." Matt turned. "You be careful."

"I will."

As he entered the house, Dana came out onto the porch carrying a brown paper bag and a thermos. She jogged to Bree's SUV and handed over the bag. "I made a sandwich for Matt too, and made sure that Luke ate before going out in this weather."

"Thanks." Bree took the bag and opened it. The smell of leftover roasted turkey burst free. "What is it?"

"A turkey and mashed potato sub from last night's leftovers. I would have added gravy, but I figured you'd be eating while you drove." Sadly, Dana was correct.

The scents saturated Bree's nose, and her stomach rumbled. "That smells incredible."

"It's as close to the Gobbler that I could make under the circumstances." The Gobbler from the Wawa convenience store chain was a famous hoagie made with all the trimmings of a Thanksgiving dinner stuffed into a torpedo roll. Luke bought them weekly during the holiday season. But at his age, he could burn the calories.

Dana shrugged. "You'll probably skip dinner. You miss too many meals when you're working a big case." She offered Bree the thermos. "Cappuccino." Her former partner had worked enough homicide investigations to understand the exhaustion, and to know it would likely get much worse each day until the case was solved or declared cold.

Bree set the thermos in her cup holder. "You're the best."

"I won't argue with that." Dana stepped back.

Bree bit into her sandwich as she drove toward Harrison's place. Hopefully, Zucco would have made contact with the cleaner by the time Bree returned to the station.

The landscape was rural between her farm and Harrison's mother's place. Bree cruised past forests and meadows. Mashed potatoes fell out of the roll and landed on her uniform pants. Good thing they were dark. Setting the food aside, she fished in the bag for a napkin to mop up the mess. A black-and-tan movement in the field to her left caught her attention. She slowed the SUV and scanned the landscape. A dog loped across the tall grass.

Turbo?

Can't be. Matt had said his GPS tag was at the creek, which was a couple of miles away. Could it be another dog that resembled him? She was no canine expert. There was only one way to find out.

She slowed the vehicle and lowered the window. "Turbo!"

The dog slowed and stopped. It turned its head, tongue lolling. Lean body. More tan than black, like him.

"Turbo!" she called again.

With an exuberant bark, he turned and ran toward her. Bree hesitated, her hand on the door handle. What if it wasn't him? What if it was a random, strange dog with Belgian Malinois / German shepherd type markings? Her old fears brimmed in her throat. Her pulse accelerated.

The scars from her childhood mauling on her shoulder and ankle itched. She knew the sensations were psychological, but the reminder stood firm. The dog had crossed half of the meadow, barely a hundred feet away now. His ears were forward, and she could feel his focus. Fear prickled the back of her neck. Even if it was Turbo, could Bree manage him? So far, only Matt had been able to handle the dog.

Stop it.

A strange dog wasn't likely to come when she called, and Turbo had never shown any signs of random aggression. Still, she had to force herself to open the door and get out of the SUV. Facing the approaching canine, she froze. What now? She didn't have a leash. She didn't know all his commands. Even if she did, would he listen to her? She tried to remember any of the times she'd watched Matt or Cady work with Turbo and other dogs. Turbo loved his tennis balls. Bree didn't have one of those. But Cady used food as a reward for the rescues. Bree broke off a small chunk of the hoagie and waited until he jumped over the roadside ditch, landing ten feet from her.

She tossed it onto the ground a few feet ahead. Turbo came to an abrupt stop and scarfed the food in one gulp. She recognized the red collar and tags. Definitely him. The green collar with the GPS chip was missing. He raised his head and shifted complete attention to her. His focus—and the intelligence in his eyes—was disconcerting. He waited for a command, but it was clear by the rigidity of his posture that he wouldn't wait long.

Bree tore off another piece. "Setzen." Matt trained K-9s in German.

His butt slammed into the ground. She tossed him another piece. "Good boy."

He vibrated with excitement, and for just a second, she thought absurdly, *What if my deputies were this obedient and focused?*

She stifled a nervous laugh as she opened the back door of the SUV. The dog leaped in effortlessly. She closed the door with a relieved exhale. *You're ridiculous.* The dog had been nothing except friendly toward her. He was a pain in the butt, but he wasn't vicious.

Bree went to the rear of the vehicle and found a section of nylon rope. Then she climbed into the driver's seat.

"You stay back there." She crossed her fingers that he would. She could tie the rope to his collar as a makeshift leash when she reached the station, but she couldn't restrain him in the vehicle by the collar. An accident would break his neck.

She had no harness, so she would just have to hope for the best and be very careful not to let him out when she opened the vehicle door. She split the remaining bit of sandwich with him, tossing his chunk over the seat. He finished it, then sat, seemingly happy to look out the window. He was miles from home. Dirt crusted his paws. He'd definitely found some mud. Stickers, leaves, and twigs were stuck in his fur. But Bree wasn't comfortable enough with him to pluck them off. "Looks like you had quite the adventure."

Panting, he looked like he was smiling. *Best day ever?*

She tapped the steering wheel to call Matt. He and Luke needed to know she had the dog.

Matt answered. "What's up?"

She spoke into the Bluetooth speaker. "I have Turbo."

"What?" Matt exclaimed. "We're halfway to the creek. I'm still picking up the GPS signal there."

"The collar might be at the creek, but the dog is in the back of my SUV," Bree said.

"Where was he?"

Bree looked ahead and spotted an overpass on the horizon. "I'm on Route 13, near the interstate overpass."

"He must be exhausted."

"You'd think, but no." She snapped a quick picture with her phone and texted it to him.

Matt laughed. "Luke and I are about a mile away from the farm. We're turning around."

"I don't have time to bring him back to the farm."

"That's OK. Just take him to the station. I'd rather keep him with me for now. It's the only way I'll know where he is."

"He *is* a handful."

"We can put him in lockup."

Bree laughed out loud as she pictured Turbo in the holding cell. The dog's head shot up at the sound, and she lowered her voice.

"He wouldn't be able to chew through the bars." Matt sounded as if he were only half-kidding. "I'll meet you at the station."

"Turbo and I will be there."

"Are you stopping for Harrison's receipt?" Matt asked.

Bree checked her GPS. "Yes. I'm only a few minutes from the farm now. I was planning to run by the liquor store too."

"Don't leave him in the SUV too long. He might eat it," Matt said, then he ended the call.

Bree pulled out onto the road, one eye on the dog in the rearview mirror. Turbo wagged his tail, peered over the seat, and gathered his muscles as if to leap into the passenger seat.

"No." Bree gave him a firm command. "Sit."

A depressed sigh heaved through his sleek body as he planted his butt again.

"Yes," Bree mimicked Cady's positive dog training cue. Cady usually followed up with a treat, but the sandwich was gone. Bree tried praise. "Good boy."

He stretched out on the back seat, lowering his head and resting it between his paws. His big amber-brown eyes blinked up at her. He could look so innocent—right before he wreaked complete destruction.

The SUV approached the overpass. Bree spotted a vehicle pulled over, the hood up, on the road above. The guardrail blocked most of the view, so she couldn't see the make or model. A piece of white cloth fluttered from the closed window. She reached for her radio to call in the disabled vehicle. As she passed underneath the overpass, something large and heavy dropped onto her SUV, denting the hood and breaking apart, chunks bouncing into the windshield. *A cinder block?* Cracks spiderwebbed across the laminated glass.

The vehicle swerved.

With no control, Bree watched the ditch approach.

Chapter Twenty-Four

Morgan picked up Olivia Cruz at her little white bungalow in Scarlet Falls.

Olivia settled in the front seat. A slim, dark-haired woman in her forties, she wore a snug black skirt and knee-high heeled boots in black suede.

Her blue overcoat gave Morgan envy. "That coat is gorgeous. Is it wool?"

"Cashmere."

Of course it is. Morgan sighed. "There are too many sticky fingers in my life for anything other than black wool."

"Someday." Olivia smiled.

"Thanks for helping today." Morgan put the minivan into gear.

"I don't mind translating. Besides, you've piqued my interest." As a writer, Olivia and her PI boyfriend, Lincoln Sharp, were a perfect match. Together, they were the nosiest couple in town.

But Morgan had to look out for her client first. "As my agent in this interview, you'll be bound by the same client confidentiality as I am."

Olivia held up a hand. "I understand."

"I appreciate it." Morgan turned onto the main road. "We're meeting at my client's house. He asked them to come and help him with something. I tried to text and call directly, but she wouldn't respond. Troy didn't say what he needed, so our request will be a shock. She'll likely assume it has to do with a cleaning issue."

"Should be interesting, then."

Morgan drove to Troy's house. All stone, wood, and glass, the building looked like it belonged in the forest. "We're early. I wanted to be here before the cleaner."

"OK."

They went inside, where Troy was pacing the huge kitchen. He paused as Morgan introduced Olivia.

Minutes later, a chime sounded throughout the house.

"That's the driveway alert," Troy explained. "She's here."

The cleaner was a slim woman of about forty, with long black hair pulled back into a neat ponytail. Troy let her into the house and led her into the kitchen. "Coffee?" He gestured toward the fancy machine on the counter.

Maria moved as if to make it, but he stopped her. With a glance at Olivia, he said, "Tell her I'll make it for her."

Olivia translated, then indicated that Maria should sit at the table.

Maria seemed uncomfortable with the role reversal, but she did as she was asked. Troy brought four demitasse cups of espresso to the table, along with sugar and cream. He sipped his black. Morgan doctored hers but nerves kept her from drinking. The next fifteen minutes would determine if her client had an alibi for the murder of his ex-girlfriend.

The second such killing within a week.

He needed to be cleared of suspicion in Janet's case. Having a solid alibi for one of two identical killings would make his involvement with the first seem less likely. Conversely, not having an alibi for either murder would make Morgan's job very difficult.

Morgan and Olivia had discussed their approach at length, so as soon as everyone had their coffee, Olivia jumped right in.

Morgan knew a little Spanish and caught the basic introductions. Then the conversation moved too quickly, and all she could do was wait. Though she didn't understand the language, she sensed that Olivia was beginning with small talk, assessing Maria's situation and willingness to make a legal statement. Olivia's skill at putting people at ease was apparent in two minutes.

The cleaner nodded, then sipped her coffee while Olivia summed up their conversation for Morgan and Troy.

"Her name is Maria Zelaya. She and her husband, Emilio, came to the US seven years ago. She says she will help. Mr. Ryder has been very generous to her. He always gives her a big tip at Christmas, lets her have his old clothes for her teenage son, and donates to the food pantry at her church."

"Gracias," Morgan said.

Maria set down her cup. "I have green card. I pay taxes." She sounded proud.

Olivia said, "She and her husband are taking classes and working toward citizenship. She says that telling the truth for Mr. Ryder is her duty. She was here cleaning his house from twelve thirty to three thirty on Thursday. He was home the entire time."

Relief settled Morgan's stomach, and she reached for her coffee. Over the next half hour, Morgan typed a formal statement that Maria signed. Morgan also made her aware that the sheriff would be contacting her to do an interview. Olivia offered to go along and translate. She and Maria pulled out their phones and exchanged numbers.

Morgan tossed back the remaining espresso. "Thank you again, Maria. We'll be in touch."

Maria said, "You are welcome" in heavily accented English.

"I have to make some calls." Morgan went outside to call Bree, but the sheriff didn't answer her phone. Morgan left a message. "I have something important to discuss. Please call me back."

Caffeine buzzed nicely through her bloodstream. One murder accusation was far better than two, but she still had her work cut out for her proving Troy hadn't killed Kelly. It wasn't enough to keep him from being charged. He had a life and a business. He needed to be completely cleared.

So tonight, Morgan would go home, put her children to bed, and go back to work.

Chapter Twenty-Five

Bree's heart catapulted into her throat as she straightened the wheel.

Fissures spiderwebbed across the windshield, completely obscuring the view.

Fuck!

Disoriented by the lack of visibility, she pulled her foot off the gas pedal. Before she could stomp on the brakes to slow the vehicle, a tire blew out. The SUV fishtailed. Bree fought to keep the wheel straight, but the vehicle didn't respond. The SUV careened, out of control, the movement sending Bree's body weight sideways. The seat belt snapped tight. Tires skidded. The SUV shimmied. A wheel—or two—lost contact with the pavement. Bree could feel the vehicle start to tip.

No. No. *No. Don't roll!*

She turned into the skid, hoping she was going in the right direction and that no cars were approaching in the other lane. Her maneuver leveled the vehicle, and the tipping sensation disappeared. She avoided the rollover, but the car continued to slide sideways. She was powerless to even slow the momentum as it crossed the oncoming lane and slipped over the shoulder into the roadside ditch.

As soon as the wheels left the road, Bree knew she could no longer steer. She was helpless as the vehicle plowed along the ditch. Debris and foliage thwacked the window. Metal scraped, bent, and screeched. The tempered glass of the side windows shattered. Glass pebbles rained through the still-moving vehicle. A sudden explosion around Bree struck her in the face and side. Pain slammed through her nose. Her nostrils filled, and something warm and wet gushed down her face.

The vehicle came to a shuddering stop. Everything went abruptly still and quiet, except for a ticking sound emanating from the direction of the engine.

Bree held still for a minute, getting her bearings. She was alive.

The SUV had come to a stop in the ditch, tilted on the driver's-side door at a nearly ninety-degree angle. She was lying on her side, the seat belt digging into her collarbone and abdomen. The airbags had deployed. The pain in her face told her it might have broken her nose. Blood smeared the deflated airbag draped over the steering wheel. She touched her face. When she lowered her hand, it was covered in blood.

She moved her arms and legs. Her limbs felt heavy and shaky, but she didn't think anything was broken. A whining sound from behind the seat made her head swivel. She ignored the burst of pain in her head and neck as she tried to see into the rear of the vehicle.

"Turbo?" she croaked.

The dog poked his head over the seat and licked her face. Bree twisted sideways to run one hand over his head and neck. No blood. She couldn't reach the rest of him. She was pinned by the wheel and taut seat belt. She tried to release the seat belt, but the button was jammed. But the dog was conscious and on his feet, so she took that as a good sign. Her gaze skimmed over the smashed passenger window. Would the dog bolt? If he did, she couldn't stop him.

She scanned the vehicle interior for her phone, which had been in a cup holder when she'd crashed. She didn't see it, so she tapped her lapel mic and reported the accident to dispatch over the radio.

"Are you injured, Sheriff?" the dispatcher asked.

"Just superficially," Bree answered. "I think."

"10-4. Deputies and EMTs are en route," the dispatcher said. "ETA eight minutes."

Bree didn't like the trapped feeling. She didn't want to wait in the vehicle, suspended by the seat belt, until help arrived. She reached for the console, where she kept a multi-tool. She'd need to cut the belt and climb out through the passenger window. Powder from the airbags triggered a cough. Pain seared through her face.

Ow. Fuck, that hurts.

She wheezed and swallowed, trying hard not to cough again. Her face throbbed as if it had its own heartbeat.

If I sneeze, I'll spray blood and possibly pass out.

She was lightheaded, and the thought made her bizarrely giddy.

Not good.

Stuck in a vehicle, vulnerable. Could the car catch fire? Behind her, Turbo growled. Bree went still. Did he smell smoke? She couldn't smell anything at all.

He slunk forward, his eyes focused on the shattered passenger window. Bree heard the sound that triggered him. Footsteps on gravel. A passing motorist?

The dog growled again, the warning rumbling low and deep in his throat. Defensive and growly wasn't his normal disposition. Matt's voice rang in her head.

Trust the dog.

Bree's pulse ramped up again. Something was wrong. Not just wrong. Turbo was acting as if there were a threat outside. An image of the broken-down vehicle on the overpass flashed through her mind. Had the motorist thrown something onto her vehicle? Bree's bones went cold. She was trapped.

Her hand went to her duty belt, but her awkward position jammed her holster between her hip and the vehicle seat. She yanked at her duty belt, trying to shift it.

The footsteps came closer. Turbo climbed over the seat, crawling on top of her. One rear paw stepped on her face, sending a fresh burst of agony through her nose into her forehead. More blood flowed over her mouth and chin. She breathed through her mouth and tried to remain silent.

Turbo stood awkwardly, two paws on her body, one foot planted on the center console, and another on the broken dashboard computer. He placed himself between Bree and the open window.

Between Bree and the threat.

Outside the vehicle, a shoe scraped on gravel. Could it be an innocent person who'd stopped to offer assistance? But then why weren't they hurrying or calling out? No. The footsteps were deliberate, almost cautious. Bree could feel the sinister intent in her marrow. She knew in her bones that whoever was outside the vehicle had caused the accident. Were they coming to see if they'd killed her? Maybe finish her off?

Another scrape sounded. This one closer still. Bree shoved her elbow past the dog's back leg to work on her weapon again. But the dog on top of her limited her movement. She forced her holster forward and slipped off the safety strap. But before she could slide the gun out, Turbo leaped upward toward the window like a canine superhero, as if he were truly turbo-powered. All he needed was a cape.

Dog nails scratched for purchase as he climbed through the open window. Boots skidded and scrambled. The dog barked as he clambered for his balance. More footsteps sounded, but this time, they were running away from the vehicle. Would Turbo give chase? No human could outrun him. If he pursued, he would catch whoever he was after. Would he bite and injure someone?

But a few seconds later, dog tags jingled, and he leaped onto the outside of the passenger door. He stuck his head through the open window. His tongue hung three inches out of his mouth, flapping with his breaths. Her hero was also a goofball.

"Good boy." Bree finally jerked her gun free of its holster. *Way too late.* Turbo lifted his head and scanned the surroundings. On guard. She watched him. Soft body posture. No growling. The threat he'd perceived was gone.

Bree stuffed the gun back into the holster and reached for the console. When she flipped open the lid, the contents fell out. Three pens, a pad of sticky notes, a protein bar, a compass, and the multi-tool dropped onto her. She opened the knife and cut through the seat belt. Once free, she fell against the driver's door. Pain rattled her hip, and she couldn't wait to shower and count her bruises.

With the pressure on her collarbone and across her hips released, she breathed in relief for a minute. Except for a potentially broken nose, she didn't sense any major injuries. Of course, adrenaline could mask pain in the short term, but her hands and feet were working just fine, and she could breathe, so her ribs were probably intact. The vehicle had slid sideways, with less impact than if she'd hit the ditch nose-first. Still, everything would hurt tomorrow.

She eased her ass onto the driver's door, then got her feet under her body. From a crouch, she climbed across the console and passenger seat, using the same grips that the dog had, although Bree's exit was far less graceful. Turbo moved aside as she clambered out the window. Thankfully, the shattered glass was tempered, and the broken bits dull, because she couldn't avoid them all.

Once her body had cleared the window, Bree scanned the area. No one in sight. She climbed off the passenger door and scrambled onto the shoulder of the road as nimbly as a fawn dismounting from a balance beam. When her feet hit the road, her balance faltered. Her brain lost track of up and down. Her knees buckled, and she ass-planted. Pain zinged up her tailbone. Great. Another pending bruise.

Turbo was at her side in a second, whining and licking her face. She rested her forehead on him. As soon as the dizziness passed, she lifted her head. "Are you OK?"

She brushed her hand across his back and sides, probing for cuts or tender spots. She checked his legs and the pads of his paws. The worst injuries she found were an abrasion on the bottom of his rear paw and a small gash on his foreleg. "We'll have a vet check you out."

He whined and licked her face again. It was gross, but she didn't resist. She plucked a sticker from his ruff.

Now that they were both safe, she replayed the accident in her head. The cinder block dropping onto her vehicle. The tire blowing out. It hadn't been an accident at all. Before she looked up at the overpass, she knew what she would see.

The disabled vehicle was gone.

The motorist had thrown the block off the overpass. Had they come down to see if the vehicle crash had killed her? If it hadn't, had they planned to finish the job?

If the cinder block had struck her windshield instead of the hood of the SUV, it could have killed her. A shudder ripped through her. Nausea followed as adrenaline ebbed. Turbo leaned on her. Or was she leaning on him?

She slung an arm over his shoulders. "Thanks. I'm pretty sure you just saved my life."

Chapter Twenty-Six

Matt drove past Todd and Juarez taking measurements on the road. Their patrol vehicles were parked on the shoulder. Matt's Suburban screeched to a stop behind an EMS unit. When he spotted Bree sitting on the tailgate holding an ice pack to her nose, relief flooded him, stealing his breath for a few seconds. Turbo sat on the ground at her feet, intently watching the medic take her pulse.

The medic had one nervous eye on the very focused dog. "Lean forward, not back, to lessen the bleeding."

Matt gathered himself for a minute. Dispatch had called to tell him about the crash, so he'd known she was OK. But it would be like her to minimize her injuries. He'd needed to *see* her to believe her. He'd also heard her between-the-lines message. This had not been an accident.

He grabbed a leash from the back seat and climbed out of his Suburban. The medic was shining a light into Bree's eyes. Letting him finish his assessment, Matt crossed the road and stared at the sheriff's SUV on its side in the ditch. The hood had a giant dent in the center. The tires were flat. The side windows had shattered, and the only thing holding the windshield together was the lamination. He stood on his toes and peered into the interior. The airbag was smeared red. The sight made him queasy. He wasn't squeamish, but that was Bree's blood, and a very bright reminder that she could have died.

He spotted her cell phone crammed between the console and the driver's seat. Carefully, he climbed onto the door, then lowered his torso through the window and grabbed it. A crack cut across the screen but it powered up when he touched it. He shoved it into his pocket and climbed off the vehicle.

Turning back to Bree, he saw the medic rummaging in his kit. Matt walked toward them. Bree lowered the ice pack as he approached. Bloody, folded gauze pads fell away. Dried blood splotched her face and saturated her uniform shirt. Her entire face was red and swelling, and she'd have double black eyes tomorrow. She looked like hell, but she was also the best thing he'd ever seen.

He winced in commiseration and looked for a safe place to kiss. He settled for the top of her head. Then he guided the ice back onto her nose. "That looks like it hurts."

"It's not too bad. Yet." Her voice was hoarse.

The medic handed Bree fresh gauze. "I'm pretty sure your nose is broken, but the bleeding seems to have stopped. If you bump it or sneeze, it'll start up again. Your vitals all look good, but injuries don't always make themselves known right away. You should go to the ER to get checked out."

"Yes," Matt said.

At the same time, Bree said, "No."

He gave her a *really?* look.

"Can't your dad just come over?" she whined, her voice nasally as she placed the fresh gauze on her nose and followed with the cold pack.

He shook his head. "He doesn't have a portable X-ray machine."

"Fine." She sulked, crossing her arms. "He should get one."

"I'll talk to him about it." Matt's dad was a mostly retired family physician. He no longer operated his own practice, but he kept his license current, volunteered at clinics, and ministered to family and friends, whether they wanted him to or not. "I can guarantee he'll be over to check on you later, though."

A half smile twisted the corner of her mouth.

He said, "You're going to have a Rocky Balboa face tomorrow. Black eyes and everything."

She grimaced. "I don't have time for this. I need to get back to work."

"The normal, human response would be *I want to go home*."

She lifted a shoulder, then winced.

"I know you're not normal." He kissed the top of her head again. "But you need your nose splinted first." And X-rays, maybe a CAT scan. "I'll run you to the ER."

She shook her head. "You have to take Turbo to the vet. He must have slammed into the back of the seat. He should get looked at too, and I don't trust anyone else with him."

Matt noticed she didn't say, *I don't trust him with anyone else.* Her relationship with the dog had changed.

"You seem to have him in hand, but yeah, I'll take him." Matt knelt on the ground and felt the dog's body and legs. Turbo didn't flinch, not even when Matt probed a gash on his leg. Matt didn't feel any broken bones, but internal injuries wouldn't be so obvious.

"You won't believe what he did." And she told him. "I'm not sure if it was the person from the overpass or not, but he seems to think he's my personal bodyguard."

 "Turbo was sure. Dogs have senses we don't."

"I trusted the dog," Bree said.

"That's what I would have done." Matt rubbed behind the dog's ear. "Good boy. You earned some of the shepherd's pie Dana is making tonight."

Turbo's tail thumped on the ground.

"What do you remember about the vehicle that was parked on the overpass?" Matt asked.

"Not much. The guardrail blocked the view of the vehicle below the windows."

"So, a sedan?"

"Yes." Bree closed her eyes as if concentrating. "The hood was raised. It was a neutral color. Light. Maybe gray, beige, light silver."

"White?"

She opened her eyes. "I don't think so."

The medic was packing up his kit with a pointed expression. "I have another callout. Do you think you're all right?"

"I'm good." Bree slid off the tailgate of his SUV. "Thanks."

She looked steady on her feet, but Matt took her arm anyway. A fall on blacktop wouldn't help matters. Deputy Zucco pulled up in her patrol car, and Bree waved her over.

Zucco got out of her vehicle and gaped at Bree's face. "Wow."

"Yeah. Need you to run me to the ER. Then you can pick up a receipt from Harrison Gibson and stop at the liquor store on the receipt for the corresponding surveillance footage."

Zucco opened her passenger-side door and cleared the seat of the organizer that held her ticket book, forms, and clipboard. Ice pack in hand, Bree slid into the passenger seat. "Did you contact Troy Ryder's cleaner?"

"Yes, ma'am. I texted her. No response yet." Zucco rounded the front of her vehicle, slid behind the wheel, and closed the door.

Bree mouthed, "I love you" to Matt as she closed the passenger door.

As Zucco pulled away, Matt could see Bree was still talking but her eyes were closed. Most people would put the job aside for a while at this point. But she wasn't most people.

Matt looked down at the dog. "You ready?"

Turbo stood and waited for a command.

"Matt?" Todd called from about twenty feet away.

Matt walked over. Todd was sketching the scene on a clipboard, and Juarez was taking photographs.

"What happened?" Matt asked, scanning a row of skid marks.

Todd lowered his clipboard and led Matt to the side of the road. Pieces of a shattered cinder block were scattered on the ground. "Someone tossed a block off the overpass onto the sheriff's vehicle as it passed underneath them." He pointed to the road. "They'd already set up a spike strip in the shadows so the sheriff wouldn't see it."

Matt glanced back at the vehicle. "If that cinder block had landed on the windshield and gone through, it could have killed her."

"They wanted her to crash, though, and the cinder block could have missed. The spike strip was a second line of attack."

"It worked. You can't steer with blown tires." Matt thought of Bree hearing footsteps. "Did she tell you about the person approaching her car?"

"She did." Todd looked grim. "Did they want to see if she was still alive, or did they want to finish her off?"

"Considering they already tossed a cinder block onto her vehicle and boobytrapped the road with a spike strip, their intentions definitely weren't good." Matt's hand rested on the dog's head. "Good thing Turbo didn't let them get close."

"We need him on the force."

"I agree." Matt turned to the dog. "I'm going to take him to the vet."

Turbo waved his tail. He liked the vet as much as he liked everyone else. Matt opened the rear door, intending to pick up the dog, but he leaped inside like a gazelle. Matt drove to the vet clinic in Grey's Hollow, where the vet took him into the back to run some precautionary tests.

A half hour later, the vet returned Turbo to Matt. "He's banged up, but we didn't find anything broken and there's no sign of internal injuries. He has a few stitches in that front leg. I'm going to send you home with some anti-inflammatories and a sedative in case he needs it. Keep him quiet. Crate him if you need to. I don't want him to tear out the stitches. Bring him back in five days, and we'll remove them."

Matt took the dog back to the car. "You heard the vet, right? You need to rest."

Turbo didn't even limp, and he launched himself into the back seat before Matt could lift him. Matt checked the stitches, which seemed fine. "Seriously, you have to take it easy."

Turbo's entire body shuddered as he shook off the day's stress.

"You did good today." Matt rested his hand on his shoulder, gratitude filling his heart. "You'll be a K-9 if I have to pay for your training myself. Hell, I'll buy the department a new vehicle too. You're going to make a hell of a cop."

Turbo wagged his approval.

"Let's go get Bree." Matt drove to the ER, dug Brody's old K-9 harness out of his emergency kit, and put it on Turbo. Then Matt walked him right through the hospital sliding door. If anyone asked if he was a working K-9, Matt couldn't lie. But no one challenged them.

For once, the ER wasn't busy. They found Bree waiting for discharge papers. A splint was taped across her nose, and she held an ice pack in one hand. She raised a brow at the dog. Matt put a finger to his lips.

Turbo stood on his hind legs and placed his paws on Bree's thighs. She stroked his head. "Thanks again." She touched the edge of Turbo's bandage and looked up at Matt. "He's OK?"

"A few stitches and some bruises. He should be good as new in a week. How's the nose?"

"Fractured but not displaced. No concussion. Ice and ibuprofen." She sounded—and looked—as if her nasal passages were swollen shut.

"Let's get you two home, so you can both rest." Matt needed to gather them close tonight. Now that the crisis had passed, his nerves were on edge.

A nurse delivered her discharge papers and a fresh cold pack for the road. Matt steered Bree and the dog out to the SUV. When everyone was settled in the vehicle, he said, "Oh, I forgot. I found your cell phone." He almost didn't want to give it to her, but she held out a hand. He placed her phone in it, immediately regretting that he'd even mentioned the device. She wasn't out of the ER for five minutes before she was working.

Bree tapped and scrolled. "I have a callback message from Morgan Dane."

Matt drove while Bree made the call. She kept the ice pack pressed to her face throughout.

"Morgan? You're on speaker. Matt is here as well."

Morgan didn't waste time with niceties. "I spoke with Troy's cleaner today. She signed a statement that she was at his home and that he was there between the hours of twelve thirty and three thirty on Thursday. She has permanent resident status and is willing to testify as well. If you don't have a translator, Olivia Cruz has volunteered to assist."

"Would you ask your client for a list of all the women he dated over the past year?" Bree asked.

Morgan responded with her own question. "What are you thinking? We've established that my client has an alibi for Janet's murder."

"I'm not making any assumptions at this point," Bree said. "But your client is the only link we have found between the two victims."

Matt did not want to find more dead women. Bree didn't say this to Morgan, but the attorney was smart enough to know why they wanted the names.

"I'll call him now and get right back to you." Barely three minutes passed before the phone buzzed. As soon as Bree answered, Morgan said, "Troy said he has dated three women other than Kelly and Janet over the past year. Their names, from most recent to least recent, are Barbara James, Claudia Ferguson, and Candy Simpson. Troy had only one date with Candy. He dated Barbara and Claudia for a month or two each."

The inability to develop and maintain a relationship seemed to be a pattern for Troy.

"Do you know how he met the women?" Matt wanted to make sure the list was complete, and that Troy didn't leave anyone out.

Morgan answered immediately. "He met all of them through the dating app Date Smart."

"Thank you," Bree said and ended the call.

"So, Troy didn't kill Janet," Matt said. "But he's still on the prime suspect list for Kelly's murder. We could have a copycat. What if someone wanted to off Janet and wanted to make it look like she was murdered by the same person who killed Kelly?"

Bree lowered the ice pack. "What if this isn't about Kelly? What if someone wanted to ruin Troy?"

Matt turned into the driveway and parked. He glanced at the list of names Bree had typed into the note app on her phone. Worry built in his chest. "We need to make contact with these women."

Were Barbara, Claudia, and Candy future targets?

Chapter Twenty-Seven

Sitting at the desk in her home office, Bree felt like she'd been run over by a bulldozer. Ibuprofen hadn't made a dent in the pain in her face. She'd barely managed a few mouthfuls of Dana's shepherd's pie, which was a damned shame. It was one of her favorite winter meals. A sedated Turbo was sleeping in Brody's old crate in the living room while Luke watched TV. She envied the dog a little. A deep sleep would feel amazing.

Matt sat in a leather chair on the other side of her desk, scrolling on his laptop. "I backtracked through Troy's social media account to identify the other three women he dated. The names match the list Morgan gave us: Barbara James, Claudia Ferguson, and Candy Simpson. Back when he was involved with them, he posted a couple of selfies of each one of them and tagged them. From there, it was easy to match their photos with their driver's licenses. We have addresses and phone numbers for all three. Do you want to call them or have a deputy ride by?"

"They need an immediate warning." She called each of the numbers, but none of the women answered.

"No one under the age of sixty-five answers a call from an unknown number."

Bree glanced at the time on her phone. 10:10 p.m. "A lot of people use Do Not Disturb at night too. Let's ride by their places, just to make sure they're all right." She stood, the motion and increase in heart rate pulsing in her face.

"You're in no shape to be working."

"I'm OK." Bree realized as she said the words how ridiculous they sounded. Her head felt like a sandbag, and she looked like she'd been whacked in the face with the same. Even her voice was weak, hoarse, and nasally.

Matt met her gaze with his own.

"Fine. I'll send a deputy." She called dispatch to send one of the on-patrol deputies to perform wellness checks on the three women.

She tried to read the email in front of her, but her eyeballs refused to focus. She blinked hard, which sent a wave of pain radiating through her face. The screen remained stubbornly blurry. "I need another set of eyes. Mine aren't working."

"It's no wonder with all that swelling." Matt rounded the desk. "Go sit in the chair. Ice your face. I'll read your emails to you."

They switched seats.

Matt leaned over her laptop. "Rory sent a list of all the women Troy dated via the app over the last year. There are three. He's requested account profile details on all of them."

"But the number of women matches the information from Troy."

"Correct," Matt said. "Zucco forwarded a copy of the liquor store receipt and video."

"Let's review the timeline for Kelly's murder."

"The ME says Kelly was killed between noon and six p.m. on Monday. Troy was seen at his cabin on Blackbird Lake around noon. He had plenty of time to kill her."

"Harrison's day is more complex," Bree said.

"The food delivery driver confirmed that Kelly was alive at 3:05 p.m. Harrison left the trampoline park at 3:32. He says he dropped off

Marina's kids before going to Kelly's house. He was seen at Kelly's door between 4:06 and 4:55 p.m."

"What time did he arrive at the liquor store?" Bree removed her ice pack. Condensation was dripping down her face.

"5:10." Matt watched the screen. "The video of him paying for the beer is pretty clear. His clothes look clean."

Bree's brain hurt too much for math. "How long is the drive from the trampoline park to Marina's house?"

"My GPS says twelve minutes, which gets him to Marina's house at 3:44." Matt typed. "He says he went inside, but we have no proof of that."

"And he's lied extensively."

"And talked Marina into lying for him as well, so there's no point in asking her. Let's say he didn't get out of the car. According to GPS, the earliest he could have gotten to Kelly's house is 4:09. He didn't get to the liquor store until 5:10." Matt paused. "What if he went to Kelly's house to get his ski gear? He and Kelly fought. He grabbed the box cutter and killed her."

"Which wouldn't take long," Bree said.

"I'd say it would be quick." Matt rubbed his beard. "I know he was behind her, but there was a lot of blood on the floor. It appears like he's wearing the same shoes as he's leaving the trampoline park as when he's entering the liquor store."

"Maybe he has more than one pair," Bree suggested. "Or he managed to avoid getting blood on himself."

"But the crime did look impulsive. Would he be focused on staying clean?"

Bree's mind chugged slowly, but it chugged. "We thought it was impulsive because the box cutter was in her kitchen and because it seems as if she let in her attacker."

"But she knew Harrison was coming over, so she let him in to get his ski gear." Matt followed her train of thought. "Maybe he knew she'd have tools on hand. He was aware of the renovation project."

"So he could have planned it, and it still wouldn't look premeditated."

"Yes."

Maybe the smack on the nose had shaken something loose in Bree's brain, because a new thought suddenly occurred to her. "I feel like we're spinning our wheels trying to prove Harrison or Troy killed these women. What if it wasn't either of them?"

"Who are you thinking, Jeff Burke?" Matt asked. "I could see anger, jealousy, and general impulsiveness getting the best of him with Kelly. We've seen him erupt into violence. But why would he kill Janet? Did he even know her?"

"I wasn't thinking of Burke." Bree checked the time and reached for a bottle of ibuprofen on her desk. She downed two with water. "Who else benefits from Kelly's death? Indirectly anyway?"

Matt tapped his forehead. "Marina Maxwell. But wasn't she with her kids when Kelly was killed?"

"Harrison said he dropped off the kids around 3:44 p.m., and we know from the food delivery driver that Kelly was alive at 3:05. Does that give her enough time?" Math was downright painful.

Matt shook his head. "Considering the distance between Kelly's house and Marina's, even if Marina killed her at 3:10, she didn't have much time to drive home and make sure she wasn't wearing any blood before Harrison and the boys got home."

He was right. That timeline was implausibly tight.

Matt swept a frustrated hand across his skull. "Do we agree that the murders are linked?"

"Both women were killed in the same manner. Both women knew Troy. Having two very similar crimes committed in the same week would be a coincidence beyond belief." Bree knew in her bones that the murders were connected.

Matt propped his elbows on the desk and dropped his head into his hands. "Yet it doesn't seem as if any of our suspects could have committed both murders."

Wait. Why hadn't she seen it before?

"What if one person didn't kill both women? What if the murders *are* connected and were *also* committed by two different people?"

Matt's head snapped up. "Two people working together? Like a team? Harrison and Marina?"

"She and Harrison started dating when he was still married to Kelly. Marina told us the same lies that Harrison did in his interview. We assumed he called her and coached her about what to say, but what if they planned the whole thing together? She would have known exactly what to say. She was pretty good with a knife in the kitchen too. Think about it. Kelly's death solves all her problems too. Harrison can sell Kelly's house, collect the insurance money, and give Marina the happily ever after she thinks she deserves."

"So, they set up Troy?"

"All the pieces fit." But were there other ways to put them together? Bree's head ached with the effort. "They thought they'd planned it so well, we'd arrest Troy immediately, and they'd be in the clear."

"But we didn't."

"No. Maybe they didn't expect us to arrive at his place to search so quickly. We surprised whoever was in the Porsche, and they did the only thing they could. They tried to evade us. Maybe crashing the car was an impromptu plan B. Or maybe they intended to crash the car all along. Who knows? Either way, one could have been behind the wheel while the other waited at a predetermined location."

"Then when we didn't arrest Troy right away, and continued to pressure Harrison, they thought they'd better shore up his defense. Create a second murder that he couldn't have committed. Marina killed

Janet while Harrison was at the station being interviewed. His alibi for Janet's murder doesn't get any better than that."

Bree's brain sorted through the evidence, all the pieces sliding into place. She met Matt's gaze. "Tomorrow morning, we bring Marina in for a follow-up interview. We go hard on her lying to us about Harrison's timeline, and we use the threat of potential felony charges for making a false statement. We might even be able to push an aiding and abetting charge. Except that any decent attorney would say she was mistaken about the time Harrison dropped off her boys on Monday. Harrison's lawyer already argued exactly that. We need evidence, not just a theory, no matter how good that theory is."

Matt stood and stretched. "But guilt can make a person very uncomfortable, and she might slip up. Harrison kept jabbering long after he should have shut his mouth."

"Marina seems smarter, but we won't know until we bring her in and apply some pressure." Bree shifted her jaw. Even her teeth hurt, but the ibuprofen was starting to kick in. "Tomorrow, we should have the forensics report on Janet Hargrave's murder. We'll review it, then bring her in."

"We need to know where Marina was when Janet was killed."

Chapter Twenty-Eight

The ringing of the phone jolted Bree from sleep. Blurry headed, she fumbled on the nightstand. Holding the screen in front of her face, she tried to read it, blinked, then tried again. She'd slept with her head on two pillows to minimize the swelling. Between that and the judicious application of ice packs, her vision was clearer than when she'd gone to bed. Zucco's number displayed on the screen.

"Yes," Bree said, her voice as husky as a 1-900 operator's.

"Ma'am, I just responded to a call from Barbara James's address. She's one of the three women who dated Troy Ryder. She's all right, but someone tried to break into her house."

Bree lowered the phone to check the time. Just after four thirty in the morning. "Are you still there?"

"Yes, ma'am," Zucco answered.

"We're on the way." Bree ended the call and sat up too quickly. The room spun for a second, then settled.

Matt sat up. "Seriously, why not let me and Todd handle this?"

"No." Bree knew she was being stubborn but didn't care. It was *her* case and *her* county, and *her* responsibility to protect the citizens of it. "Todd shouldn't leave Cady alone at night when she's this close to delivering."

"Then I'll handle it." Matt was already on his feet, stepping into his tactical cargo pants.

"No. I need to be there." Bree went into the bathroom. Operating on autopilot, she turned on the faucet to splash water on her face until a glance in the mirror reminded her of the splint on her nose. *Holy . . . Her face . . .* Thank goodness the swelling wasn't any worse. But the bruising was another story. Just wow. She glanced at an ancient tube of concealer, and a maniacal laugh started to rumble in her chest. She tamped it down. Exhaustion and pain were wearing on her.

Keep it together.

No time to dwell. She brushed her teeth and applied deodorant. When she emerged, Matt took her place. His frown said he wasn't happy with her but had accepted her determination.

She dressed and stuffed the bottle of ibuprofen in her pocket. Matt grabbed protein bars and water on the way through the kitchen.

The porch light stabbed Bree in the eyes. "You drive."

Matt slid behind the wheel of the patrol car a deputy had dropped off. In the passenger seat, Bree contacted the deputy assigned to watch Troy Ryder. The deputy said that Troy hadn't left his house all night, then confirmed his presence at home by ringing the bell.

"Stay on him," Bree said.

Matt and Bree arrived at Barbara James's house to find lights blazing from every window. Bree's eyes had mostly adjusted, but she still didn't love the brightness. They walked up to the front door. Inside, a large dog barked.

Zucco opened the door before they had time to knock. "Juarez came out here last night to warn her. He briefed me before he went off shift. The intruder attempted to gain entry through the back door."

A short, stout Staffordshire terrier with a coat of blue-gray fur rushed them like a cannonball as they crossed the threshold.

"She's friendly," Zucco said. "Her name is Meatball."

Matt shifted to move in front of her, but Bree motioned for him to stop. She appreciated his protective nature, but if he stepped in every time she faced a strange dog, she would never truly feel recovered from her past. She braced herself as the staffie sniffed her feet, its tail whipping back and forth. She was built more like a sausage than a meatball, but Bree relaxed at her soft body posture.

She held out a tentative hand. Meatball dropped to the ground and presented her belly. Bree crouched and gave it a quick rub. As she stood, she spotted a small pile of empty beverage cans by the door.

The dog followed as the deputy led them into a kitchen, where a slim woman of about forty sat on a stool, her hands wrapped around a can of sparkling water. She wore flannel pajama bottoms, a sweatshirt, and a pair of sheepskin booties. A canister of pepper spray sat on the table next to her drink.

Zucco introduced them. The dog went to the woman and lay on the floor at her feet. More empty cans were lined up on the counter.

Barbara gaped at Bree. "Are you all right?"

Bree's hand unconsciously went to her nose splint. She looked truly terrible if the crime victim was concerned for her.

"It looks worse than it is," Bree said. "What happened?"

Barbara cleared her throat. She lifted the can to her lips and took a small sip, as if fortifying herself against reliving the memory. "A deputy knocked on my door around ten thirty. Scared the hell out of me. I thought someone died." She breathed and sipped. "If my brother wasn't out of town, I would have gone to stay with him. But he's in Aruba." She reached down and scratched the dog. "Which is why Meatball is staying with me." She paused to lean over and kissed the staffie on the top of her broad head. "Thank God."

"The dog alerted you?" Matt guessed.

"Yes. After the deputy's visit, I was on edge, you know, tossing and turning. I checked every window and door to make sure the house was locked up tight. I don't have a security system. I raided my recycling discards and stacked empty cans against the doors. That way, at least I'd be warned if someone broke in. I took my pepper spray to bed with us too. Around three forty-five, the dog's head went up. I didn't hear anything, but Meatball is usually a sound sleeper. Not much bothers her, so I knew something was up." She exhaled, wrapping her fingers around the can. "We went out into the kitchen. I saw a shadow through the glass. Meatball went ballistic, barking, growling, throwing herself at the door." She pointed. "You can see the scratches." She shuddered. "She's never done anything like that before."

Bree studied the back door. The top half of the door was glass panes. On the bottom half, scratch marks showed where the dog had clawed through the white paint to the wood underneath.

Barbara continued. "The shadow disappeared. I heard someone running away. If the deputy hadn't stopped by earlier, Meatball and I might have been sleeping harder. We might not have heard. They might have gotten in." Her hand strayed to the dog again. "I didn't think Meatball had it in her. Usually, she's the calmest dog. She loves everybody she meets. But she would have tried to protect me, and maybe they would have hurt her." She met Bree's gaze. "So I owe your department a huge thanks."

"Someone tried to pry open the back door." Zucco went to the kitchen door and opened it. The door had a sturdy dead bolt, not an easily pickable knob lock. Deep gouges showed where the intruder had used a tool, maybe a crowbar, to try to force the door open. "They didn't count on the dog."

Who isn't usually here.

Bree went outside onto the patio and scanned the yard. Matt followed, turning on his flashlight and playing the beam across the grass and shrubs. Barbara's neighborhood was on the edge of Grey's Hollow town proper. The lots were small, but mature trees and foliage provided plenty of privacy. No one would have seen a person at Barbara's back door. Bree clicked on her own flashlight, and they searched the ground.

A stamped concrete walkway led all the way around the side of the house to the driveway. The chain-link fence gate didn't have a lock, just a U-shaped latch. Metal scraped softly as Matt lifted it. The gate opened with a faint squeak. They walked through the side yard to the driveway without their boots leaving concrete.

Matt said, "No point looking for footprints. The intruder could have parked anywhere and walked here."

"Agreed."

They checked the rest of the doors and windows. Matt shined his light on a window above the air-conditioning unit. "I see scratches on the frame. Looks like they tried to get in here first but couldn't get the window open."

The house was elevated by several steps. Without the AC, reaching the other windows would have required a ladder.

Bree and Matt walked down the driveway to the sidewalk and scanned the street. Most of the driveways were short and narrow, barely wide enough to fit one car. Vehicles parked along the street on both sides of the lane. A line of trees grew between the sidewalk and road. Spreading branches blocked much of the light from overhead streetlamps. Visibility was poor overall. It was a great setup for sneaking around without being seen.

Bree focused on the front of Barbara's house. "I'll have Zucco dust the gate latch and back doorknob for fingerprints." She would follow procedure but felt the futility in the act. She didn't have much hope of finding anything. If the attempted intruder was the same person who had killed Kelly and Janet, they weren't new at committing crimes. They knew enough to wear gloves.

Lights illuminated the windows of the house next door. Bree saw two men standing behind the glass of their storm door. "Looks like the neighbors are up. Let's see if they saw anything."

The men in their fifties stepped out onto their front stoop as Bree and Matt approached. Both men went wide-eyed at Bree's face but were too polite to say anything. Bree introduced herself and Matt.

"I'm John." The blond man tapped the redhead on the arm. "This is my husband, Gary."

Bree gestured to Barbara's house. "Someone tried to break into your neighbor's house tonight. Did you see anyone?"

"No," said John. "But I'm a super light sleeper, and I heard the dog barking next door. A couple of minutes later, a car engine started up and drove away. I got up and looked out the front window, but I guess whoever it was had gone by then."

"I slept through the whole thing." Gary lifted an apologetic shoulder.

"Do you have a doorbell camera?" Bree asked.

"We do." John turned and pointed to it. "But we turned off the motion camera. There's too much foot traffic here, and it goes off nonstop. Besides, this is a quiet block. Nothing ever happens."

Until tonight.

"Did you notice any unusual activity in the neighborhood recently?" Matt asked.

"No." John shook his head.

"How about this evening? Anyone you didn't recognize walking? A vehicle cruising too slowly down the street?"

"Sorry. It's too cold for me to be outside. In the winter, I rarely leave the house after I get home from work." John lifted his phone and read the screen. "It's almost six. No point in trying to sleep. Tell Barbara we're up. I'm making coffee and breakfast. She and Meatball shouldn't be alone over there."

Bree agreed. "Thank you. I will." She and Matt turned away. Lights shone from the windows of several houses. People were rising. The sun would be up in an hour. "I'll get a deputy out here to knock on doors. Maybe someone else on the street saw a strange vehicle or has a camera that covers the street."

"We don't even know where they might have parked," Matt pointed out.

"We have to keep trying." Frustration bubbled through Bree as thick and nasty as black tar. "I'm calling in additional deputies to canvass the area and dust for prints. We're going to see Marina Maxwell."

Chapter Twenty-Nine

Matt scanned Marina Maxwell's street. At seven thirty, the sun was peering over the horizon. He double-checked the license plate number of Marina's minivan.

They drove past the address, and Matt steered the vehicle around the block. He looked for the minivan. "I don't see her vehicle."

"No lights on either," Bree said.

Marina's house didn't have a garage. The minivan had to be on the street. They parked at the curb and walked to the front door. Standing to the side, Matt listened. Silence blanketed the house. No murmur of a TV, voices, or running feet. In his limited experience with kids, they weren't quiet.

"Where could she be?" Bree asked. "She works retail. They're probably open on Saturday."

Matt checked his notes for the boutique's name. "The store doesn't open until eleven."

"No school on Saturday. Not much is open at this hour." Leaning on the armrest, Bree peered out the window. The early-morning light shone on her face, highlighting her bruises. Her gaze looked clearer than the night before, but her eyes reflected pain. Contemplating the front of Marina's house, she opened a protein bar and took a bite. Matt had eaten his bar an hour before.

Bree washed her bite down with a swig of water. She chewed slowly, wincing as if the motion were painful. "Kayla gets up with the sun. Maybe her kids do too. They could have gone to breakfast. The diner is open. Or maybe one of the kids had an early activity. Some sports start stupid early."

"True." But Matt's gut swirled with doubt.

Bree finished her bar in a minute, then downed two ibuprofen. "Let's knock."

As they stood at the door, the house felt empty and silent. No one answered Bree's firm rap or the chime of the doorbell. Matt cupped his hands over his eyes and peered through the narrow window next to the door. He could see the tiny living area. "Nobody's home."

They stepped away and returned to their vehicle.

"I'm going to call her." Bree pulled out her phone and punched in Marina's number. Matt heard a few rings, then the call flipped to voicemail. Bree pocketed her phone without leaving a message. "I'll try a text." She used her thumbs to send a message and showed him the screen. "Notifications silenced."

Where is Marina? Where are her boys?

"I'm worried about the children," Matt said.

"Me too." Bree paused, her hand on the door handle, and gazed at him over the roof. "Unfortunately, we don't have any evidence that Marina is involved, just a theory."

"Let's drive by Harrison's farm and see if his vehicle or Marina's is there," Matt suggested. Without additional evidence, they couldn't get a search warrant. Harrison lying to them wasn't sufficient. They needed to establish probable cause. Considering Burke's attack on Harrison and the threats of harassment, the judge would demand proof before he signed off on any warrant. Regardless, Matt would feel better if he knew where both Harrison and Marina were at the moment.

"We can also check up on the other two women Troy dated in the last year and update them on the situation. They should know what happened to Barbara this morning."

He drove to the Gibson farm. As the engine idled in front of the property, Matt scanned the parking areas. He spotted Harrison's Corvette, the old pickup truck, and the Ford Taurus. The same vehicles that had been present during their initial interview with Harrison. "Marina's minivan isn't there."

"Unless they hid it inside one of those outbuildings." Bree used the dashboard computer to search vehicle registrations. "The pickup and Ford belong to his mother."

"So where is Marina?" Matt tapped a finger on the wheel. "When we were here last, the garage was full of tools and heavy equipment. We couldn't see inside the barn, though."

"It looks big enough to hide a minivan," Bree said.

"If it was dark, I'd sneak up on foot from the back of the property and get a look inside the barn."

"And if you got caught, you could render any evidence inside meaningless, not to mention getting the county—and me—sued. Then it would be even harder to get a warrant if we find some evidence. We have to follow the letter of the law. If we get into a courtroom, we don't want Kelly's killer to get off on a technicality."

"I know," Matt said. "Let's warn the other potential victims. Where do they live?"

Bree tapped on the dashboard computer keyboard. "Claudia Ferguson is on Maple Street in Scarlet Falls. Candy Simpson lives in that new apartment complex near Walmart."

"An apartment in a complex would be harder to break into. Walls are thin. More people around. An intruder might get caught on surveillance cameras or be seen by other residents in a general-use parking lot."

"I agree. Let's talk to Claudia first."

Matt headed for Scarlet Falls.

Bree worked the computer while he drove. "The house Claudia lives in is owned by a man named Connor Jones. He bought the property seven years ago."

Matt drove up to the house and parked at the curb. He and Bree stepped out of the vehicle. Side by side on the sidewalk, they stared at an older brick Colonial home on a corner lot. The small development of approximately twenty homes sat in the middle of rolling fields. Houses were farther apart, with fewer trees and shrubs and better visibility than in Barbara's neighborhood. A white picket fence surrounded the rear yard. Inside the house, several large dogs barked.

Matt said, "Breaking in here would be riskier. You'd be out in the open."

"No one would sneak past those dogs either. They started barking as soon as we drove up." Bree headed up the driveway. The two-car garage was turned to the side. One of the overhead doors was open. A Ford Escape and a Honda Accord were parked inside.

They turned left and continued to the front door. Bree knocked. Two German shepherds appeared in the front window. The dogs raced back and forth from the window to the door.

"The garage is open, so someone should be home," Matt said.

"If they are, they definitely know we're here." Bree pressed the doorbell. At the sound of the chime, the barking intensified, punctuated by a few howls.

Footsteps sounded inside, and a man's voice yelled, "Leave it!"

The dogs quieted. A door opened and closed. Footsteps approached, then a man of about forty opened the door. Bleary-eyed, he wore pajama bottoms and a gray T-shirt. His hair stood up on one side, and stubble covered his jaw. The man's annoyed expression shifted to surprise when he took in Bree's uniform, then settled on her face. "Is something wrong?"

Bree introduced herself and Matt. "We'd like to speak to Claudia."

"She went to work hours ago." The man rubbed his face.

"And you are?" Bree asked.

"Oh, sorry. I'm Connor Jones. I worked until three a.m. I was out pretty hard when you rang the bell."

Matt pictured the open garage door and two vehicles parked inside. "What does Claudia drive?"

"A Ford Escape."

"It's in the garage," Matt said. "The door is open."

Connor's brows furrowed. "Can't be. What time is it?"

"Just after eight," Bree said.

"She left at six fifteen." Worry creased Connor's face as he stepped out of the house barefoot. Hugging himself, he led them back down the walkway. "She's a nurse at the hospital. Her shift started at seven." At the open garage door, he came to an abrupt stop. Then he rushed forward, past the Accord to the driver's side of the Escape. "What the hell?"

Right behind him, Matt took in the scene. Between the vehicles, just outside the driver's door, a purse and cell phone lay on the concrete. The purse strap was broken, and the zipper had been pulled half-open. A key fob, lip balm, and small bottle of hand sanitizer lay scattered on the concrete.

"Where is she?" Connor asked.

Matt circled both vehicles. "Not in the garage."

"Please step back." Bree crouched and studied the floor. She pointed to the ground next to the left rear tire. "Look at this."

Matt peered over her shoulder. The floor was clean for a garage, except for three dark-red spots on the white concrete. "Have you used red paint recently?"

Connor's face went white. "No."

Matt exchanged a look with Bree.

"I'll call the hospital and make sure she isn't there." Bree turned away, her phone in hand.

She wouldn't be. Matt knew it in his soul. His insides had gone cold.

"What was she wearing?" Matt asked.

"I don't know. She wasn't dressed when I saw her. But probably scrubs. She works in pediatrics, so most of hers have cartoon characters on them."

Bree shoved her phone in her pocket. "She isn't at work."

"She never calls out."

Connor reached for Claudia's phone.

Matt stopped him. "Let me." He snapped a picture, then tugged on gloves and picked up the device. He tapped the screen to wake it. "Do you know her passcode?"

"Yeah." Connor gave it in a disbelieving monotone.

Matt entered the digits. The screen brightened. Several messages popped up, all labeled VICKY. "Who's Vicky?" There was also one from Connor from late the previous night telling her that he'd be very late getting home.

"Her supervisor." Connor shoved a hand over his short hair.

"Was everything normal this morning?" Bree asked Connor.

He said, "Yeah. I only saw her for about fifteen minutes. I got home between four thirty and five. She was just getting up for work. She cooked me eggs while I showered. I ate standing over the sink. Then I went to bed, and she got ready for work."

"What do you do?" Bree asked.

"I'm an ER doctor. We had a doc call out last night, so I covered half his shift." He looked away for a few seconds, processing something. "It was an ugly shift. We lost a patient. By the time I got home, I was so tired, I was asleep when my head hit the pillow."

"Do you work at the same hospital?" Matt asked.

Connor nodded. "That's where we met in August."

"And she moved in with you already?" Bree asked.

His eyes went misty. "It sounds cliché, but it was love at first sight. Her lease was up, so why not? I knew the first time I saw her that I was going to marry her." He wiped at his eye. "Where is she? What happened?" His gaze went to her purse on the ground. "'Cause it looks like someone took her."

"I don't want to panic you," Bree said, her voice forced calm. "Did Claudia ever mention a man named Troy Ryder?"

Connor tilted his head. "She dated some guy named Troy before me."

"Do you follow the news?" she asked.

Connor shivered. "I've been working a lot for the past few weeks. The ER has been swamped with sick people. I've been asleep when I haven't been at work."

"Did Claudia mention that a deputy stopped here last night?" Bree asked.

"No." Connor shook his head. His lips flattened. "But she knew I'd had a rough night. She probably didn't want to worry me. Why would a deputy need to talk to her?" He blinked, as if just remembering something. "Is this about those two women who were murdered?"

"Possibly."

"Did this Troy guy come after Claudia?"

"Where were the dogs when Claudia left?" Matt asked.

Connor paused. "In the bedroom with me. She said she would feed them and take them out before she left so I could sleep." He choked back a sob.

"Did you hear the dogs bark when she left?" Matt asked.

"They always bark when she leaves," Connor said. "They bark whenever anything happens."

"So you wouldn't have noticed anything unusual if they were barking at that time, and I doubt anyone could have gotten into the house with the dogs inside."

"Definitely not. They're good dogs, and they would protect her if someone tried to get in. They love Claudia," Connor said. "I have to call Claudia's mom." He turned toward the house. His bare feet were red from the cold.

"Matt?" Bree squatted on the concrete. "There are some white fibers stuck to the zipper of Claudia's purse. If she resisted, and they struggled . . ."

"Neither Kelly nor Janet had a chance to fight back, but it looks like Claudia put up a fight." Matt glanced around. From where they stood in the garage, they had a clear line of sight to the front of the house next door. "Kelly likely knew the killer, and they sneaked up on Janet. They had privacy inside the house." He pointed to the neighbor's home. "Maybe they were interrupted or they just changed their mind and took her instead of killing her. Given the state of her purse, it looks like Claudia at least had a chance to resist."

"But why change their MO?" Bree asked.

"Because whatever the motivation for the crimes, a quick death wasn't meeting their needs anymore."

Bree brushed a hair out of her face.

Matt pulled his phone from his pocket. "I'll call Rory and see if there are any similar fibers at either of the first two crime scenes."

"I'll have a deputy go to Candy Simpson's apartment. She needs to be protected."

He dialed Rory's number. The tech answered immediately. Matt explained about the third potential crime scene and the white fibers Bree had found. "Can you see if there are any white fibers found at the first two scenes?"

Rory said, "I'll pull the reports now and call you back. I'll also get the status on the analysis from the lab."

Matt paced while Bree continued to search the scene and call in reinforcements. Rory called back in less than fifteen minutes. "There were white fibers collected from the first crime scene. I contacted the lab to expedite the testing. We need to get the new sample to the lab immediately for a comparison."

"I'll have a deputy deliver it."

"Perfect," Rory said.

But even expedited tests would take time. Time that Claudia Ferguson might not have.

Chapter Thirty

"I hate waiting." Bree leaned on the conference table and stared at the murder board. The answer had to be somewhere in all those columns of information. *But where?*

Next to her, Matt drank from a bottle of water. Todd walked in, carrying his laptop and a take-out espresso cup. Dark circles underscored his eyes.

Worried, Bree asked, "Everything OK?"

"Cady was up last night, but it was just a few false labor pains." He downed his espresso like a shot of tequila. "Nerve-racking, though."

"Should you be at home with her?" Bree asked.

"No," Todd said. "She's sleeping, and her mom is with her. They'll call if anything happens."

But Bree didn't like it.

"I'd rather take my PTO after the baby is here," he added. "I can't really do anything, and it could be another week or two before she actually goes into labor."

"That makes sense."

Todd rubbed his eyes and blinked at the board. "Where are we?"

Bree summarized the attempted break-in at Barbara's house and Claudia's early-morning disappearance. She and Matt had knocked on every door on Claudia's street. No one had seen anything. Houses were too far from the street for doorbell cameras to pick up motion from passing cars. They'd put out a BOLO on her, but without a vehicle description, the chances of her being spotted were slim. A deputy had checked on Candy Simpson—she was fine—and escorted her to her job hostessing at a busy restaurant. She promised to stay there until the end of her shift. Her father—a former marine—would pick her up and take her to her parents' home, where she would stay.

The conference room door opened, and Jager walked in. "What is happening?"

Bree gave her a brief summary. "We're assuming Claudia was kidnapped. I'll do a press conference and put out a picture of her."

"Good idea," Matt said.

It was Bree's only idea, other than to wait for lab results that might or might not be relevant. Claudia could have brushed up against someone at the hospital and picked up those fibers there. They might be meaningless.

"We need a current photo," Bree added.

Matt nodded. "I'll bring up her social media account and text Connor to approve the picture."

"I'll make the calls." Stepping away, Jager whipped out her phone and started tapping on the screen.

Bree reviewed evidence while Jager called the media. Todd left to deal with a scheduling issue. Matt typed up reports from the callout to Barbara's house and Claudia's disappearance.

Reporters came running at Jager's call, and an hour later, Bree stood in front of the press. "Claudia Ferguson went missing from her home around six fifteen this morning. She is five feet, six inches tall and weighs approximately one hundred thirty-five pounds. She has shoulder-length brown hair and brown eyes. Claudia is a nurse and was likely wearing scrubs when she went missing. We have a recent photo of Claudia to distribute. We believe this incident is related to the murders that occurred earlier this week, so time is of the essence." Bree reviewed the names and locations of the previous murders and showed photos of Kelly Gibson and Janet Hargrave. "Anyone with information regarding these crimes should call the tip line immediately. We need to find Claudia Ferguson."

Jager stepped forward with a few words of praise for the sheriff's department and concern for the families of the victims. "We're calling on every citizen to help find Claudia Ferguson."

Bree took a few questions and ended the session.

Back in the conference room, she stared at the murder board.

Matt brought her coffee and a muffin from the break room. The muffin was a no go. Too little sleep and too much caffeine had left her wired. Bree sipped the coffee anyway.

As far as physical evidence went, they had very little. "Do we think Harrison and/or Marina took Claudia?"

"That's our best line of investigation until we have results from the lab," Matt said. "The tip line hasn't panned out."

"Let's consider the Marina/Harrison pairing for a few minutes." Bree scratched an itchy piece of tape on her nose. "Why would they take Claudia?"

Matt frowned. "In this scenario, Harrison killed Kelly for the money. The house sale and the insurance policy payout would leave him in a very nice financial position."

"Right," Bree said. "And Marina killed Janet while Harrison was here to throw us off."

"Why Claudia?"

Bree had nothing. "It doesn't make sense. Where could they take her? To the farm?"

"Out into the woods to dump her body?" Matt asked.

"I don't think so. The other victims were left in their homes. Those deaths each served a purpose that required them to be found. Why hide this one?"

Matt scrubbed a hand down his beard. "We don't know the motivation for the crime, so who knows?"

Frustration tightened in Bree's gut. Marge knocked on the doorframe and peered in. "Something interesting just came in on the tip line. A woman called in to say she saw someone at Kelly Gibson's house on Monday afternoon. Her name is Paisley Babcock. I have her address. She's expecting you."

"I'll grab my coat." Bree ducked into her office and met Matt at the back door.

He handed her an envelope. "Photo array."

"Good to be prepared." Bree put the envelope in her pocket.

While Matt drove, Bree checked out Paisley Babcock on her dashboard computer. "No criminal record. Not even a parking ticket. Brian and Paisley Babcock have owned their house for eight years."

Paisley opened the door before Bree had a chance to knock. Bree introduced them as they walked back to her kitchen. They passed two young boys watching TV.

"I'm so sorry I didn't call earlier in the week. I didn't know. Between the kids and work, I don't have much time during the week. Saturday morning is my time to catch up on the news." Paisley kept her voice low. "I saw you on my Facebook feed this morning and called right away."

"We appreciate that." Bree copied her soft tone. "You said you saw someone at the Gibson house?"

"Yes. I saw a woman going into Kelly's house around three forty-five on Monday afternoon."

Marina? Anticipation roiled in Bree's gut, as if her instincts could feel the case breaking. "You're sure of the day and time?"

"Positive," Paisley said. "Ryan has band practice on Mondays. The late bus drops him off at three forty-five. I always walk to the corner and wait for him. I can see the Gibsons' house from there."

"How well do you know Kelly?" Matt asked.

Paisley glanced through the doorway, checking on the boys, who were still focused on the TV. "We saw each other at neighborhood events, but we didn't socialize. Most of our friends have kids the same age as ours."

"But you're sure it was Kelly's house?" he confirmed.

"Yes." Paisley nodded emphatically. "Last month, my son had to sell overpriced wrapping paper for his basketball team. We went door-to-door in the neighborhood. Kelly bought a few rolls."

"Can you describe the woman you saw?" Bree pulled out the envelope with photos of Marina and four other random women with similar features.

"Oh, yes," Paisley said. "I've seen her before. Tallish, stout, midsixties, gray hair."

Bree froze. Shock rippled the hairs on the back of her neck. "Gray hair?"

"Yes," Paisley said. "I don't know who she is, maybe Kelly's mom."

Or mother-in-law.

She and Matt exchanged a look. "Are you thinking what I'm thinking?"

"Is there anything else to think?" he asked.

"Do we have a photo of her?"

Matt pulled out his phone. "There must be a photo of her somewhere. Give me a minute and I'll pull a few comps for an array."

"Check her son's social media accounts," suggested Bree.

"Good idea." He typed and scrolled for a few minutes, then straightened suddenly. "We're in luck. She has her own account. Damn. Her profile picture is an alpaca." He scrolled for another minute. "Got one on her son's account." He worked on his phone for two minutes, then slid the phone in front of Paisley. "I'm going to show you five pictures. Tell me if you see the woman who was at Kelly's house." He advanced the photos one by one.

On picture number four, Paisley touched the face on the screen. "That's her."

The woman in the photo under her fingertip was Elaine Gibson.

Chapter Thirty-One

Drizzle and darkness bathed the Gibson farm by the time Bree had her warrant in hand. The judge had been exacting with the affidavit and hadn't signed until Rory had called and identified the white fibers found on Claudia's purse as alpaca wool. The second piece of evidence had clinched his decision.

Frustrated that the delay had made the search more difficult, Bree scanned the property. Both the pickup truck and sedan were parked between the house and barn. Elaine's sedan was gray, Bree noted, a light shade like the disabled vehicle parked on the overpass when the cinder block had struck her SUV. No lights shone from any of the buildings. There were plenty of places to hide on a farm, and her team would have to operate in the dark.

Matt stopped just short of the top of the driveway. Patrol vehicles parked behind theirs. Bree, Matt, a half dozen deputies, and one K-9 team assembled in the road. They did a two-minute check of earpieces and equipment. Bree tugged down the knit cap she'd donned.

Todd held the battering ram. Matt carried a rifle. Bree drew her Glock, checking the light mounted to it. She took a deep breath and held it to slow her heart rate. With a long, controlled exhalation, she signaled the team to move forward. They jogged up the driveway. Bree slipped in a half-frozen muddy rut but caught her balance before going down in the slop.

As they'd previously planned, the team divided into three groups. Juarez and Zucco circled to the back of the house to peer through windows and block any escape. Todd, Bree, and Matt crept to the front door. The remaining deputies and the K-9 headed behind the house to begin scouting sheds. The dog's superior vision and hearing would prove useful in the dark. The words SHERIFF DEPT glowed in silver on Greta's body armor in the same font as on Matt's vest.

Bree crept to a double window to the left of the front door. Matt crossed to a matching window on the other side. Bree used her cell phone on a selfie stick to peer inside. The rooms were slightly darker, and rain spotted her phone screen, so she couldn't see much. But she didn't notice any movement. She motioned toward the door. Then she and Matt flanked it. Bree switched on her gun light. Her heartbeat thrummed in her ears.

Staying clear of the center, Todd swung the battering ram and struck the door next to the dead bolt. The old wood jamb gave on the first hit. The door flew open, and Todd stepped aside to trade the battering ram for his long gun. Matt and Bree swept in, crossing the threshold with speed. She shined her light into the left corner of the space. Matt took the right.

Empty.

They moved through the living room. Todd veered toward the dining room. Matt headed for the bedrooms. Bree continued down the hall, checked two storage closets, then proceeded to the kitchen. Three closed doors loomed ahead. Bree opened the first, flashing her light into a pantry. Empty.

Matt emerged from the second doorway and mouthed, "Bedrooms are clear."

Bree could see Juarez and Zucco at the back door. Bree spoke into her mic. "We're almost done here. Help the rest of the team with the outbuildings. The dog will find someone before we will."

Juarez and Zucco turned and jogged across the grass.

Todd approached the third door. Matt covered him as he pulled it open. The beam from Todd's light cut through the darkness to illuminate narrow wooden stairs leading downward. He flipped a light switch on the wall, but nothing happened. They waited, listening for breathing or the rustle of fabric, but Bree heard only the *whoosh* of a furnace turning on. Hot air rattled from a vent near the baseboard.

Bree's pulse hammered as Todd started down the stairs, leading with his lighted weapon. Stairwells were called fatal funnels because you were trapped and vulnerable to ambush on the way up or down, so Todd didn't dawdle. He moved steadily, peering into the space as he descended. Matt stepped into the doorway to follow him. When Todd hit the fourth step, a crack sounded, and he plunged downward, disappearing into the darkness.

Chapter Thirty-Two

Matt's heart stuttered. He yelled into the space where Todd had been standing two seconds before. "Todd!"

No answer.

Matt shined his light downward. Todd lay on his side on the packed dirt floor. Debris from the stairs covered the lower half of his body. Fear clogged Matt's throat. He called out again. "Todd!"

Nothing.

Matt's flashlight beam settled on saw marks on the frame of the steps. "This was intentional. A booby trap. I'm going down." He slung the rifle onto his back.

Bree shined her flashlight onto the remains of the basement stair frame, and Matt climbed down. Behind him, Matt heard her calling for EMTs, an ambulance, and backup from surrounding state and local law enforcement. She also warned the other members of the team to watch for potential booby traps. He jumped off a wooden beam, landing next to Todd.

Matt scanned the space with his light. The basement was empty except for some shelves full of boxes and a few pieces of random junk. No killer with a razor-sharp chef's knife. Matt took an intentional breath. "Clear."

The ceiling was low. Todd had only fallen about eight feet. Matt pointed the light at Todd's face. Blood smeared his forehead. "Looks like he hit his head on the way down."

Matt pressed two fingers to Todd's neck. Relief flooded him when he felt the steady rap of a pulse. "He's alive."

"ETA on EMS is thirteen minutes," Bree said. "I'll grab the first aid kit." She disappeared.

With his rifle on his back, Matt pulled a flashlight from his cargo pocket and set it on the ground, illuminating the debris pile. Then he started clearing wood treads and risers from Todd's legs. Matt grabbed a section of several steps and lifted with his legs. Muscles straining, he hoisted it to the side. Then he did the same with another piece. As he moved the last section, he heard steps overhead. He swung the rifle into position, ready to defend Todd. Aiming the weapon to the open door above, he stood in front of Todd's still body and waited.

"It's me." Bree's face popped into the beam of his light. "I have a first aid kit and a blanket." She tossed them down.

Matt caught them. "I'll stay with Todd. You go. Find Claudia." He hated to separate—he always wanted to have her back—but their team was already down two. Bree's deputies needed her.

She mouthed, "Love you" before she turned away.

Matt covered Todd with the blanket and began feeling for broken bones. He couldn't let anything happen to Todd, not with Cady so close to delivering their child. *Damn it.* She and Todd deserved to be happy.

He should have gone first. He shouldn't have let Todd take point.

Matt's pocket vibrated silently. As he pulled out his phone, he knew exactly what he would see. He tapped the screen, and a text from his sister appeared.

In labor. Headed to the hospital.

Fuck.

Matt returned the phone to his pocket and tapped Todd on the cheek. "Hey, man. You have to wake up."

Chapter Thirty-Three

Still overly warm and nauseated from watching Todd plummet into the basement, Bree ran outside and grabbed the battering ram before jogging to the rear yard. She gulped cool night air and welcomed the cold rain on her face.

Focus.

She put aside her worry about her chief deputy and tuned in to the task at hand: finding Claudia. She had to trust Matt to take care of Todd until EMS arrived.

But she cursed Elaine Gibson as she ran.

"Team three, talk to me," Bree said into her mic.

A deputy responded, "First two sheds are clear. Heading for number three."

"Roger that." Bree spotted Zucco and Juarez emerging from behind a tractor and approaching the barn. She joined them. The barn door wasn't locked and slid open easily. Inside, chickens clucked, and larger animals rustled their bedding. Something screeched, and Bree whirled.

"What was that?" Juarez said in her ear.

Zucco's voice sounded next. "For all that's holy . . ."

Bree aimed the weapon into the darkness, the beam of light cutting a narrow swath and illuminating . . . alpacas nervously pacing the aisle.

One animal lifted its head and emitted the same high-pitched alarm, somewhere between a scream and a bleat.

Bree exhaled, her heart rapping against her breastbone, then said in a low voice, "It was just an animal."

"Fuck," muttered Zucco.

Beyond the alpacas, framed wire panels formed spaces the size of large horse stalls. Chickens fluttered from roosts, clucking in confusion. Bree and her team moved slowly through the darkness, checking behind every partition. Zucco opened a door with care. Something crashed to the ground and broke. Bree spun. In the beam of Zucco's light, broken pieces of cinder block lay on the floor of a storage room. Bree remembered a similar concrete block bouncing off the hood of her vehicle.

Elaine Gibson liked her cinder blocks. She'd balanced one on top of the door. Had she known they were coming? Booby traps would slow them down.

Zucco frowned at the pieces of block on the floor. "Good thing I didn't rush in." She peered into the room. "Clear."

"Let's be extra careful. We don't know what other surprises she left for us," Bree said.

Zucco provided cover as Juarez scaled a ladder, testing each rung before transferring his weight. At the top, he scanned the loft, climbed down, jumping the last few feet. "Clear."

"Let's check the garage." Outside the barn, Bree picked up the battering ram from the ground and handed it to Juarez. The ram required some heft to swing. If using it proved necessary, he could do the job more efficiently.

She checked the knob. Locked. She stood aside. Juarez moved into place and used two swings to open the door. When it burst inward, Bree gestured for the team to wait. Normally, she'd send in the K-9, but after the booby trap in the house, they needed to be wary. She didn't want Greta to trigger a trap that could endanger them all.

Bree searched for a light switch but didn't find one. She played her gun light across the space. Discarded household items filled the expanse, roughly placed into rows with little apparent organization. Though she couldn't see over the rows of junk, by following the high ceiling, she estimated the building was large enough to house five cars. The clutter made for too many hiding places and a building-clearing nightmare. Signaling for Zucco and Juarez to take their positions behind her, Bree checked above the door for a cinder block—or worse—before stepping inside. Zucco and Juarez filed in behind her, covering the corners and staying low.

She slipped around two rusty lawn mowers, a fence-post digger, rolls of chicken wire, and sacks of animal feed stacked on pallets. A workbench and pegboard full of tools occupied one bay. In the next, Elaine's pickup sat, the truck bed partially loaded with gear. The license plates were out of state. Had Elaine swapped her own for stolen ones?

She was planning to run.

Zucco and Juarez approached two closed doors. Bree headed between two rows of junk piled head high, old feed tubs, discarded chicken roosts, random pieces of furniture, and a broken sink.

"Clear," said Zucco.

A few seconds later, Juarez echoed her statement.

Bree stepped around a highboy draped in cobwebs. Something tapped the side of her head. She flinched and whirled, brushing at her head with one hand. Her fingers encountered a string dangling from the ceiling. She pointed her light upward, looking for a booby trap. The string hung from a light bulb. Bree pulled it, and the bulb cast a puddle of light for six feet in each direction.

Zucco cursed from Bree's right.

"What happened?" she asked, shining her light in the direction of her deputy.

Zucco came around the corner, blood dripping from her hand. "Brushed against some skinny knives jammed through a board."

"How bad?" Bree asked.

"I can keep going," Zucco said.

Adrenaline would block the pain for a while.

Bree took another step. The toe of her boot caught, and she almost fell. She glanced down to see a trip wire extending across the aisle between two pallets piled with straw bales. Dread curled up in her belly as she poised to run.

"Look out!" Zucco yelled as she dived forward, taking Bree down.

The impact with the ground knocked the air from her lungs and sent waves of white-hot pain through her broken nose. Her deputy landed on top of her. An elbow caught her in the ribs. Pain zinged through her midsection. Their guns skittered across the floor, the beam from the mounted lights playing in crazy arcs over the room. Bree caught movement in her peripheral vision and turned her head. A sledgehammer swung from a rope, passed a few feet above their heads, and smashed into the garage wall, leaving a three-inch hole in the drywall.

Had Elaine set all these traps today? Or was this the normal state of the Gibson farm?

Sprawled on the dirt floor, Bree nudged her deputy off her.

"Sorry," Zucco said, scrambling to her feet and turning in a circle, clearly looking for her gun. She moved toward the straw bales with purpose.

"Don't apologize. You saved me from getting bashed in the head," Bree whispered back. Her palms and knees burned as she got to her feet. She spotted her own weapon six feet away, just a few feet from Zucco's. She took a step toward it.

"Oh, no, you don't." Elaine Gibson stepped out from between an armoire and a bookcase. She held a pump shotgun aimed at Bree's chest. "Hands up."

Bree froze, her heart hammering. *Fuck.* She slowly lifted her hands, palms out. Zucco did the same. Elaine had already killed two women and kidnapped a third. She clearly wouldn't hesitate to pull the trigger.

"Where's the other one? The man?" Elaine moved sideways. She kicked their guns farther under the pallet.

Bree didn't respond.

"Where are you, Deputy?" Elaine called out. "Come out with your hands raised or I'll shoot your sheriff. Maybe I won't shoot the deputy, though." She laughed at her own joke. "Who am I kidding? I'd kill both of them in a heartbeat."

Bree didn't know exactly where Juarez was, but if she distracted Elaine, maybe he could get into position. "Where's Claudia?"

"Don't you wish you knew," Elaine said in a mocking voice. "I'm not going to make it easy for you."

"Drop the shotgun!" Juarez aimed his AR-15 at Elaine from behind a stack of hay bales.

Elaine laughed. "I guess you got me." Her tone didn't sound scared or even angry as she tipped the gun barrel toward the ground with a *my bad* vibe.

Bree's instincts went on alert. Elaine was too calm. Did she have another booby trap set up? Bree scanned the space, looking for potential risks. Zucco stepped forward and disarmed Elaine. Bree walked toward the spot where she'd last seen her gun and Zucco's. Crouching, she looked under the pallet, but the weapons had slid out of reach. She looked around for a stick to retrieve them and spotted a broken broomstick. She grabbed it.

A gunshot went off.

A bullet struck a hay bale next to Juarez. He dived behind it. Bree dropped to the ground and crawled behind the highboy. Zucco scrambled behind the hay bales.

Who was shooting at them? Harrison? His sports car was parked outside. He'd grown up on a farm. He could probably handle a weapon.

Elaine darted between the armoire and bookcase, disappearing the way she'd come.

Damn it.

Bree picked up the broomstick, put her hat on it, and stuck it out from behind the highboy. Another shot sounded, and a bullet slammed into the furniture, sending chunks of wood flying. Zucco returned fire with Elaine's shotgun, blowing a hole in the wall.

Footsteps retreated. Bree thought it sounded like more than one person running. A door opened and slammed shut. Shots rang in the night outside. Bree waved her hat on the stick again. Nothing. She peered around the furniture but didn't see a shooter. Her heart skipped as she crept out from behind the furniture.

No one shot at her. Bree swept the broomstick under the hay and pulled out her gun and Zucco's.

Collins's voice sounded in her ear. "Two people just exited the garage. They shot at me and missed. I returned fire, but they ran across the field."

"We're on the way out. Wait for us to pursue." Bree, Juarez, and Zucco raced out the door.

Collins was struggling to hold on to Greta, who strained at the end of her leash. Collins pointed out over the meadow behind the barn. "They went that way."

Bree checked the map app on her phone. Then she called dispatch to notify the backup officers en route of which way the suspects were headed. Maybe they could cut them off by vehicle. Then she assigned three deputies to secure the house for the arrival of EMS. They thought Elaine and her accomplice had run out into the meadow, but they didn't know if one or both of them had circled back to the house. There could be additional shooters.

"Let's go." She started forward with Zucco and Juarez at her side. Collins gave the dog her command.

Greta didn't need her nose to the ground. She had the suspects' scents in her nose, and the trail was fresh. Bree heard sirens approaching.

She used her radio to contact dispatch. EMS could not enter the house until law enforcement deemed the premises safe. She could not risk EMTs being injured. As much as she hated to do so, she told them the house wasn't secured, and that they'd encountered booby traps all over the property. Two suspects had fled into the woods, but they didn't know if there could be more. A responding state trooper responded that they'd assist with clearing the house for EMS.

EMS will get in. Todd will be OK.
He has to be.

Chapter Thirty-Four

Kneeling at Todd's side, Matt heard the sirens and Bree's commands in his earpiece. He understood. She was doing the right thing. She couldn't risk the EMTs' lives. They had to wait until deputies and troopers determined the situation was safe before allowing the medics to enter the house.

But helplessness floored Matt. He wanted to secure the house himself, but he couldn't leave the basement for fear that one of the shooters would attack Todd while he was vulnerable.

And right at this moment, Cady was in the hospital, in labor with their child. Matt couldn't even consider the chance that Todd wouldn't get there. After all his sister had been through, that would break her.

He checked Todd's pulse again. Still beating. Matt tugged the blanket higher. There was nothing else he could do, and the forced inactivity gave him anxiety.

He stared up at the open doorway, willing help to arrive.

Chapter Thirty-Five

Jogging steadily, Bree watched the K-9 team work ahead of her. There was no guesswork. No creeping along, shining a light on the ground, looking for tracks. Greta made the pursuit easy. She probably would have caught the suspects already if Collins hadn't been holding her back, wary of a booby trap or ambush. Though they were all moving too fast to be truly careful in the dark. If Elaine had set traps in the woods, she would probably lead them right into them.

The rain intensified, pouring through the forest, soaking Bree's hat and dripping down her back. The woods seemed to get even darker—and colder. Bree shivered.

She pictured the blood on Claudia's garage floor. Was she injured? Was she even still alive? The temperature would continue to drop throughout the night. Was Claudia somewhere warm or out in the elements? Hypothermia could set in quickly on a wet, frigid night.

Greta barked. A shot rang out ahead. A bullet slammed into a tree next to Bree. Bits of bark exploded. She rolled behind a fallen tree. Next to her, Zucco and Juarez dropped to the ground. Collins stumbled and fell. She dropped her flashlight and Greta's leash. The dog—still on the scent—bolted into the trees. Her black coat vanished into the darkness.

Collins cupped her hands around her mouth and yelled out a recall command in German, but the dog didn't return. Had the rain drowned out the command? A female scream split the wet air.

More shrieking, then a gunshot. Collins levered to her feet and ran toward the sound. Bree lunged forward and followed.

"Circling around," Juarez said in her earpiece. "Don't shoot me."

In her peripheral vision, Bree saw Zucco follow him to the right.

"Shoot it! Shoot it!" Bree heard Elaine Gibson shout, her voice panicked.

Collins and Bree surged forward. Jogging had been hard enough, but the full-out sprint challenged Bree's wind. She struggled to suck in oxygen through her swollen nasal passages. Her lungs heaved. Lack of oxygen made her lightheaded. She kept her legs pumping through sheer force of will.

"There!" Collins said and veered to the right.

Bree shined her gun light onto two shifting shadows. Greta had Elaine by the calf. The dog's head shook back and forth as she tried to drag the suspect backward, to Collins, to her handler. Her black coat rendered her nearly invisible against the dark forest floor.

"Shoot it!" Elaine was shrieking now, her voice high with pain and fear.

Bree arced her light in a semicircle.

Ten feet away, Marina Maxwell held a handgun, pointing in the direction of Elaine and the dog. "I can't. I can't see. I'll shoot you. I'm not that good."

Marina? Where's Harrison?

"You're useless!" Elaine's flailing hands closed on a stick lying on the ground. Grabbing it, she swung it at the dog, striking her in the side. The dog didn't react at all.

Bree pointed her weapon at Marina. "Drop the gun, Marina!"

Instead, Marina pivoted, the gun's barrel swinging toward Bree. Before she could squeeze the trigger, a gunshot sounded. Bree flinched, then froze, waiting for the bullet to strike her, for the searing pain of the gunshot. Nothing? No pain. She looked down at her torso. No red blotch. No holes. *Did she miss?*

Someone gasped. Bree's head snapped up.

Marina's mouth gaped. Her eyes widened with horror and pain. She dropped to her knees, revealing Zucco standing behind her, weapon raised. The gunshot Bree had heard was Zucco shooting Marina. Juarez skirted around her, kicked Marina's gun away, and handcuffed her.

Greta resisted Collins's command to release, and the handler had to drag the K-9 off Elaine. Bree moved forward while Collins praised her dog. Bree reached for the cuffs on her belt. She stomped toward Elaine. "Don't move."

"You won't take me to jail," Elaine snapped. She rolled sideways, pulled a knife from her coat pocket, and slashed her own throat. Blood gushed.

Fuuuuck.

Bree wanted Elaine to be held accountable and for the families of the victims to have answers and closure. Death was too easy. She rushed forward and kicked the knife to a safe distance. Juarez turned away from Marina and shined a light on Elaine. Bree dropped to her knees and tried to stem the flow of blood with both hands. It wasn't going to work. She needed a towel or something.

The corner of Elaine's mouth curled upward in a satisfied *gotcha* sneer.

"Oh, no. You're not going to die on me," Bree said. Elaine was wearing a scarf. Bree removed it and used it to stanch the blood flow. She applied pressure. "Give me more light."

Juarez changed the angle, highlighting the wound.

Elaine's face contorted in an angry snarl. She writhed, trying to evade Bree's hands on her neck.

Bree leaned on her hands, increasing the pressure. "Where is Claudia?"

"You'll never find her," Elaine whispered. "She's going to die." She choked, then mouthed, "Fuck you" before her eyes rolled backward and she lost consciousness. She was still alive, though. For a brief second, Bree contemplated not trying so hard to save her life. Bree had killed bad people before in the line of duty. Their deaths didn't keep her up at night, something she wasn't proud of. In fact, her lack of guilt often disturbed her. But this was different. If she let Elaine die, it wouldn't be an act of self-defense. It would be a choice. She'd be issuing judgment, which wasn't her job.

Apparently, she had lines she couldn't cross. *Good to know.*

"Cuff her while I keep pressure on this wound," she called to Juarez. "Is everyone OK? How is Greta?"

"The dog seems fine," Collins said, relief in her voice. A repetitive high-pitched squeaking noise indicated Collins had rewarded the dog with the stuffed hedgehog toy she loved. "Maybe a little sore on one side. Her armor protected most of her."

"Marina?" Bree asked.

"Shot in the upper arm," Zucco yelled. "Putting pressure on it. I have a tourniquet on my duty belt. I'll secure it."

Juarez handcuffed Elaine and searched her pockets.

"Is Marina conscious?" Bree asked.

"Yes," Zucco said.

"Marina, where's Claudia?" Bree yelled.

Marina didn't respond.

Bree shouted, "Where's Harrison?"

Still, Marina refused to answer.

Bree cursed, then updated dispatch and requested aid. What a fucking mess. Was Harrison still out there? Armed?

Where is Claudia?

"Juarez, take over here." Bree moved aside as his hands replaced hers. He'd pulled latex gloves from his duty belt. Bree hadn't had time. Her fingers were coated with Elaine's blood. But the flow coming from the wound seemed to be lessening. The scarf wasn't completely saturated. She didn't see any gushing or spurts of blood that would indicate an arterial spray.

"Help is on the way," Bree said. "I'm going back. Collins, is Greta good to work?"

"Yes, ma'am," Collins responded. "She won't quit."

Juarez nodded. "Zucco and I can handle things here."

"I know you can." Bree stood, wiping her hands on her pants. "Collins, let's go. We have a victim to find."

Chapter Thirty-Six

It took Bree and Collins ten minutes to run back to the house. The property was lit up with roving flashlights. She'd announced their approach over the radio, so no one shot at them.

A state trooper greeted her. "All buildings are clear. No sign of the missing woman."

No one had seen Harrison either.

Matt appeared. "Todd is on his way to the hospital. He regained consciousness as they pulled him out of the basement. My sister is in labor. Not an ideal situation, but at least they'll be at the same hospital."

Relief weakened Bree's knees. She told him about Marina. "Now, if we can just find Claudia . . ."

Matt pointed to the dog. "If she's here, Greta will find her."

Bree hated to make the dog work after being struck with a stick—Greta should be evaluated by a veterinarian. But Bree had no choice. She reminded herself that the dog was a tool, not a human. Her purpose in the department was to save human lives. So Bree made the hard decision, but she didn't like it.

If Claudia was on the farm, she was well hidden, and the temperature was dropping. If she wasn't on the farm . . . Bree refused to entertain that idea. One step at a time.

Collins had brought one of Claudia's socks, supplied by Connor. She held it out to the dog now. Greta gave it a long sniff and began circling around the property. Head up to sniff the air. Nose down to trail along the ground. She paced and spiraled. Then her head snapped up, her nostrils working the wet breeze. When she moved forward, it was with purpose.

"She has the scent," Collins said.

They followed the dog, who led them behind the house toward the barn, then past it. She hesitated at a tree stump covered with a dark substance. Feathers and an axe on the ground indicated this was where Elaine slaughtered chickens.

A person who slaughtered animals would be accustomed to using a knife.

Then Greta moved on, around the building to where the tractor was parked on the other side. She stopped next to the heavy equipment, sat, and whined.

"Under the tractor!"

"Somebody find the keys!"

Ten minutes later, the tractor keys were located on a rack in the barn storage room. A trooper started it up and moved it forward. It rumbled and shook for thirty feet, revealing the door of a root cellar.

"Be careful opening that!" Bree called out. "We've encountered booby traps here."

The troopers lifted the door and waited. Nothing happened. They lit the stairwell with floodlights.

"Let me." Bree moved forward. They all understood that she wanted to see the search through, no matter what she was going to find.

She held her breath and approached the opening. "Claudia?"

A weak voice sobbed.

Greta barked and wagged her tail. Bree tested each tread with her weight on the way down, but they all held. She shined her light into the darkness. A woman crouched. Her hands were bound behind her back, and a burlap sack was tied over her head.

"She's here!" Bree called out as she moved forward. Setting down her light, she removed the sack. Claudia Ferguson blinked at her. A tight gag pulled at the corners of her mouth. Bree worked it loose. Claudia sagged forward, crying, in Bree's arms. Her skin felt as cold as meat in a locker. The light jacket she wore was soaked through and no match for the cellar's chill. Bree turned and yelled, "She's here, and she's OK. Somebody get a blanket."

"Thank you. Thank you thank you." Claudia's weak and raspy voice was one of the best sounds Bree had ever heard.

"We've got you." Bree helped her to her feet. "Can you walk?"

"I'll crawl if I have to," Claudia said, her voice strengthening.

"Dim the lights," Bree shouted. "I'm bringing her out."

A collective cheer sounded outside.

Claudia had been blindfolded and in the dark for long hours. Bright lights would be painful.

The crowd of law enforcement officers parted, pointing their lights to the ground, as Bree led her out. Greta rushed forward.

"She found you," Bree said.

Claudia bent down to wrap her arms around the dog's neck and sobbed harder. Greta looked over the woman's shoulder, her gaze meeting Bree's with uncanny intelligence. Her tail thumped on the wet ground in a happy cadence.

Someone wrapped a blanket around Claudia's shoulders and led her to a nearby vehicle to get warm.

"More ambulances are on the way," Matt said.

Bree checked in with Zucco and Juarez. "Elaine is still alive."

"Good. A quick death would be too easy for her. She needs to pay for what she did. Marina too."

"Marina isn't talking. Yet." But Bree had all the questions. Was Harrison involved at all? Where was he? Where were Marina's boys?

"I want to be at the hospital when Marina gets there," Bree said. "She needs to answer questions."

"She didn't seem worried about her boys. I suspect they're safe."

"I hope so," Bree said. "On another note, we really need another dog. Turbo would have been a big help tonight. Poor Greta had to do it all."

"She did good," Matt said. Collins joined them for the long walk down the driveway. Greta kept pace, but she was limping. Collins loaded the dog into the K-9 unit and headed for the vet.

"Turbo will go to the academy. I'll make it happen," Bree said. "I know just how to do it."

At the end of the driveway, she walked forward to where the press was waiting. "I'd like to thank my deputies and the state troopers who helped stop Elaine Gibson and Marina Maxwell—and save Claudia Ferguson tonight. I'd also like to specifically mention K-9 Greta, who went above and beyond to protect her fellow deputies and find Claudia Ferguson. We would not have succeeded tonight without her."

Reporters surged forward.

"Do you have an update on the injured deputy?"

"What is the condition of the killers?"

Bree held up a hand. She wasn't taking questions that she didn't have answers for. "I'll give you more information as soon as I have it."

She rejoined Matt and they walked toward their vehicle. "And when I do that update, I'll announce that we'll be adding another K-9 unit to the department. Let Jager refuse to fund the budget then."

Matt laughed. "Ask for forgiveness instead of permission?"

"That's my plan." Bree would turn Jager's philosophy right back on her. "But first, we have to find Harrison."

Chapter Thirty-Seven

As it turned out, it was harder to slash your own throat than someone else's. At nearly midnight, Matt and Bree approached Elaine Gibson's hospital room. Matt nodded to the deputy on guard. Personally, he couldn't have cared less if the murderer lived or died, but Bree wanted answers. She had legal threads to tie. The DA, the press, and the public all had to be satisfied. Marina had refused to talk, so Bree was left with Harrison's mother.

"She'll be angry with me. She wanted to die, and I didn't let her," Bree said. "So I'd like you to be Mr. Nice Guy. Get her talking."

Matt sighed. "You always make me be the good cop."

"You're better at it than I am. People *want* to talk to you."

"It's a curse." Matt always felt a little slimy after an interview when he agreed with killers and stroked their egos.

"We still need to find Harrison and Marina's boys," Bree reminded him. "I'll bet Elaine knows where they are."

They'd put out a BOLO on Marina's vehicle, but so far, it hadn't been spotted.

"Right." His job wasn't to punish Elaine. His goal was to get information.

Elaine's skin was the color Matt would expect after losing a bunch of blood. She had missed the artery, though. The blade had been rotated, and most of the damage had been superficial. Messy, but superficial.

They entered the room. Elaine was awake and handcuffed to both bedrails. She'd already tried to rip out her stitches. With both hands restrained and her neck heavily bandaged, she could only roll angry eyes at them as they stepped up next to the bed.

"What do you want?" she snapped in a raspy voice. "You already ruined everything."

"What did I ruin?" Bree asked.

"Harrison's future." Her eyes went white around the edges.

"Where is he hiding?" Bree asked.

"He had nothing to do with this," Elaine spat. "I did it all."

"I don't believe you," Bree said. "Maybe you're just protecting him."

Elaine's eyes went small and angry. "He isn't shrewd enough to make and carry out a plan this complicated."

That Matt could believe.

"Convince me or I'm bringing Harrison in with you," Bree said.

Elaine coughed. "If I tell you everything, will you leave him alone?"

"Yes," Bree said, clearly lying. If the evidence pointed to Harrison, Matt knew Bree would not let him walk away. It was perfectly legal for a cop to lie to a suspect.

"Fine," Elaine snapped.

"Why did you kill Kelly?" Bree asked.

"I did it for Harrison. So he and Marina could have a good life. Kelly was trying to destroy their future."

"How so?" Bree asked.

"Harrison made all the money that paid for that house. He deserved it. Not her."

"But they were married for many years. She raised his children. Your grandchildren."

Elaine's shoulder jerked. "They're just like their mother. Weak. They don't want anything to do with their father or me."

"They're already angry at him for leaving their mother," Bree said. "Maybe they would have forgiven him in time, but now . . ." She didn't add that they'd never forgive Elaine for killing their mother.

Elaine didn't look sorry. "Kelly didn't deserve their devotion. She stopped caring about her husband's needs. She was all about herself." She cleared her throat and nodded toward the water pitcher on the table next to the bed.

Matt stepped up. He reached for the cup and brought the straw to Elaine's lips. "So you wanted him to have a second chance."

"Exactly." Elaine licked her lips.

Matt set down the cup. "Because he deserves it. He's worked hard."

"He has. And Kelly was an ungrateful bitch. He chose the wrong woman the first time. He should still have the chance at a happy life."

"And Marina was the woman for him?" Matt asked.

"She's the first woman to love him as much as I do. She is devoted to making him happy."

She'll have to do that from a prison cell now. Matt felt bad for her little boys. Who would raise them?

"Was killing Kelly your idea or hers?" Bree asked.

Elaine rolled her eyes. "Mine. Marina is sweet. She's a great homemaker, but she isn't exactly a genius."

Sweet?

Elaine continued. "In fact, it took me a while to convince her to help. But she's exhausted and getting a little desperate to make ends meet. When Harrison had to pay an emergency room bill for her son's stitches last month, she understood. She and Harrison need and appreciate each other. Really, they're a perfect match."

Her praise was disarming. How could anyone rationalize murder for money? Matt thought one thing was for certain: Marina wasn't going to be a great wife and homemaker from prison.

"And Kelly just let you in?" Bree asked.

"Sure," Elaine said. "Why wouldn't she?"

Who would expect their senior citizen mother-in-law to slit their throat with a box cutter? Elaine's bluntness turned Matt's stomach.

"I gave her a chance to change her mind." Elaine wet her lips with her tongue. "I said, 'Kelly, you have to let all this go. Sell the place as is. You've dragged this out too long.' But she wouldn't. She insisted she had every right to maximize her profit from the house sale." Elaine made a *tsk* sound. "I panicked for a minute when I couldn't find her knife block. I'd planned to use a chef's knife. I hadn't been in the house since the previous spring. I didn't realize she still had all her good knives packed away. The renovation should have been done months ago."

"So you just killed her?" Matt was horrified that this grandmother had killed two women in cold blood. Had she always been a psychopath? How many people like her were walking around, seemingly normal, until they snapped?

Elaine lifted a shoulder. "Yes."

"Did you or Marina kill Janet?" Bree asked.

Elaine sighed. "As usual, I did all the real work, though Marina did provide logistical support. She did some of the initial scouting. For example, Harrison mentioned that Kelly was dating Troy. I decided her new boyfriend would be the best person to frame. Marina and I took turns watching his house and following him around. If one of us did all the spying, we might have been spotted."

"How did you get into his house?" Matt asked. "We couldn't find any evidence of a break-in."

Elaine looked satisfied, almost smug. "I watched him enter the garage door code through a pair of binoculars. My original plan was to leave the box cutter in the house, but then I thought maybe you wouldn't get enough evidence to get a warrant. I had to make it more accessible to you. I was going to crash the sports car in the woods anyway. I just didn't plan on you chasing me. I had to improvise the rest of that day."

"And the sock?" Matt tried to sound interested.

"I didn't want an arrest or conviction to be dependent on one piece of evidence. So, I left Kelly's sock in the hamper because—once you found the box cutter in his car—you'd get the warrant and search his house. You'd find the sock. I thought that would be the end of it. Why didn't you arrest him? That should have been enough proof."

Maybe for a TV show.

"The blood on the sock wasn't Kelly's," Bree said.

Elaine looked thoughtful. "I nicked my finger while I was killing her. I didn't realize it bled that much. Is that why you wouldn't arrest Troy?"

"Among other reasons," Bree said vaguely. "Why did you kill Janet?"

Elaine frowned. "Because you wouldn't arrest Troy, and you kept going after Harrison. I figured I'd give him the best alibi ever. He'd be with you when Troy's second girlfriend died."

"That was clever." The praise felt like a bone lodged in Matt's throat.

"Except Troy also had an alibi for Janet's murder," Bree said.

Elaine shook her head. "Bad luck on my part. Usually, he's home alone. The man has no social life."

"How did you find Janet and Claudia?" Bree asked.

"Social media," Elaine said. "People post way too much about their personal lives."

Truth.

"Why did you kidnap Claudia? You killed the others."

Elaine nodded. "In hindsight, that was a mistake. But I felt like I had to do something to get you off Harrison's back. I wanted to kill her, but Marina talked me out of it. Like I said before, she's sweet. I didn't think it through. I was frustrated. I acted on impulse."

"Where is Harrison? I'm sure you wanted him out of harm's way," Matt said. "In order for the whole plan to work."

"Yes." Elaine nodded. "I sent them to an indoor water park place for the weekend. A future stepfather and sons bonding trip. The boys were really excited." She gave them the name of the resort. "I guess you have to call them. It's a shame to ruin their fun."

What the actual fuck?

She had murdered Kelly and Janet. She'd kidnapped Claudia and tried to kill her. And she was worried about ruining Harrison's weekend?

"I suppose he took Marina's minivan?" Bree asked.

"Yes," Elaine said. "The Corvette doesn't have a back seat, so Marina won't let the boys ride in it. She's such a good mother." She narrowed her eyes at Bree. "So, you'll leave Harrison alone?"

Bree made a noncommittal noise.

The nurse came in to change Elaine's bandages. Bree wrapped up the interview. They walked into the hall. In the elevator, Matt said, "That might have been the weirdest Q and A ever."

"She was so . . . casual about killing two people and kidnapping a third. Like their lives meant nothing compared to Harrison's comfort."

"Makes you wonder, doesn't it? Has she always been a complete sociopath, or did something snap later in her life?"

"Who knows?" Bree shook her head. "Doesn't matter. She's going to prison."

"Do you believe Harrison had nothing to do with it?"

Bree lifted a shoulder. "We'll interview him for sure, but verifying his alibi for Claudia's kidnapping should be easy enough. The hotel and water park will have cameras. He was at the station while Janet was killed, and Elaine confessed to Kelly's murder. Barring a confession from him or solid physical evidence that proves he was involved, I doubt the DA would be willing to charge him."

Matt sighed. "What we think isn't important. All that matters is what we can prove."

"But I can believe that he isn't cunning enough to have planned Kelly's murder. He's a jerk, but he's no criminal mastermind."

Matt snorted. "There is that."

They took the elevator to the maternity floor. Matt needed an emotional palate cleanse.

They'd stopped at home to shower and change before coming to the hospital. Bree was in uniform, and no one stopped the sheriff. Matt's mom and dad were in the waiting room.

His dad's smile was a mile wide. "You're just in time! The baby was born about thirty minutes ago. A strapping baby boy! Ten pounds, six ounces."

"Whoa! Flynns don't mess around," Matt said, kissing his mom on the cheek. "Get him shoes. He can walk out."

"Does he have a name?" Bree hugged his parents.

"Cady wants to tell you." Matt's dad, George, had tears in his eyes. "Go on in."

"Are you sure?" Matt said. "I don't want to intrude."

"She's waiting for you." His mom smiled. "I told her you were on the way when you texted me."

Bree hung back. "One person at a time."

Matt heard his dad asking Bree all the medical questions about her nose as he walked away. He stopped at the closed door and used hand sanitizer. Then he knocked softly.

"Come in."

Cady rested on pillows. Todd sat in the chair next to her, his head bandaged. Scratches covered his face.

Cady looked exhausted but also the happiest Matt had ever seen her. And the baby in her arms . . .

Matt leaned over and kissed his sister's head. "He's perfect."

"He is." Cady beamed.

"How are you?" Matt asked Todd.

"OK. Concussion, but OK."

Cady grabbed for his hand. "He's allowed to stay here as long as he remains in the chair."

Todd squeezed. "I just made it in time."

"Good," Matt said.

"Come closer and hold your nephew." Cady scooted over, wincing slightly.

Matt perched on the edge of the bed, and she transferred the bundle into his arms. Navy-blue eyes squinted up at him from a wrinkled red face. He looked a little like Yoda. "He's perfect."

Cady settled back on the pillows. "Meet Matthew George. MG for short."

Matt didn't bother to stem the tears.

MG was definitely perfect.

Chapter Thirty-Eight

Sunday afternoon, Bree was in her office buried under reports. The law didn't stop for weekends. She spoke with Morgan Dane, letting her know that Troy was cleared of all charges. She was setting down her phone when Madeline Jager walked into her office in a snug navy suit.

Should have closed the door.

Not that a closed door would have stopped Jager.

"Nice work." Jager crossed her arms. "You caught the killer and saved Claudia Ferguson."

Bree leaned back and touched the bridge of her nose. The swelling was down, but she knew the bruises had gone full eggplant. Her face looked like bruise-colored camo, like someone had tie-dyed her skin with purple paint. "I wish I'd caught her before she killed Janet Hargrave."

"You once told me that you can't stop a crime before it happens." Jager perched a hip on the edge of Bree's desk.

"It's true, but I still don't like it." But Bree hadn't even had Elaine Gibson on her suspect list. Harrison's mother had never been on the radar at all. Who expected a senior citizen to commit a violent, bloody murder?

"You expect yourself to be perfect," Jager said.

Bree looked away. "When I'm not, people die."

"Look on the bright side."

"There's a bright side? Two women are dead."

"You're getting a new K-9." Jager didn't even look peeved. "You outmaneuvered me on that one. You're learning. Kudos."

"It's not a game."

Jager shrugged. She totally thought it was. Her eyes lit with triumph. "But now you have to admit that my tip line worked. Go on. Admit it."

"Fine," Bree said. "It worked. But that was a once-in-a-million shot."

"Still worked." Jager grinned.

Bree clenched her teeth. Of all the narcissistic . . .

Jager examined a fingernail. "People might say I helped solve the case."

"People" being yourself.

Jager stood and straightened her skirt. "I like that we're partners now instead of adversaries. We're a good team."

Bree had no words other than *please no.*

Jager sauntered toward the door. "I'll make a politician out of you yet."

Bree sincerely hoped not.

Her phone rang. Marge. "I know it's a Sunday, but I thought you'd want this information ASAP. I found the woman in the drawing. Her name is Phyllis Sanders. She was a social worker for Randolph County for twenty-five years. She's retired now, but she says she remembers your mom and you're welcome to stop by her house." Marge read off an address in Grey's Hollow.

Bree's throat tightened, and she couldn't speak for a moment. She'd wanted this information, yet having it felt almost overwhelming. She swallowed and cleared her throat. "Thanks, Marge. I couldn't have found her without you." Bree reached for her jacket.

"I know." Marge ended the call.

Now that Bree had the information, she had to follow up immediately. She'd waited too long. Her stomach roiled with nerves as she drove to a little ranch-style home on a neat lot. Phyllis Sanders opened her door and gave Bree a smile.

Bree started to introduce herself, but Phyllis cut her off. "I know who you are. I've been following your career. Your mom would have been so proud of you."

Bree felt tears pressuring her eyes. She blinked them away.

Phyllis took her by the arm and led her into a cheery yellow kitchen. "I'll make you some tea. Then we'll talk."

Bree dropped into a farmhouse chair.

Tea was served, and Phyllis faced her over the steaming mugs. "You drink, and I'll tell you everything. I met with your mother at least six or seven times. She wanted to leave. She knew she was in danger. But she also knew leaving would be risky. Men like your father don't let their women go. They feel like they own them."

Bree knew this. Statistically, victims of domestic violence were at the greatest risk when they left. They instinctively knew it, which was why they were afraid to go. Every memory of her parents' marriage—all the violence—spoke to her mother's fear and the very real danger running away would bring.

"She was making plans, though, and I was helping her. I was looking for a spot in a shelter for all of you. There weren't enough shelters. There still aren't." Phyllis paused and sighed heavily. "I don't know if he found out or not, because he killed her before I could find a place. I'm so sorry. I wish I could have done more."

A quick flash of that night played in Bree's mind. The very last time she'd seen her mother. The gun. The rage in her father's eyes. Her mother pinned against the wall, distracting him, her eyes pleading for Bree to take her younger siblings and run.

She'd sacrificed herself so her children could live.

Because she'd loved them.

Bree couldn't process all the information over a sip of tea. It was a lot to take in. Did her father find out that her mother was planning to leave? Was that why he killed her? Maybe he would have killed her anyway. Maybe his escalating violence had triggered her mother's attempt to leave him. She would never have all the answers, and she would have to accept that.

Bree's voice was rough when she finally spoke. "None of what you told me is a surprise, but it's good to know she was trying. I know she loved him, though, as hard as that is to believe."

Phyllis raised a hand. "You don't have to tell me anything. I've seen it all. Your mother isn't the only woman I lost." She reached across the table and took Bree's hands. "She loved you more, though. All she wanted was to protect her children. She just didn't know how. She was terrified for you three, not for herself."

Unable to speak, Bree simply nodded.

Phyllis squeezed Bree's hands. "I'll say it again. She would be so proud of you."

Exhaustion felt like a weighted vest when Bree stood, thanked Phyllis, and left. She sent Adam a text that she needed to talk to him—he deserved to know. Then she drove home in a mental fog, changed into jeans and boots, and went to the barn. She was too wired to nap. Some time with Cowboy would be her therapy.

The rain had stopped early in the morning, and Cowboy was covered in mud when she brought him in from the pasture. After closing the door against the chilly wind, she snapped him onto the cross ties. "Did you find every mud puddle on the farm?"

He butted her with his head, and she fed him a carrot.

The barn door slid open, and Adam stepped in. "Got your text."

Bree leaned on Cowboy's rump. Over her horse's back, she told her brother everything Phyllis had said.

Adam nodded solemnly. "Not a huge shock, right? But still, this kind of feels like a closure of sorts."

"It does." Bree had come home to Grey's Hollow reluctantly. She hadn't wanted to revisit her past. Yet, in doing so, she felt . . . healed. Had she worked through the worst of her pain, or would there be more? There always seemed to be more, but she was tired of living in the past. She needed to focus on moving forward. Her mother's murder would always be a part of her. But the burden felt lighter now.

"Then what I have to say seems appropriate." Adam patted Cowboy's back. Dust billowed. "My last two paintings did pretty well."

"Pretty well?" Bree snorted.

Adam laughed. "Yeah. I used to not value money. But it sure is nice to be able to help people. The kids and the farm are taken care of. I've put aside some for you too." He held up a hand. "I know you don't want it, but you're not going to want to put your life on the line forever. I want you to be able to quit whenever you choose without money being an issue."

"Thank you," Bree said. "That's a comfort to me." Because he was right. She wouldn't chase criminals forever. Sure, Matt had money, but it was a relief to know she was independent.

"I've even spent a little on some fun things." Adam had bought a nice car and built himself a real house instead of living in his converted barn studio. "So, now that those needs have been met, I have another plan. I don't remember Mom. I was just a baby when she died. But I want to make her proud. What would you say to opening the Mary Taggert Women's Shelter?"

Joy flooded Bree. She had no answer except to walk around her horse and throw her arms around her brother. "I think that's the best legacy you could give her."

"I figured I can't help her, but I can help other women like her."

"You might even save some lives." Bree hugged him harder.

"Yeah." Adam cleared his throat. "You give back every day in your job. I want to do something too."

"She would be proud of us," Bree said.

"I hope so." Adam leaned back. His eyes shone with moisture. "I'm also going to take Zucco on a nice vacation—somewhere warm—as soon as she can spare the time."

"I'll approve her vacation days." Releasing him, Bree wiped a happy tear from her cheek. "She's more than earned it, and you deserve some happiness. I know sometimes it's hard to remember that. She suffered. We suffered. But that's all in the past. We can't change it, and we deserve to be happy."

Later, when she and Matt lay in bed, their legs intertwined—not with each other but around two dogs and a cat with an attitude—she didn't want to talk about the case. She told him about the shelter. "I didn't want to come home almost two years ago."

"I know."

"But I'm glad I did. My whole life is something I never imagined."

He reached over Ladybug, took Bree's hand, and brought her knuckles to his lips.

"The baby is still good?" she asked.

"The baby is perfect."

"Do you ever think about having one of your own?"

"You mean one of *our* own," Matt corrected. "Because I would not want a child with anyone else."

"One of our own then."

"I do, but I'm a happy man right now. I don't need a child to complete me, and I feel like Kayla and Luke are mine anyway." Matt shrugged. "You?"

"I don't feel the overriding need for a baby—especially not a ten-pound one. That's just not right."

Matt laughed. "Cady is almost six feet tall, so . . ."

Still . . . Ouch.

"I want to make sure I'm not keeping you from something you need," Bree said.

Matt stroked her arm. "I'm not in a rush to make any irreversible decisions, and holding little MG makes me realize how permanent that would be. My sister and Todd made a *person*."

"What would you say to an almost-as-permanent decision?" Bree rolled over. The dogs protested with groans. Vader hissed and bolted to the nightstand, where he cleaned his paw and looked offended.

"Like what?"

We deserve to be happy.

So, why was she putting off something that would make her life even better?

"Marry me?" Bree asked. The question felt like an impulse, but it wasn't.

"Tonight?"

Bree laughed. "I'd rather wait until I don't look like I lost a prizefight."

"I will marry you any day, anytime. Do you want to elope?"

"I think your parents will want to be there, don't you?" And Bree suddenly knew she wanted both their families around them. Friends too. Their joy was something to be celebrated. With her past—and his—they'd earned their happiness.

"I do." He grinned and leaned forward to kiss her. "We can keep it small, though. If you don't want to do the work, I'm sure my parents would host it at their house."

"Maybe. Here at the farm would be nice too." Bree would feel closer to her sister here at home. "I've wanted to marry you for a while."

"I know."

"Ha ha." Bree rolled her eyes. "But now I feel ready to marry you. Like I've finally put some things to rest mentally so I can move forward unencumbered, or at least, less encumbered." She shook her head. "It's not coming out right."

Matt shifted, leaning forward to kiss her. "I understand."

Brody sighed and jumped off the bed. Ladybug didn't budge, but she did give them an *I'm sleeping* side-eye.

"Do you want me to get down on one knee?" Bree asked, laughing. "I don't have a ring."

"Kneeling isn't necessary. I've seen the bruises on your legs. I don't need a ring either." Matt kissed her again, one hand sliding to her hip. "All I need is you."

His fingers squeezed gently, and she felt the need for him: heart, soul, and body.

I *deserve to be happy.*

And she was. She really was.

She cupped the side of his face. "Back atcha, big guy."

Acknowledgments

Special thanks to all my writer friends: Rayna Vause, Kendra Elliot, Leanne Sparks, Toni Anderson, Amy Gamet, and Loreth Anne White. Writing is a solitary business. I'm grateful for my virtual support system. Cheers, ladies! I love you all. As always, credit goes to my agent, Jill Marsal, for her continued unwavering support and solid career advice. My continued thanks to the entire team at Montlake, especially my acquiring editor, Anh Schluep, and my developmental editor, Charlotte Herscher, along with the copyeditors and proofreaders who all love Bree and her crew. As far as teams go, I am lucky to have the best.

ABOUT THE AUTHOR

Melinda Leigh is the #1 Amazon Charts and #1 *Wall Street Journal* bestselling author of *She Can Run*, an International Thriller Award nominee for Best First Novel, *She Can Tell*, *She Can Scream*, *She Can Hide*, and *She Can Kill* in the She Can series; *Midnight Exposure*, *Midnight Sacrifice*, *Midnight Betrayal*, and *Midnight Obsession* in the Midnight Novels; *Hour of Need*, *Minutes to Kill*, and *Seconds to Live* in the Scarlet Falls series; *Say You're Sorry*, *Her Last Goodbye*, *Bones Don't Lie*, *What I've Done*, *Secrets Never Die*, and *Save Your Breath* in the Morgan Dane series; and *Cross Her Heart*, *See Her Die*, *Drown Her Sorrows*, *Right Behind Her*, *Dead Against Her*, *Lie to Her*, *Catch Her Death*, *On Her Watch*, *Track Her Down*, and the short story "Her Second Death" in the Bree Taggert series. Melinda has garnered numerous writing awards, including two RITA nominations; holds a second-degree black belt in Kenpo karate and has taught women's self-defense; and lives in a messy house with her family and a small herd of rescue pets. For more information, visit www.melindaleigh.com.